I0654162

AFTER AVALON

Curated by Nicole Petit

AFTER AVALON
An 18thWall Productions book published by
arrangement with Nicole Petit
verba mea in minibus
desiderium meum
Cover by Barbara Sobczyńska
Design by Elisgraphics
Text Copyright
The May Hawk's Daughter © Colin Fisher
Sir Gawain and the Quest for Merlin's Tree © Leigh Ann Cowan
Hour of Their Need © Amy Wolf
Paste-bones and Ragdolls © Thomas Olivieri
Bel Nemeton © Jon Black
Knight of the Ice Moon © Patricia S. Bowne
Mordred Beguiled © Claudia Quint
The Saga of Freydis Beastsbane © David Wiley
The Confession of Mrs. Fay © Christian Bone
The Hammer and the Spear © Patrick S. Baker
Forsaking All Others © Elizabeth Zuckerman

All rights reserved.
ISBN-10: 1-946033-00-6
ISBN-13: 978-1-946033-00-0

PUBLISHERS NOTE
This is a work of fiction. Names, characters, places, and incidents either are the products of
the author's imagination or used fictitiously. Any resemblance to actual persons, living or
dead, business establishments, events, locales, public figures, private figures, and fictional
characters is entirely coincidental.

Table of Contents

The May Hawk's Daughter

Colin Fisher

I

"This was Broceliande," the man said, and laughed. He slapped
the rough timber. "Not much left for Lords and Ladies now, but
stout enough to prop up this old place." The boy was wide eyed.
He couldn't reach it, but he could draw it down with his eyes.
The dark oak, ridges like ripples spreading across the flat plane
of wood, had the patina of iron. A crust of centuries lay upon it.
He thought of it upright, still leafed, crowding close with its
brethren on hills and plains and deep, hidden troughs where
sunlight never fell and the law of a Christian land held scant
weight. Canopies of light and shade held fast to secrets and
enchantment.

"How old is it?" He heard rain falling on broad leaves,
pattering hard on stones and empty chapels. It was just the wind
against shuttered windows, the crackling of logs in the wide
fireplace, but for a moment he was lost in the stories he'd heard
at his Grandmother's knee.

"That?" The innkeeper swept the table clear and picked up a
handful of empty tankards. They looked like thimbles in his huge
fist. He glanced at the beams as if seeing them for the first time.
"Bloody old." Then, "'Scuse my language," and glanced at the
boy's Father, counting coppers out at the bar. "Inn's been in my
family for a hundred years, and it's said the timber was salvaged
from another building on the same site."

"What's left?" The boy looked out of the great bay window
of the inn, although dusk had fallen and little could be seen.
"What did they find there?"

But the innkeeper had moved away, clunking his tankards
down on the scarred surface of the bar. The boy's Father spoke
to him, and the Innkeeper glanced back, but smiled and shook

his head before disappearing into the building's inner chambers.

The boy sat thinking all evening, while his Father spoke to others of how the fishing had gone, of storms that wracked the coastal villages, of how he had seen a troop of the King's soldiers riding north to search for brigands on the borders. While they in their turn shared news of the towns and villages they knew. Yet the boy thought only of the long wide roads, grown now with weeds, that they had travelled, tall trees always ahead of them on the horizon. He imagined them echoing with the iron tread of horses weighed with knights in bright armour.

Eventually, he grew tired. His Father remained deep in conversation with his men, and those of other villages they had come to trade with, so he returned to their own room to tell himself stories of the High Kingdom that had fallen with the death of Arthur and his knights. The inn was large, with several wings and galleries, and he struggled to remember the way. Finding himself lost, he turned to retrace his steps along an unfamiliar gallery. As he did so he passed an open door.

He had gone several paces before something half glimpsed prompted him to turn, and creep back to peer through the crack in the door. A girl in a black gown sat straight-backed at a table. Golden hair cascaded over her high collar from a circlet that gleamed like molten silver. She was turned away, looking out the window at the dark shapes of lone trees moving in the wind. The boy could see them through the glass, silhouettes bowing and dancing like graceful giants. On the table before her sat a skull, pitted and stained. Red light from the fire moved across it and hid in the empty orbits. On the crown was the jagged black scar of a wound, inches long.

"I never knew my Father," she said, without looking at him. "But I met the man who carried his head along the corpse road against the High Downs." She raised her hand, pale and ringed, and touched the side of the skull with long fingers. "They say he killed a hundred of Medraut's knights before he fell, though he had a Saxon axe embedded in his head. I do not know the truth of this, but truth can be strange." She turned her head, and stared at the boy. "I am sorry for you."

He backed away. She was beautiful, but her eyes were black as the night sky and directed an unfathomable sadness at him. His throat tightened as if he fought back tears. Scolding himself for having been caught spying, he hurried away to his room.

Later, he heard a commotion outside. Horses turned in the inn yard, and men dismounted and called out. Others joined them, and they pointed back along the road, to the town and the river crossing. There was a coming and going of servants. They were taken inside, and their voices became muffled. Eventually silence returned.

He was woken by his Father entering the room. "There has been a raid," he said. "A farmer killed. His wife taken. And cattle."

"Who?" He sat up, wide-eyed in horror. "Not Saxons?"

"Cutthroats from the Forest, almost certainly. They'll be heading back to the border. Lordless scum. There have been raids here before. There are villagers arrived, after hunting them down and seeking help from willing travellers."

"Will you go? Are you to arm yourself?" The boy glanced out of the window, "You cannot hunt in the dark!"

His Father sat on his own bed. "In the morning. There are men here who are not a'feared of bandits. And some of our own men are veterans. I'll lead them out with others from the village."

"But…" the boy stammered, "What of our wares? What of market?"

His Father looked at him, then knelt and blew out the candle. His bed creaked as he stretched out with a groan. "We'll reach market. Now let me sleep. Day will come soon and the ale here is strong."

The boy lay in the darkness, thinking of the Forest, and who might have come from it. He thought of the crags, and the High Moor, and how far they were from the King's Guard. Even the Shire Reeves were a two day ride away. But most of all he thought of the golden haired woman, and the broken skull, and the deep, flickering light in its cavernous orbits.

He woke before dawn to see his Father moving about the room, lighting candles. He watched as the man laced up his boots. "It's still dark," the boy said, "are they gathering so early?"

The man stood, and put his hand on the boy's shoulder. "Son." His grey eyes searched the boy's face for acceptance. "I need to walk out my thoughts."

"What thoughts? What is it?" The boy thought of the previous night's conversations in the Common Room. "More decisions?"

"Aye. Things are turning. We've heard some news here. Lots of travellers pass through. The north isn't what it was." He shrugged himself into his cloak, heavy and crusted with the salt of the biting sea. "There are Kings there now, so-called Kings, and they're looking south. And the Irish on our own shores. They're fierce, and cold, and the sea won't stop them."

"And the Saxons?" The boy looked fearful.

His Father gave a half smile. "Well, the Saxons took a hiding, and the one's that came after, they were better at letting us be, or mebbe they'd just learned their lesson. But who knows? There are more behind, and behind them are deep forests and wide plains. Even the Empire never went there, and now it's a memory in most parts. There are wild and hungry men, and eyes that look to rich lands like ours."

"Perhaps the King will come back?" The boy couldn't keep the eagerness from his voice. "When the need is great, he'll return from sleep to reclaim his Kingdom."

The man paused in lifting down his stout staff from the high shelf. "Maybe he will, and maybe he won't. But look here," and he touched his staff to the dark beams that ran overhead, and framed the doors of the great inn. "This here was his Kingdom. Logres. This wood, all its knots and grain. Its secrets, and its high castles. All the lords and ladies in their finery. And neither the King, nor his knights nor his champions could save it from the axe, and the fire. He didn't come back to save them when the barbarians came. Small kings and Saxons, Scots and Picts, aye, and our own lords some of them. Chopped it down and carried it off for timber. Why, our own boats were made of ash from the great Forest. His precious Round Table so much kindling, and his castles broke and sunk in grass. He didn't come back. He's dead, or dreaming, or lost and the world has turned. And Christian men like you and me must make our own way, and protect our own people. Aye," and again he put his hand on his son's shoulder, but this time he squeezed it hard, "men like you and me. You're not a boy any longer. Hear me. If tomorrow I don't come back, those same decisions are for you to make. The men will listen to you. It's their livelihood, but they'll listen to you."

The boy was puzzled. "You'll come back. It's just outlaws."

"Oh, I shall." His Father straightened. "I've every intention of doing just that. Likely these are just disorganised raiders skulking in what's left of the Forest. You'll see. They'll turn tail soon enough when they see a score of determined men with bows and axes. You'll see. But for now, I'm going to walk up and see the dawn rising against the hilltops. I'll join the men when they gather on the south track. We'll talk tomorrow." And the boy watched as his Father opened the chest at the foot of his bed, and took out the gleaming sword that had been handed down in their family since time beyond memory, from a soldier who returned home after long service in the Empire's wars to become a leader of men in time of peace. The sword had been kept keen and bright, and even if no-one could now read the proud letters that ran the length of the short blade, all in their family knew the words by heart. *As duty demands, so courage grants.* No other man in their small town possessed such a thing, and all looked to his Father for wisdom, and guidance, because he was skilled in both, and because he carried the Centurion's sword.

Then he hugged his son, which he hadn't done since the boy was a child, and the boy nodded awkwardly in his Father's embrace, and hugged him back. And then his Father left, and his boots thumped softly down the long corridor into silence.

But the boy's Father didn't come back that day, nor the day after. The boy sat with those of his Father's men as had remained, and listened to their talk, and spoke as if his head were full of the catch, repairing nets, and preparing their boats for summer. He listened to them speak of the taxes that became ever greater to pay for the King's wars, and whether and how their kin along the coasts might band together to prevent raids. Yet all the while he watched the road that lay hard against the great moor and the heaving forest. But as days passed, and men came and went, still no-one came over the hill or along the road with news.

Each evening as the boy made his way to his room, he tried again to find the room of the lady with the skull. He retraced his steps to the floor that seemed to him to be the right one, but none of the doors seemed familiar, and most stood empty and unlocked. He hadn't seen her depart, and didn't believe that someone of such obvious standing and authority would be travelling without an entourage, so knew that she must be staying somewhere in the inn. He couldn't have explained why he wanted to find her room, but if pressed might have said that she was a puzzle that took his thoughts from the hours of waiting, and the emptiness of the road outside.

At breakfast on the third day a rider came gasping to the inn. By his livery and demeanour it was plain that he was a messenger from the King. The innkeeper and his guests, the boy among them, crowded around him as he dismounted in the yard and called for ale. There had been a battle. Westward, a large band of Irish raiders had been caught inland by knights of the King's household. The recent attacks had been scouts foraging for food and captives, and their pursuers, having followed them towards the old Roman road, had been surprised and ambushed when they came upon the main force. They had no chance against a well-armed force of several hundred men, and had been slain as they fled. None survived. The raiders had still been looting their bodies when the King's men came upon them, and they in turn were surprised and slain as they fled hither and thither across the heath, or into the boggy terrain of the High Moor.

There was other news. One of the slain had been a son of King Amalgaid of Mumhain. There would be more attacks in reprisal. The coastal villages would become dangerous. But the boy heard little, and said less. He and the remaining men stood, hearts turned to stone, as the messenger delivered the news they secretly dreaded.

As the messenger was led forward into the inn, fielding a dozen questions, the boy pushed forward, and stayed him with a touch on his arm.

"None survived?" he asked, keeping his face a mask because he knew his Father's men would gauge his reaction, and their respect thereby hung in the balance.

Even though not yet full grown, the boy was tall for his age, and the man stopped. He shook his head, then shrugged. "It's not likely, lad. Their horses were rounded up by squires. They matched the number of bodies. All will be taken north to Caer-Baddan and buried with honour."

"The old road runs by Broceliande. Some may have ridden to safety beneath its eaves."

"Maybe." The messenger was doubtful. "The bodies were scattered about Rook Tor—it looked like they made a stand there, by the giant's stones." He looked at the faces of the remaining men, etched with pain. "Come to Baddan. You may count the dead, and be certain."

The boy stepped back, and let the throng move inside. Their voices became disjointed, their sense carried away by the wind. He felt a hand on his shoulder, and he started, remembering his Father's grip. It was Einion, Captain of his Father's fleet.

"We'll go together," he said. "All of us. We'll take the news back, and sell our goods along the way. The town needs to hear. And there will need to be a council." He looked uncomfortable. "You must stand in your Father's stead, and make the decisions he intended to make. You're head of the fleet now, Annwyl. People will look to you for leadership."

The boy gave him an empty stare. The words broke around his head, and fell to the ground. Leadership. He wasn't Leader. His Father—strong, with a grip of iron whether on the tiller or the spear—was Leader. He thought of him at the prow, his black hair stiffened by the sea, as they sailed along the coasts of Powys under a shimmering sun.

"Annwyl." Einion shook him. "The men are inside, now. They are afraid, and they are grief-stricken. They must ride back and tell wives and mothers and children what has befallen here, and those voices that said we should leave, that we should take our boats and sail for Armorica, will grow louder. Devin will say he was right when he defied your Father—that there's nothing left for us. The Saxons are on the march again, and the Irish, and our northern cousins are caught between them and the Picts and cannot come to our aid. What the men need now is command, a strong voice. This…this slaughter…God knows it is bad and we have to find the strength to come through it, but it is not the end. The raiders have been caught and killed. Bledric is rebuilding the defences at Caer Uisc, and is creating new knights. The Kings at Caer Baddan, Caer Ceri, and Caer Gloui are forging a new alliance. The men need to hear all this, now, at their lowest point."

"Small Kings and Saxons," the boy said, shrugging the man's hand away.

"What do you mean?"

"That's who we stand between. Our Kings are at each other's throats, and the godless pagans are waiting to seize the spoils. Logres has fallen."

"Logres?" Einion shook his head. "You fill your head with nonsense, boy. Now get in there and put some steel in these men's backs." He pushed the boy ahead of him into the inn.

As he stumbled forward, the boy looked up, and saw, standing on a balcony above, the woman in the black dress. She was dressed in a green cloak and hood, her hair hidden, but the glint of silver still shone from her brow. She looked at him without expression, then turned her gaze away. Across the yard, toward the winding, weed strewn road, and the dark forest beyond. The boy set his jaw, and stepped into the inn.

It was not the chaos he expected. Men stood in sombre groups, their eyes downcast. Others sat dejected. Some stood with the King's messenger, talking urgently. The boy walked forward, and the men parted respectfully. One or two touched his arm, but he hardly noticed them. Gradually the men stopped what they were doing, and waited. With Einion behind him, he walked to the end of the room, and turned to the hopeless faces. He felt foolish, that he had no words to offer them. There was a tightness in his chest, as if he were caught in a vice, or the fist of Cormoran the giant. It crushed the words in his throat. He took several deep breaths, to try and free them. His heart hammered in the hush.

"We have all lost friends and family. We have come from our home, under the protection of the King, to buy and sell. To feed our families. To keep them safe. And safety we were promised. Yet that has proven false; here we stand while those who rode beside us are food for crows, slain by evil men that roam freely upon our once civilised land."

There was murmuring. Men looked at each other.

"Annwyl." Einion was behind him, a warning in his voice.

"Aye, freely!" The anger that was trapped in his chest surged forth. "The Kings do not protect us, they are too busy feasting behind their walls! And when they're not feasting, they fight amongst each other. What of High King Caninus? His sons have torn his Kingdom apart, and Saxons push against divided borders. Irish reavers attack our coasts, sail our rivers with impunity. What has King Bledric done? Where were his knights when my Father…" he stumbled over his words, "when our kin died defending his Kingdom?"

A stocky figure with braided hair and a jutting beard leapt to his feet. "They died because of your Father's recklessness!"

"Devin." Enion's voice was a warning growl. "Best keep your peace."

The man pushed to the front, and leaned forward. His knuckles whitened as he gripped the table. "At whose command, Einion? Yours? This stripling? This wasn't our fight until Galwyn made it one!" He turned to face the other men. "You all know what I think, what I've been saying for the last twelvemonth. We take our boats and we take our families. We join our kin in Armorica. Or stay here and be butchered in our beds!"

Other men shouted. Some in agreement, some against. Einion pushed forward and seized Devin's arm, but the other man shrugged him off and leapt on a chair.

"How many more have to die? The raids will only get worse, and there is no-one who can stop them!"

"Arthur will stop them." The boy's voice was drowned out by the roar of angry men. Some turned to look at him or cupped their hands to their ears as if trying to hear, but shook their heads and simply added their voices to the growing cacophony. His heart pounded in his chest. Men were beginning to push and shove each other, but he needed to be heard. He clambered on the table. "King Arthur will stop them!"

There was silence. Einion turned to him, his mouth open. Devin smirked, the two of them raised above a crush of bitter men. His face wore a look of scorn.

"What's that you say, boy? King Arthur? Are you mad? The Bear and all his hopes have gone into the dirt. We'll join them if we don't leave!"

"The King will come back! At the hour of our most desperate need, the King and his knights will wake and ride forth to defeat our enemies!"

One of the men—the boy recognised him as one of his Father's boatwrights—tried to help him down. "Come down, lad. Don't tarnish your Father's memory."

The boy knocked his hand away. "My Father has ridden into the Forest! I know it! In all likelihood he seeks the King's help, even now. He promised he would come back, and he shall!"

He saw Einion looking at him with a mixture of grief and pity, but it did nothing to quiet the raging in his head. He knew he was right. "Go now to Baddan. Honour our dead. Einion and I shall ride to Broceliande."

Arguments broke out again on every side. Einion shook his head, and turned away. "Listen to me! We will all ride to Baddan, and then home. Just listen!" He strode to the bar. The boy heard his voice raised above the hubbub as he banged for silence. As the noise and the arguments gradually subsided, the boy jumped to the floor. Ignored, he stole from the gathering, and returned to his room. If he could not persuade Einion to join him in his quest, then he would go alone. He would take the path to the Forest and the King. Hurriedly, he began to pack.

II

He met her at the turn in the road, where the eaves of the forest shadowed the line of the hills as they marched north. There was a tumbledown hut, a shepherd's croft or a farmer's store, and her grey mare stood beside it, tugging mouthfuls of grass from a broken wall. She sat astride her horse, not side-saddle, as if preparing for an arduous journey. She was cloaked, and a bow was on her back.

He had taken what he needed from his room while the men were still arguing. It wasn't much—his staff, the broad bladed knife given him by his uncle, and his Father's pack, sturdy and still half full of bread and apples and strong cheese. Then, leading his horse *Guaire* from the stables, he pulled his hood over his face and clattered from the yard out to the great southern road. No one stopped him, and he left a message in his room instructing Einion to take the men on to Baddan, where he would join them. God willing in company with his Father.

She watched him approach. "I am Nyfain," she said, as he drew level, "My Father was King of Gododdin. Walganus he was to those who spoke the tongue of the Emperor, in whose lands he was raised. He is called here *Gwalchmai*, the Hawk of May, and I am his daughter."

"I am Annwyl ap Galwyn," the boy said, self-conscious. He had never seen a woman so beautiful, or clothes so rich. "And I ride to find my Father. He and I shall seek Arthur the King, and raise him from slumber to save his Kingdom."

"Whereas I ride to lay my Father to his slumber. I would lay one to sleep, you would rouse one." The woman looked him up and down. "Do you think he will heed one such as you? You have neither knightly garb, nor fair raiment, nor bright weapons."

The boy bristled. "He will heed my Father, who is mighty, and a leader of men. I believe..." the boy faltered, "I know he is lost within the Forest."

The woman laid a hand on her saddlebag. She looked serious, but her eyes held a touch of humour. "Fathers can be troublesome. Even in death our love obliges us to follow them."

"My Father is not dead," Annwyl said.

There was silence. The Lady nodded, and looked up the road. A hundred yards ahead it forked. One path turned south east, heading for Bledric's capital at Uisc, the other sloped upward, cutting through crags. The old legions had made no concessions to the ancient stone, but grass and heather had crept back in the centuries since their departure, and it appeared now as if the road ascended between the knees of a gnarled, squatting giant. Beyond, the morning mist had yet to burn off as the sun rose higher.

"We should go," the Lady urged her horse past Annwyl to the road. "They will come after you."

"I left a letter. Instructions. Einion may want to, but the others will persuade him to ride for Baddan."

"Nevertheless. You are his Lord's son. He is responsible, and he will answer to your kin, to your sister."

"She is a baby. Others have charge of her."

"She will not always be a baby. Einion will understand this. We must answer to the future, as well as the past." She looked back at him. "We must go."

They took the path that turned through the crag, and together they rode through the defile. Moss-covered rock rose high on either side, twisted trees clinging with roots like claws, lost in a mist which surged about them, muffling their horses' hooves and erasing the path. The boy strained his ears for pursuit, but could hear nothing, and the crags and the mist woke strange echoes from their own passage so it seemed as if other riders wove in the air above them or moved, just out of sight, beyond each turn in the road. Beside him, the Lady sat straight in her saddle, her form blurring as if seen through the edges of sleep. Her bare hands, loose on the reins, looked ghostlike, as if she were taking on the form and substance of the grey mist.

For an hour they rode in silence, following the path's twists and turns. In truth the boy couldn't say if they travelled between stone, or had emerged onto open moorland, such was the density of the mist and the strange patterns within. Only the echoes, close to their side, or high above, suggested walls still confined them.

"The sun will burn this mist soon," said the boy, "and we shall see what the road brings."

The lady nodded, but did not speak or look at him, and he wondered indeed if she had slipped away to leave only her own echo pacing phantomwise beside him. He swallowed hard, ashamed of himself. He wasn't a child, and he knew that in Arthur's day many a knight had ridden with firm heart through the gates of Broceliande to adventure. He sat up straighter in his saddle. He would not be cowed.

"Where do you seek?" He looked at his companion. He could just make out her profile within her hood, lips upturned as if with humour, but a determined set to her jaw. She glanced at him, and he noticed for the first time a golden light in the dark of her eyes, as if the sunlight lost somewhere above were imprisoned in them.

"Where? I would lay my Father's remains beside his kin."

"But where is that? I shall search for my Father within the Forest's boundaries westward, where he may have ridden from pursuit. Its margins are not broad at this point. Further south, it grows deeper, and when I find my Father then we shall seek there the true King's domain."

"I will seek where the King lies sleeping, and ravens circle without rest." She shrugged. "It is in a cave, or upon a land across water, or in the pillared hall of a lonely castle. Gwalchmai will sleep beside him, and gather his strength."

"Then our paths lie together. But how shall we find it?"

She halted, and held up her hand. Her horse stamped. The sounds about and above them had gone, replaced by tall shapes that stood immoveable and dimly seen. "The mist clears," she said. "The Forest has found us."

He looked about, and gasped. She was correct. Even as they spoke the mist thinned and vanished. There was no sign of the moorland crags. About their path stood ancient trees, tall beyond wonder, their trunks thicker than he could have embraced were his arms twice as long. Great oaks massed about the path, their limbs sweeping above their heads as if reaching out to each other. Each might have concealed a host of men within their foliage, and it seemed as if the two riders sat amidst a green tunnel bored deep through the woodland realm. The boy could not see the sky beyond shards of blue that seemed cut in the high canopy by thin shafts of sun that fell, dappling the forest floor here and there with golden light and shadow. The trees stretched in all directions. Before them the road drove straight, its flagstones weathered and cracked, worn smooth in many places or pushed apart by weeds and creeping growth. The forest lay utterly still.

The Lady spoke, startling the boy. "The old road will carry us for a league onward, and then we will come to a crossroads. Beyond this is the clearing where Calogrenant took counsel with the giant, and by his words thus found *Le Val sans Retour*, the Valley of No Return. There we shall find the Fountain of Barenton, and summon its Guardian. The valley is sacred to the fey, and there are many strange wonders therein, but with luck we may find guidance."

He frowned. "My way lies further north. I think it is not many leagues to the edge of the Forest, where the Irish drove my Father's men to battle. I would search for his path there."

She spoke as if she had not heard him. "Beyond the Fountain we will find Loudine's Castle. Perhaps your Father sought sanctuary there. We will see how the Forest stands, and in which direction he might have journeyed. In any case, we can take shelter, and food." She urged her horse forward.

"Why is it called the Valley of No Return?" he called after her.

She spoke without turning round. "Only the faithless may have fear. It is a witching place, but those who have kept faith, as we have, will come to no harm."

With a twitch of the reins, he hurried to catch her up. The silence of their initial entrance had given way to birdsong, and the rustle of creatures in the undergrowth. The air had grown warmer, and small clouds of insects buzzed in the shafts of sunlight. He kept a look out for game they might catch, although he knew it was unlikely that they would be in the wood for more than a day or two, so greatly had it been reduced by the depredations of woodsmen, and the axes that sought ever more timber for the King's castles and hilltop fastnesses.

"Are you in truth Gawain's daughter?" he asked as he drew level with his companion. "In tales he has only sons."

The Lady looked at him. Her eyes, which had appeared so fathomless a black in the shadows of the inn, held again sparks of gold deep within that seemed to burn like the brightest of fires. Without a word, she lifted a bow that was hitched to her saddle and, in one swift movement nocked an arrow and lifted it toward him.

He caught his breath, and made to dodge, but she continued raising it, and loosed her arrow at a bough that twisted like a mighty serpent above his head. With barely a whisper, the shaft sank to its feathers in the ancient wood. He stared at it, heart pounding, and then looked back down at the Lady. Her eyes flashed with merriment as she replaced the bow at her side.

"Not for nothing was my Father called 'the Maiden's Knight.' My mother was Princess Aigneis, daughter to King Tradelmant of Wales. The May Hawk seduced her, and left her shamed with me. She was sent to the nunnery at Deva, and I was raised by a Lady in Waiting. Yet I am my Father's daughter. His strength waxed and waned with the Sun, a gift I have inherited." She gazed up at the flickering canopy above their heads.

"Though her face is hidden from us, I know the sun is at noon for I have the strength of three!" And then, laughing, with a flick of the reins her horse surged forward into a gallop, and she raced ahead down the broad road. After a last gaze of wonder at the buried arrow, the boy followed her.

Several times, as they rode, they were forced to take detours from the path. In places tangles of undergrowth had spread across the way, and fern lapped like a tide of green water at the ankles of forest giants, obscuring the ground in all directions. At other times the trees themselves had fallen, blocking their way with sweeping limbs that had carried lesser trees down with them, littering the forest with the wreckage of gnarled trunks. Shrouds of moss hung like curtains upon them, or walls of earth and stone reared up where roots had torn from the soil like the upturned hulks of shipwrecks and now rested a score of feet overhead. At such times, as heat lay trails of perspiration down the boy's face, and thick bodied flies buzzed in emerald clouds about the close standing trunks, they spent many minutes threading their way around the obstacles, searching for the path beyond, and would often only stumble upon it by chance as they dragged themselves from clutching brambles, or spied fragments of broken stone poking from among fern or jutting from beneath the soil, and it seemed then as if it had been abandoned many centuries, not the few decades since the boy knew regular passage had ceased.

"How is this possible?" he said, after the longest of one such detour, when they had been forced to dismount and lead their horses far from their intended route, while the warbling cries of unseen birds rang high overhead. "Broceliande is barely a score of miles across at its northern edge. The Emperor's road is overgrown, but runs straight and true to the farthest borders."

Nyfain wiped her face with the hem of her sleeve. The boy tried not to look at her bare arm, slender and pale, as she did so, but he noted it was scratched from thorn and bramble. No longer did she carry herself straight, or have an air of matchless

21

puissance. He wondered how far the sun had slid down the western sky, carrying her strength with it. "The Forest has no more need of men," she said, "it is slipping back into Faeryland, drawing in its borders like the horns of a snail. It has always been perilous because of where its roots lie, but axe and fire have cut its moorings, and now it drifts back the long way to the Far Country, where mortals have no sway and little understanding. The sleepers go with it, and will dream its own dreams, not those of the realms they leave behind."

They came to the clearing two hours later. For the first time since entering the gorge the boy had a clear look at the cloudless sky. Heat fell upon them as if tipped from the blue expanse. The boy loosened his cloak, and the Lady cast back her hood. Her golden hair lay in damp strands about her shoulders. As their horses picked their way across the grass, the boy half expected to see the coarse figure of the giant rise from its rest to confront them. But they saw nothing, and heard nothing beyond a breeze that never seemed to reach them sighing in the branches.

They rode on, taking now a path that descended towards the valley. It emerged onto a wooded ridge, and then sank sharply through hawthorn and ash. Away through the trees, they could see a ruined and overgrown tower. The boy wanted to investigate, but Nyfain cautioned against leaving the path at this point, so they turned away from its brooding, ivy clad shoulders, and continued downward.

Finally, they emerged, hot and scratched from the press of ragged thorns, onto a broad meadow. A lone pine, its dark leaves casting the ground about into cool shadow, stood in the centre. At one side a long, pale stone lay where it had fallen.

Leaving their horses to graze, they approached the stone. Strange characters were engraved upon the surface, angular marks that spelled words the boy couldn't read, and the curved, looping shape of a labyrinth, worn almost to nothing. He ran his fingers through the twisting, shallow lines. Before he reached the end, Nyfain, noticing what he was doing, seized his fingers in her grasp, and lifted his hand from the groove. He was startled as much by the cool touch of her fingers as her action. He looked at her.

"Sometimes, it is best to leave the past to its dreaming. This is an ancient thing, and its thoughts are not our own." She let go his hand, and walked away. He glared at her back, feeling like a rebuked child. Then his attention was caught by a glint of light from within the tree's shadow. He glanced at Nyfain, but she was a dozen yards away, kneeling to examine something in the grass.

He approached the tree. The trunk was sticky with pine, and the air was strong with the scent of it. Above, branches shimmered in the drowsy heat, and the buzz of bees drifted down. Beside the roots was a circular spring. The water bubbled and stirred as if boiling, though no steam rose, and he felt no heat. Above his head, half hidden among the sweet smelling leaves, hung a golden basin. He reached up, and reverently lifted it down. It was a bowl with figures chased and beaten around the rim, leaping and curling around a figure that sat cross-legged by a wide tree. Horns like a stag's rose from its brow to merge with the branches, and hooded eyes like discs of gold stared into the boy's. He had never seen an object so beautiful, nor so precious.

He turned to call out to Nyfain, but she was a distance away, tugging the remains of a shield from the grass. It was tarnished and broken, and she turned it this way and that if trying to determine the device upon it.

He looked back at the marvellous basin, and struggled to remember the tales he had heard. He knelt and filled it from the spring. As he guessed, there was no fire nor heat in the water, yet still it bubbled and boiled as if alive. In the stories, water was poured upon the stone to summon the Guardian of the fountain, whom Nyfain desired to question. Thinking to find more favour with her than he had so far, he carried it back to the long stone with its graven letters and ancient patterns, and poured out the water. As it fell, it darkened the moss and bleached stone to an angry grey.

There came a long, low rumble in the sky, far off over the forest. He looked up, shielding his eyes. There was a darkness on the horizon, reaching towards them.

The Lady, still crouching, stared at it with a frown. Then her head whipped round, and as her gaze took in the boy standing by the stone, upturned bowl in hand, her eyes widened, and her hand flew to her mouth. "What have you done? Have you drenched the stone with the Fay's waters?" Her face wore a look of dismay.

"I would call the Guardian for you to question," the boy stammered, "as did Sir Yvain. Or how shall we find our path?"

"The Guardian is here!" she gestured at the ground, and the broken shield in her hand, "Did you learn naught from your Grandmother's tales?"

He made to reply, but a peal of thunder broke from directly overhead, and he flinched. A great cloud like mountains piled upon mountains rose above them, devouring the blue sky as it climbed leagues into the heavens, black as midnight and boiling with fury. Shocked, he looked at Nyfain open mouthed.

"The spell!" she shouted, "The incantation upon the stone must be recited as the water is poured! Quickly!"

I cannot read it, he wanted to say, but even as she called the light failed. It became so dark that the boy thought night had fallen. Another crash of thunder burst around them, and with it the gale howled upon them from the north, bringing sheet after sheet of rain so fierce he was drenched in an instant. Caught unawares, he was almost blown from his feet. Only the stone, against which he fell, kept him upright. The bowl flew from his hands and vanished in the darkness. "Nyfain! Lady!" he tried to shout, but the words were snatched away. Rain drove into his face as he staggered to his feet, squinting to see where she was.

24

He thought a scream was carried to him on the wind, then another, but he could not tell if it were his companion, or the sound of some unearthly creature caught high in the tumultuous air.

There came another crash, and the world lit from horizon to horizon. For a second the meadow was illuminated like a graven image, all colour and movement subsumed to the stark lightning. He saw their horses, captured in full gallop toward the treeline, scattering their possessions as they fled in panic. He saw trees yawing and pitching like ships driven on a storm-tossed sea. And thirty feet away, he saw in horror that Nyfain struggled with something in the grass that clutched her legs, and strove to climb from its broken bed to embrace her. Then the darkness fell back.

He thought he ran, but it was a stumbling, half staggered walk, buffeted from his path by the howling gale that threatened to carry him away as he forced himself headfirst into it. He drew his uncle's knife, though it was not even a foot long and the wind threatened to tear it from his grasp, forcing him to grip the hilt with both hands. Another flash of lightning broke from the sky, this time a bolt that seared his vision as it crashed amid trees to the east. Flame burst upwards from its passage, and the ground shook.

A figure fell against him. It was Nyfain, hair whipping like cords in the wind. He lost his balance, and they fell even as she clutched at his tunic and mouthed soundless words in his face. Behind her a dark silhouette swayed in the wind. It held aloft a sword, broken six inches from the point but still formidable. Even as the boy stared over Nyfain's shoulder, heart pounding and breath rasping in terror, it swung down.

Without a second thought, he pushed her to the side. The wind seized her and threw her to the ground. Arms shaking, he met the blade with his own knife. He was no fighter, and even though the blow lacked force, his hands stung with the impact. He was driven to his knee, panting. The knight took a halting step forward, and again swung his sword overheard.

The boy hurled himself away, slashing at the man's knee. It rang hollowly, and a shudder went up the boy's arm. Another flare of lightning split the meadow. The knight stood poised, armour broken and rusted. Several yards distant, Nyfain knelt amid the grass, face upturned to the merciless sky. Her eyes were closed and she was shouting into the gale with outstretched arms. Only fragments reached him, strange barked syllables that meant nothing, as if the wind were tearing them asunder and reassembling them in alien shapes. Sodden sleeves clung to her slender arms and flapped wildly in the wind. Darkness toppled over them once more, and the boy slipped and slid as he tried to stand, but it was all but impossible as wind and rain pitched and hurled like an angry sea about him.

The knight was upon him. As the boy crouched in the storm's teeth a shape loomed out of the darkness and seized his tunic. Steel fingers twisted at his throat, digging in his skin. His eyes went wide. Never had he felt such strength. He was lifted from his feet, and the fabric knotted like a garrotte about this neck. He hammered on the knight's arm, and tried to grip the man's wrist, but could find no purchase on the slick metal. It felt as immoveable as an oak.

He began to choke. He couldn't twist from the knight's grasp. Air wheezed through his straining lungs. Light sparked across his vision, and the sky and the trees and the rain began to wheel in his sight, anchored by the dark, implacable figure that stood before him, and even now drew back his arm to bring the sword down upon the boy's head.

With the last of his strength he jumped—setting both feet against the knight's chest, he pushed himself back with all his might. For once the wind was his ally, and he was hurled backwards. He flew a dozen feet, and then the ground rose, hammering the last breath from his body.

As he lay gasping, he felt the tightness still at his throat. He realised the mailed gauntlet was still entangled in the fabric, splinters of white bone shimmering amid the darkness and rain. He tore it away in horror. A few paces away the outline of the knight was bent, tugging the sword from where it had embedded itself in the earth.

Lightning flared again. The boy cried out as fury split the air between them. The ground shook as a bolt seared overhead and struck the great pine tree. With a shattering detonation it split. The boy rolled on his face and covered his head. The world was full of fire—burning arrows of wood cut through the air, and with a whoosh the tree went up in flames, casting the meadow in leaping, garish spectacle. The knight stood pierced about with a dozen flaming brands. Even as the boy watched the flames melded into one and the figure sank to its knees, and pitched forward into the grass. With another crack the top of the tree sheered away and crashed into the meadow. Leaves flared and died in the wind's teeth. The glade was ringed with the storm's burning touch.

Nyfain knelt where the boy had seen her; slumped in the lee of the stone, arms resting upon the ground. Her hair whipped like a tangle of snakes, dark and lithe. A flame still smouldered on the hem of her gown, but she seemed heedless, insensible. With a lump in his throat the boy crawled toward her. Every muscle screamed.

"My Lady! Lady Nyfain! Are you injured?" But he could not make himself heard above the onslaught, and did not know if he did more than croak. He touched her shoulder. Slowly, her head raised. Her eyes were dull, but a spark awoke in them as she recognised him.

"You are mighty indeed," she whispered, though he could not have said how it was he heard her, "I had believed the bounds of mortal flesh would burst before the Fay's reckoning. Well I chose."

"I don't understand."

"Few of Arthur's knights could withstand the forces here marshalled, now the time of men is past. The Forest abides once more in Faeryland, and it is a realm that judges men wanton. It was a mortal's death cast down the Knight of the Fountain, and you saw how its bonds could no longer hold him. Yet, fearless, you came to succour me, though the tempest stood against you."

He was abashed. "Not fearless, Lady. I could not breathe through the terror of it. Your Father would have felt no such hesitation."

She rolled over, resting her back against the cold stone. Despite her evident exhaustion, she raised a smile. "I saw no hesitation," she said, "and true courage is not fearlessness. The fearless can never be truly courageous. Do you think my Father did not quail before the Green Knight's axe? He took his courage in his hands, and fulfilled his oath, and so his deed will live on. You have the heart of a knight." She raised her eyes from his face. "The storm passes."

He looked about them. The wind was falling. The rain became no stronger than spray on the deck of his Father's ship as it harboured against an eastern wind. Minute by minute the sky lightened even as the fires about the trees shrank. He stood, and, holding out his hand to Nyfain, helped her to her feet.

It took them an hour to find the bag that held Gawain's skull. It lay some way within the wood's margins, by the trunk of a tree split and blackened by the lightning, though it was itself unscathed. Of their horses they found no sign, though they searched and called beneath the tall trees. Some belongings they found, scattered when the horses fled, but the boy could not find his Uncle's knife, and Nyfain explained Fey had likely carried it away, disliking the cold metal. They gave the blackened armour of the Knight of the Fountain a wide berth, leaving the glade to reclaim it, and took instead an overgrown path from the far side of the meadow leading by winding degrees across the valley's far side. By the time they had completed their ascent the birds had once more broken into song, and the blue sky shone undimmed through the high canopy. Looking back, they could no longer see *Le Val sans Retour*. Only the burned and blackened pine, symmetry cleft by the lightning, stood like a warning above the surrounding trees. Then they turned away, descending the far side of the ridge, and it was gone.

III

Another hour passed beneath the shadow of the trees. Nyfain stooped, back bent as dusk drew light and heat from the Forest. The boy walked before her, clutching a shorn beech limb as a tall staff. It had fallen in their path as they scrambled along another bank, and seemed well suited in weight and balance to replace the one that he had lost, and he knew it would be their only defence should more of the land's natives cross their path.

Once, he climbed a tall ash in an attempt to descry the forest's margins, and see if he could find the Castle that belonged to the Fountain's Guardian, although he no longer believed they would find anyone within. Instead, he saw the Forest spreading unchecked to every horizon, and nearly fell in surprise, for the Broceliande he knew was but a fraction of the green ocean that now harboured them, its summits lusher and more expansive than any forest he could conceive between the two seas. His eyes were wide when he re-joined Nyfain upon the forest floor, while hers shone with the secret amusement he had come to recognise.

Night had fallen by the time they reached the castle. Tall lamps wreathed in a pale, flickering light glowed on staves by the crumbled wall, reflecting from an oily water that lapped sullenly about their feet.

The boy touched the staves. They had the aspect of stone, but were warm and felt like wood. The water glowed with their strange light, the breeze forming eddies that carved the light into brittle fireflies, skating across the unquiet surface. He looked through the gates. Nothing remained intact. Streets of broken walls curved away, blocks of fallen masonry projecting here and there from the water that flowed sluggishly around them. Empty windows opened on roofless spaces. It seemed as if a lake had arisen beneath the Castle, and was slowly mounting the walls and buildings.

"The land has no more need of it," Nyfain whispered as she stepped past the boy into the Castle grounds.

Together they splashed through the streets until they reached the motte. It rose out of the water into the night sky, and the boy supposed that Loudine's Keep sat upon it, but he could see nothing but a tangle of vegetation, and a dark, irregular shape that loomed into the sky. Casting about, they found overgrown steps, and ascended.

The keep was nothing except a swaying mass of ivy. Brute, and square, the stone was hidden by leaves and crawling vines that squirmed and wrapped about the blunt silhouette. Nyfain touched the boy's arm, and pointed. A lone window, high above, was illuminated by a flickering within, as if by firelight. "The Lord's chamber. We may find answers there."

"I begin to doubt my Father ever came this way." The boy gazed at the leaping, glowing light. "Perhaps it is he, but I fear another trick of this phantom realm. Let me go first, Lady. There is no love here for those who follow in knightly footsteps."

They found the doors, once stout but now devoured by briar, and edged inside, feeling their way up the crumbling steps. The boy went first, using his staff to probe the stone as they ascended from floor to floor, wary of the tangle of roots beneath their feet. In places he could not tell the difference between wood and stone, and it seemed indeed as if the building were being transformed stone by stone into a gnarled wooden thing. On each floor they peered into rooms, but all were devoid of anything that suggested human occupancy. Root and thorn devoured the galleries and bedchambers, and only moonlight through vacant windows, or holes where masonry had plummeted to the ground, lit their passage. Twice they heard sounds from outside. The boy thought he heard something passing high in the air above them, a whirr of wings turning in a turbulent updraft, and he wondered if it arced and fell in the forest beyond the Castle. The second time there was a rattle of stones, and the rustle of undergrowth as if a body were forcing its way through the watery streets.

Each time he rushed to the nearest window, and strained his eyes to see, but the glowing lights that stood here and there about the town cast everything beyond their radiance into impenetrable darkness, devoid of sound or motion. On the second occasion, as he made to turn back, he thought he saw a sinuous line snaking through the black water that circled the foot of the motte, but it passed from sight around a half eroded bridge, and he thought not to trouble Nyfain with his fears as she stood, face lined and wan beneath the moon's silver light.

Finally, they reached the floor from which the fire had shone, and were confronted by a darkened hallway. Doors were gone, ragged holes betraying the presence of chambers that smelled of soil and rain. But at the end a pair of tall doors stood firm against the dark and damp. Light leaked around their edges.

The boy strode forward and tried to open them. They would not give in the smallest degree, but when Nyfain set her hands upon them, and pushed, they opened with ease. He looked within, and gasped.

Never had he seen such a richly appointed room. Tapestries hung in hues of red and brown and emerald, and a golden canopied bed occupied the room's centre. Logs burned high in the grate, and silver goblets sat by ornately carved chairs. A golden cage rose on a stand near the door, its occupant a nightingale that cocked its head to regard them as they stood in the doorway.

"The Lady's bower," whispered Nyfain.

"But how is this possible? The building is abandoned. This is enchantment, and we should be wary."

"We must always be wary in Broceliande," Nyfain stepped into the room, "but here, at least for now, I believe we are welcome." She went to warm herself by the fire.

"Perhaps. Yet there are things here which do not love us," and he remembered the movement of the water in the moat, and the sound of wings beating in the air. Leaving Nyfain to the fire, he opened the door to a side room, and was greeted with the sight of a chamber laid for a feast. Sweetmeats and pastries, cheeses and cold meats all stood on a small table as if freshly laid. His stomach knotted with hunger, and he reached for a freshly cut cob of bread.

Nyfain was at his shoulder. He felt her light touch on his arm. "Remember your own warning. The generosity of the Fay is rarely without condition. Food and drink especially." He put down the bread with reluctance.

"I must rest," she said. "You must keep watch upon the hall."

He looked back through the main door. The hallway was dark and ruined as they had left it. The fire's heat felt glorious upon his freezing limbs and damp clothes, and he was loath to abandon it.

"Surely no knight would compromise a Lady's virtue so?" Nyfain smiled at the reluctance on the boy's face. "I would divest myself of these worn garments, and leave them to dry awhile against the fire. There seem no others here."

Unbidden, a memory came to him; her body, curves outlined as the rain and wind smoothed her soaking gown against her. His face grew hot, and to his discomfit he saw the humour return to her lips. He clenched his jaw, and dismissed the image.

"I am no knight, but I shall watch." He picked up the staff he had leaned against a chair, and then, with a thought, tested a carving knife from the dining table. Its blade shone red in the flickering light, and the edge was keen under his thumb. With a curt nod, and with his face still glowing under Nyfain's amused gaze, he dragged a chair to the hallway, and sat, back to the door. Before he could settle, he was startled by a touch on his arm, and realised she had followed him.

"None would gainsay you that name," she said, and he saw that she bound a white scarf about his wrist, patterned with the outline of a hawk. "And for your chivalry, you may wear my favour, so all may know you for the May Hawk's champion."

He stared at it, and felt his tongue cleave to the roof of his mouth. His heart thumped in his chest, and he looked up at her again, as, smiling, she stepped back into the bedchamber, and with a toss of her hair, closed the two doors.

An hour passed. He remained at his vigil, lost in thought. His eyes became used to the scant light, but he fought to keep them open as he stared into the unchanging dark. Eventually, he rose and, pacing the length of the hall, peered into the empty rooms, their crumbling stone and mildewed furnishings lit only by moonlight. Nothing stirred, and he returned to his seat, and tried to keep his thoughts from Nyfain disrobing before the fire, or, curled, sleeping naked upon the canopied bed. Again and again, her dark eyes, shining with flecks of gold, invaded his sombre thoughts, and on such occasions he would rise, and shake his head, and walk the bounds of the ruined rooms. *Treading out his thoughts*. His Father's phrase.

At length, seated once more, he became aware of a change in the quality of the light. The silver sheen of the moon was fading, and he knew that light in the eastern sky could not be far off. And as he did so, he became aware too of a sound. Something clinking, like coins sliding across metal, and the sound of a long, slow breath that came like a wave hissing upon a stony shore. He rose. So lost in his thoughts had he been that he had no idea how much time had passed since the sound began, but it was getting louder, approaching up the stairs, a long, slow susurration that drew nearer moment by moment. With his stave in hand, and the knife thrust through his tunic he walked down the hallway to the

33

stairwell.

A smell of rancid water assailed him. The stairwell was in darkness, but something shimmered at the far end, something that caught the faint light of stars and moon and twisted it into a mosaic of shifting colour. It halted, and there came a sigh as something rose into the air and wavered, a beast taking scent before it struck. It was still some way below, and he risked a glance behind, to ensure Nyfain had not emerged from the bower.

The staff was torn from his hands, and snapped in two. The pieces went spinning back down the stairs. Rearing in front of the boy was a long, serpentine face on a sinuous neck that stretched backward into darkness. Frills like hair hung from its sides, and a thick, steaming tongue curled about ivory teeth. Eyes like emerald discs narrowed as they looked down on him.

The boy hurled himself backwards, rolling as the fanged head struck at the floor. As he did so he pulled the knife from his tunic, and in desperation dived forwards, under the weaving head that even now was raising itself for another strike. Curling himself into a ball, he rolled down the steps, and thudded into the body of the beast that curved serpentine around the stairwell. Without hesitation, he drove the knife into the creature's soft and slimy belly.

He was sprayed with ichor as it jerked backwards with a bellow. As the beast snaked back and forth the boy was caught in its escape and tumbled head first down the stairs. Together they scraped and fell to the bottom, the boy snared in a chaos of scales and limbs and a foul pungent stench. He tried to grab the knife hilt, but his hands and face were slick with blood and he could find no purchase. Then he was crushed against the door frame as the creature fled from the keep and hurled itself towards the brackish water. It was only then that the boy realised the cords of his tunic were caught about the knife, and he was dragged after the beast.

He hit the ground with an impact that drove all the air from his body, skidding across the wet turf as he tried to dig in his heels and slow his progress. Light had grown around them, and he caught glimpses of the whole sinuous form of the scaled creature as it slid down the motte, half lizard and half snake, with cruel and curving teeth, short arms and the long, lashing body of a great serpent. He heard a shout from above, and guessed that Nyfain had come to the window. Before he could notice more, he was plunged into the freezing water.

He had thought the water not deep—they had walked calf deep through it—but he was submerged in an instant, and felt as if the creature were diving fathoms down. In truth, it could have been no more than a scant few feet before he scraped upon the decaying flagstones of the sunken street, and more air was crushed from his lungs.

He felt the creature twist and buck as it tried to loosen him. Jaws closed inches from his face as he wrestled to pull his knife from the beast's hide. Razor claws slashed at him, and all the while his lungs burned as he wrenched it this way and that, seemingly to no effect. He felt it grate deep in bone.

Taking a different tack, the creature surged back into the air. Wings unfurled, dark green scales dripping with water glowed in the light of the rising sun. The boy fell gasping against a broken wall as its head shot toward him. He jammed his arm into the jaws as they tried to seize him. Eyes huge as plates stared into his own as its jaws came closer and closer and his arm and shoulder screamed in agony. With all his might he wrestled to pull the knife free, but the handle was slick with weed and blood, and he succeeded only in slicing his own hand.

With a last resolve, he drew back his arm, and hammered his fist upon the knife hilt, driving the blade further and further until the hilt was buried in the hide. The creature shrieked, covering the boy in phlegm and rancid breath, and then launched itself upward. Its whole bulk exploded into the air as wings unfurled to their full extent, dragging it upward. The boy was torn from his position by the fallen wall, and hurled aloft, feeling as if the cord would cut him in two. Somehow it had become tangled around the monster's forelimb, and he now trailed from a tangle of knots. He spun into the air as wings pounded and claws dug at the sky, helpless in the grip of the creature's terrible strength. Higher and higher he was carried.

With a twang, an arrow shot passed him and split the cord. The monster sprang upwards, and the boy fell back, tumbling with a cry into the water. He rose to the surface, coughing and spluttering, heaving to spit the foul liquid from his mouth. Feeling as if a dead weight of iron held down his limbs, he dragged himself to the motte, and hauled his aching and bloodied body upon the grass. Then he lay flopped over onto his back, and watched the great serpent vanishing high over the trees westward, in a loping and erratic flight that he hoped was caused by the injury he had done. He drew deep, shuddering breaths.

"Again, you emerge victorious." He shaded his eyes with his hand, and saw Nyfain standing, midday between him and the tower. He thought of his ruined clothes, and what miserable aspect he must present. For once, he did not care. He had saved her from the serpent. She stood in the rays of the rising sun, hair aflame and eyes shining. Her rich gown and cloak showed no sign of having ever been soiled by storm or contest. Her left hand held her bow, which he had thought lost in the *Valley of No Return*. He clambered to his feet and stood, swaying, dripping weed and water. Blood ran from his scored arms and dripped from his battered brow. Somehow, it did not matter. He straightened. Every bone ached, yet she spoke truly. He had fought, and won.

"And you have conquered beneath my favour." She looked into his eyes; in hers the strange golden glitter moving once more amid the black. He raised his arm, and saw her device was still there, though bloodied and torn. "Thus you are my

Champion indeed. And therefore shall I name you, by my right. I call you *Annant*. From the waters. For twice you have fought amid inundation, and twice you have prevailed. Water carries you, and water shall succour you, and no water shall you or your kin fear to the hundredth generation." And he wondered then, for it seemed her stature and her bearing was greater than his own, and her face more yet more beautiful and mysterious than he remembered.

"But come," and she smiled, and held out her hand. "Water may not harm you, but it may discomfort. The fire still burns above. You must dry yourself, and we must prepare for our final trial."

"Trial?" The boy shook his head. "My trials here are over. We have sought the Valley, and the Castle, and in neither have we found your answers or my hope. I will dry my clothes, and then we shall head for the Forest's edge, in whichever direction that may lie. I have avoided my duty for too long. Einion has need of me, as does my sister Grania."

"Nay, you have avoided nothing, for we have both answers and hope. The dragon has shown us the way. Come, and witness." And smiling, Nyfain took his hand, and led him back to the high chamber.

The boy was full of doubt, and weary beyond belief, but the light of her smile, and the touch of her warm hand, sent a thrill through his body, and he seemed to gain new strength, following her willingly. In the room the fire burned as bright as the previous evening, and he stood and warmed himself whilst she drew back the shutters on the western window, and pointed. He joined her, and looked out.

Far to the west, in the direction that the dragon had taken, a hill rose from the mist. Around the summit a great shape like unto a serpent was carved from chalk upon the green sward, shining in the dawn. Above the serpent, upon the crest of the hill a long mound stood, capped with tall stones. As they watched, the sun rose higher and its rays wove gold strands upon the granite blocks. A device stood out, plucked from the cold stone by some unfathomable illumination; a sword, point uppermost, clutched by a slender hand that rose from water.

"The dragon shows the way, to those that sleep."

IV

It was noon when they reached the hill. The boy no longer questioned that the path which snaked about the tall trees was suitable only for travel by foot. No other paths rose to distract them. The deep woodland, shadowed by beech and elm, looked as impenetrable as a trackless wilderness. They walked side by side while Nyfain shared whispered stories of the Fay, and the shifting, perilous land of which they had become a part. The boy kept cautious watch through the trees, and in the blue sky, for a winged, hissing shape, but Nyfain, on noticing, told him that the dragon had served its purpose, and had now returned to the land of which it was made.

"*It is a symbol of the Forest,*" she whispered, "*our desires give such things substance, and so Broceliande is dangerous for mortals.*"

The boy protested that he had no desire to fight almost to death with such a terror, but Nyfain had merely looked sideways at him with her golden eyes, and burst into laughter. He scowled, and remained silent for long minutes after.

They reached the hill through a stand of hawthorn. The path curved into their twisting shadows, and as Nyfain and the boy clambered around the gnarled and thorn laden limbs it seemed as if they had entered some ancient dance in which they were required to perform certain steps to reach a place of safety. Birdsong ceased, and the heat soared. Again and again they were snagged on branches. The path all but vanished, but they could see the hill rising ahead of them, and were able to force their way through clutching limbs and beneath boughs that hung heavy and unwelcoming, until at last they stood at the hill's foot.

The sun was high when they emerged. A broad bank surrounded the base of the hill, rising a score of feet. They followed the curve to an entrance at the south, and the path took them over a ditch to another path that wound steeply up the hill's flank, tracking them backward and forward as they climbed toward the summit. They passed clumps of agrimony and gorse, pods crackling in the still, warm air, and the lazy, fluttering wings of green and white butterflies were the only signs of movement as they sweated beneath the high summer. The boy no longer questioned how the season had turned since they entered the Forest, nor how, standing and wiping the perspiration from his forehead, the limitless expanse of trees covered the hills and valleys as far as the eye could see. There were no signs of habitation, no signs of the great swathes driven through the forest by the hands of men, no signs that the tall trees had ever given way beneath fire and axe. It was an untouched land, and only the hilltop carving, and the long mound that the two made their way toward—the boy heaving for breath and bent double at his exertions, the woman striding carelessly and without effort—showed purposeful design in any feature or place of the enigmatic land.

Finally, they stood on the dragon's head, its long snout carved in brilliant white across the summit of the hill. Before them a great tumulus stood, sides bare of grass, chalk blinding in the noon sun. The great stones they had seen from the keep blocked the entrance, alternating triangular blocks with tall fingers of stone that glittered with quartz. There was no sound; the air contracted around them until the world consisted only of Annwyl and Nyfain, side by side before the impassive rock that flung the noonday heat back in their faces. Everything seemed to wait.

They drew closer. The carving that they had seen so clearly illuminated from the keep was hard to find, worn almost to nothing, scored by lichen to blotches of white and black. Nyfain ran her fingers across the surface, and the boy marvelled at her surety as she traced the shallow grooves of the sword's edge down, down to the slender hand that rose and clutched it.

"How do we enter?" he said, for he had no doubt that this represented the end of their quest. The stone was twice as broad as he, and would have dwarfed any man he knew.

"It must move aside," Nyfain replied, "see here, and here, there are grooves upon the soil."

"But not with such strength as we can muster. I would swear a score of men must have laboured here."

"Then you and I must suffice," she smiled, "and thank my Father for the May Hawk's gift."

He looked at her in wonder as she set her bag down on the grass, and, tossing her hair from her face, set her grip about the stone's edge. Her back arched and it seemed as if her fingers clave to the stone itself as she braced her legs and wrenched the stone outward.

Inch by inch it groaned across the grass. The boy leapt forward to help, but felt as if his efforts were wholly ineffectual, and it was Nyfain, eyes closed and face rapt in concentration, who was channelling all her might and willpower to bend the stone to her will, fingers stretched like talons into the warding rock. Gradually it opened.

When they had cleared a space large enough to slip through, they let go of the stone and looked at each other. Taking the lead, the boy squeezed through the space. He felt Nyfain's warm breath on his neck as he stood within, and knew that she had joined him. The transition from warm sun to the cold grip of earth and stone was abrupt. A passage led into the heart of the barrow. The floor was bare chalk, but the walls were dry stone. Side chambers opened at regular intervals, cloaked in darkness. The boy was not surprised to see that torches in iron sconces burned at the entrance way. He lifted them, and turning, handed one to Nyfain. Then he made to enter the passage.

Nyfain spoke from behind him. "Our ways part here."

The boy gaped at her. The light set half her face in shadow. Her eyes burned with a strange intensity. "But...what do you mean? We have come so far, we must not give up."

She shook her head. "It is a separate fortune that lies before us." She held up her bag. "I will lay my Father. You have come to find yours."

The boy was bitter. "My Father is not here. Has never been here. My errand was folly and Einion was right. I have failed those who relied on me."

"No quest has been greater than the one you have undertaken," she replied. "And by your actions, you have saved, not failed, them. But now we part."

"No. Wait, no, I can help you," he stammered, his heart in his throat. "I can help you search. It is too dangerous. You cannot fight, you have no weapons."

She put her hand on his chest, as if to feel the hammering of his heart, and forestall his objections. He felt the heat of her hand through his tunic. "I have all the weapons I need, as do you. This is not a place for steel or sharp blades. This test belongs to each of us alone, and we must find our own conclusion. Now I go to find the cave of the sleepers."

"But so do I!" Desperation crept into his voice, "I have come to find Arthur the King, to wake him so he may save his country!"

Her face softened. "Do you? Is that what you have learned?" She held him with her eyes, burning gold and black in the flickering torchlight. She seemed ageless.

His gaze dropped. He was silent for long moments. He knew the truth in his heart, and shook his head. "Arthur cannot save us. We must forge new kingdoms, not return to those that have gone. It is his example that will sustain us, not his sword. The Land remembers him, and for those who do likewise, it will be enough."

There was silence. Her hand fell to her side. "Now kiss me," she said. "for it is farewell."

Shocked, he looked up. "But…I am not…you are a King's daughter," he began, but she placed a finger to his lips.

"Would you deny me the gift that Lady Bertilak sought of Gawain?" Her eyes held the same familiar amusement. "We are neither of us promised, and may therefore bid each other farewell as Knight and his Lady."

And she drew close to him, and smiled. With his heart in his mouth, he drew himself up, and, closing his eyes, leaned forward and touched his lips to hers. And his senses fled as he was assailed by her presence. She tasted of summer breezes, and orchards, and long hours of sunshine lying amid the harvest. She tasted of mint blowing on cliff tops, and the smell of heather, and pine, and the scythed grass laid fresh for the May. And she tasted of birdsong and honey and starlight. And then, shocked, he opened his eyes, and she was gone.

With joy and sadness mingled he made his way along the passage, ignoring the side turnings. He knew they did not mark his path, and so he headed on into barrow's depths, his light held high. He walked for many minutes, further he knew than the barrow stretched, and it seemed to him that he descended, and as he did so the floor became smoother, and the walls higher and made of such stones he believed only giants could lift. And other passages depended from the one he walked, and in the flickering light he thought he could see shapes move within. Eyes stared from darkness, and cold things shifted and lifted their heads, but were ancient and possessed no strength to leave their beds. On he hurried, leaving behind whispers that carried words he could not understand, faint and helpless. Yet sounds grew stronger as he went, and from other chambers he began to hear cries, and the clash of iron. Voices called out, repeating names he could not recognise, pleas to brutal men or prayers to hungry gods, he could not tell which. He stopped, and shone his torch into one chamber from which came the sound of infants crying, and harsh trumpets, but he could only see shifting shapes that seemed to struggle and writhe beyond the torchlight. Swords struck down, and the crying ceased. He hurried on.

He heard other sounds. Feet marching, and the jingle of harness. From one chamber he heard the twang of a bow, and a woman scream. He leapt inside, but saw only shelves of rock, and the jumble of bones and pots. When he turned back there was a man in the doorway, dark haired and with his face painted. He spoke, his dialect thick and his words guttural, hard to comprehend.

"Come with us boy. This is dead, join us," but the boy lowered his head, and pushed passed the figure, feeling it give way before him, and hurried on down the passage.

At another turning there were steps down into a courtyard. Paintings decorated the walls, and statues stood with water spouting from iron throats. Beyond, he could see a blue sea and cloudless sky. A family sat on benches arranged upon a floor with coloured tiles in images and patterns of strange beasts and gods. Fruit and meats covered bowls of metal, and they held goblets that he knew were of glass or crystal. He had heard of such things, but never seen one. A woman looked up at him, and gestured to an empty seat beside her. He felt an overwhelming desire to sit with them, to taste the food and drink, and rest amid those fine things he knew the world no longer possessed. He took a step forward, and the family looked at him expectantly. A man entered, and the boy started at the likeness to his own family. The two stood facing each other, and then the boy shook his head. The man gave a smile, and nodded, and the tableau faded into darkness even as he walked on.

Finally, he emerged into yet another chamber. Great horses stood, their heads bowed, upon a floor strewn with hay. On the far wall hung shield after gleaming shield. He recognised the devices of many knights—Drustan, Cai, Yvain, Bedwyr, and others. With a thrill of recognition, he saw there too the device of Gwalchmai, the Hawk of May, and wished with all his heart that he could find Nyfain within. With reverence, he approached them, and saw beyond another wide passage descending. A marvellous light shone from its depths, glorious and effulgent, and he guessed at once it led to the cave of the Sleepers. With a deep breath he walked toward it.

"Son."

He turned. His Father stood by another passage. He still wore the salt encrusted cloak the boy had watched him clasp to his shoulders a scant few days before, and carried the same staff and sword at his belt. His face was lined with the cares the boy remembered, but bore a kindly expression.

With a cry the boy ran to him, and, heedless, hugged him both as a son and as a friend, and his Father hugged him back, and smiled and looked into his face.

"So I spoke well," he said, "I left a man behind when I rode west."

The boy smiled, though tears ran down his face. "I knew I would find you. I knew you would come back."

"Aye, and through doubt and fear you never wavered. I know that. Many trials have you conquered, and you'll face more, never doubt that. But they'll not be ones you can't master. You'll see."

A thought struck the boy, and he looked around. "I didn't conquer them alone, I had help. The Lady Nyfain, the May Hawk's daughter. Is she here?" he asked eagerly. "Have you seen her?"

"She has gone to the sleepers." He nodded towards the far passage. "Her Father dreams now with his fellows."

"Then she can come with us! Let me fetch her."

Galwyn let go of his son. "You have learned more wisdom than that, I think. Some things break our hearts, whichever choice we make."

The boy stood, arms at his side. He looked around at the radiant light, and then at his Father's sombre face. His heart sank. "Neither of you may come with me?"

His Father put his hand on his shoulder, as he had in the cold night in the inn. "It is your choice, Annwyl. You may stay here, with us, or you may go forward, alone, to a world of struggle and hardship."

"Then it is the world that needs me." And he felt his Father's grip tighten, and the man nodded his approval. "May I not say goodbye?" he said, with a glance behind.

His Father smiled. "You have said goodbye, I think. Without words."

"Will I see her again?"

"That is not for me to say. Her blood is not that of normal men. You're her champion. Chivalry demands it, even as the heart desires."

The boy straightened his back. "Then I shall go back to now to our land, and our home, and help as I can."

"Come with me," said his Father, and led him to the passage that spiralled upward. By it stood his Father's horse, still saddled and bridled as if for travel. "Take Doane, he will never lead you awry. And take this also." And he unbuckled the sword that had been passed down in his family from the days of the legions, and handed it to his son, who stared at it in wonder. "This will be yours, and by its mark you will carry our leadership and truth."

And they hugged each other again, and with tears pricking in his eyes, but with a great joy in his heart, the boy took Doane's reins, and led the horse up the long wide passage way. And soon he no longer needed the torch as the darkness turned to grey, and the grey soon turned to the bright light of the afternoon sun, and Annwyl emerged from between the tall stones that ringed Rook Tor, where he knew his Father and his men had made their final stand. To the west the setting sun stood a hand's breadth above the horizon.

As Annwyl led his horse to the road, there came a shout from behind. It was Einion, and Devin beside him, riding toward them with wonder and gladness on their faces.

"By God, Annwyl, you're alive! Where have you been? A fortnight we've been looking. The men have gone ahead, but we would not leave. Devin said you might have come here, after tidings of your Father. But we could not have hoped to find you, thank God you're safe! This is not a good place to be riding alone."

The boy pulled himself into the saddle. "Not alone. I rode with Lady Nyfain, although our ways have parted. From the inn."

Einion shook his head, bemused. "What Lady? I don't recall any Lady at the Inn."

"Lady Nyfain. Gawain's daughter. She spoke of my sister. I guessed you had talked with her."

"I did not." Einion shook his head.

Devin snorted. "Not more of this. Gawain's a hundred years dead. No daughter of his is still living. More fantasy, and us risking ourselves for it. There's no Lady, and your Father fell here fighting. We've seen his body. Enough is enough, boy."

Einion held up his hand, "He's had a hard journey, Devin."

But the boy wheeled to face them, and with a stern face threw back his cloak. The sword gleamed at his waist. "I am Annwyl Annant, son of Galwyn ap Cadan. I have returned from storm and darkness and the serpent's coils. I have journeyed to Afallon and back. I ride Doane, my Father's steed, and bear the Centurion's sword his Father gave him, and his Father before that to the days of the Romans. I wear the favour of the Lady Nyfain, the May Hawk's daughter, and I will lead our people in war and in peace, and together we will make our homes and families safe and secure. And neither the Irish nor the Saxons nor the warring kings shall take from us what is ours."

And for the first time the two of them took in the horse that Annwyl sat upon, and the sword at his side, and they stared in amazement, knowing they were in the presence of enchantment and marvel, and with new respect they bowed their heads and joined him, and together the three men took the road over the High Moor to the sea.

Sir Gawain and the Quest for Merlin's Tree

Leigh Ann Cowan

After the Battle of Camlann, where the treacherous Mordred met his end

and the great King Arthur was fatally wounded, accordingly the king

contrived to journey to the Isle of Avalon to be healed of his deadly injury.

Alas! the king, most regal of rulers, was dead before he reached the shore

of the Lake where the Lady lay in wait to receive him and to soothe his hurt.

So while Arthur freed the kingdom of Camelot from the tyranny of those

enemies, he left behind his venerable legacy, vulnerable to the dreaded Saxons.

One Sir Bedivere completed his assigned task to deliver the immortal sword

forged on the Isle itself to the murky depths of Avalon, where forevermore

that blade *Excalibur* would await, until such time that the king returned.

'Twas this knight who brought back the tidings of the king's death;

dark news indeed were Bedivere's words, for they foreshadowed the fall

of Camelot and all her people. Yet the burial of King Arthur was one most grand:

celebrated was his life, mourned was his untimely demise, and highly honored

was he.
It was only at last when
their king was entombed
that the kingdom's citizens
bethought themselves doomed.

But none were more stricken with grief than Arthur's noblest
nephew Sir Gawain:
he who wore upon his breast a token of his fidelity—a pentangle,
an endless knot
that represented the good knight's flawlessness in fives: in his
senses, and in his fingers,
in the five wounds of Christ, in Mary's five joys, and in
friendship and fraternity,
in purity and politeness, and not the least of these, in pity.
Gawain—
he who kept his head from the fabled Green Knight, and ever
after wore the object
of his shame, a girdle of green given to him from the waist of a
wily lady—
for five days he lay weeping in the darkness before his uncle's
tomb. But
at last to him came an idea: were he to discover the prison of
Merlin, the sorcerer
who to the late King Arthur was once a trusted advisor, and free
him, surely
the wizard would find himself indebted to Sir Gawain, and
would help him
restore Camelot to her former glory. Therefore 'twould be only
right that Merlin,
with whatever magic had he, bring Gawain's uncle back from his
stone-cold grave,
and with the demonic powers under Merlin's control resurrect
the man Death had

stolen.

So Gawain spent another three days
deep in prayer, with hope abiding
Mother Mary might give away
where exactly Merlin's tree be hiding.

The long hours passed, and still Sir Gawain was given no answer.
Yet from the altar he did not leave; his prayers he did not cease,
for good things come to those who are faithful, and good Gawain was
determined to receive his reward. He begged the Virgin Mary to grant him
reprieve from his bereavement, asked for this task that would send him
on a journey and save him from his reckless desire to revenge his dear uncle;
but as he meditated he came to realize that his wish to resurrect
King Arthur was an impossible one. Regardless of the great power vested
in Merlin the magician, the astronomer, the engineer, the prophet, the bard,
such power to revive a lost spirit belonged only to Christ himself.
And so Gawain amended his prayer thusly: "Mine is a graceful and giving God
to grant that I may find this legendary tree which renders the great Merlin
in an everlasting sleep. I pray that Mary, thou holy mother of Christ,
hear my plea. I ask that thou help this wretched soul appease his anger—
        I pray

for love of my uncle
who so loved his domain;
I would not see it crumble
so soon after his reign."

Finally, revelation visited Gawain in the form of a dream: in it he found himself
walking through a twilit forest, hunting an elusive white hart.
Each time Gawain spotted the beast and raised his bow, the magnificent
creature did dart silently out of sight; but never went it too far.
In this way Gawain was led to a dark clearing, where for him awaited
the animal he sought. With solemn eyes and antlers gleaming, the stag
stood regally at the center; wherein the last rays of golden sun bathed it,
and as the knight entered from betwixt the trees, his bow he lowered to his side;
the sky's yellow eye closed, hiding away beneath the dark lashes of the horizon.
And then the pale face of the moon emerged quite suddenly, and the hart reared
onto its hind legs. To Sir Gawain's awe, the milky white fur changed to
shimmering robes; the body of the animal became that of an old man's, whose
long silver beard pooled at his feet. But the antlers atop his head remained,
and grew at an alarming rate, stretching upwards and outwards like the
branches of a great oak; and indeed in the next moment the man appeared as

        a tree.

This was most certainly Merlin
the great magician, who in legend old,
was born by the seed of a demon;
it was he who Arthur's death foretold.

Sir Gawain crossed himself and thanked the Virgin Mary with
utmost gratitude;
for now he knew where he was to seek Merlin in the forest of
Broceliande, where
last he was spotted. Then he called that his bags be packed with
provisions, and his trusty
steed Gringolet brought to him rigged and ready to ride; and
Gawain was dressed in
all his trimmings and trappings as he was many a year ago when
he set out
to fulfill his vow to the Green Knight; and when he called for
them his arms were
produced and laid out for his inspection, of which Gawain made
quick work.
All of this was done before the break of brilliant dawn, so that
when the first rays of light
bathed the land, Gawain upon Gringolet's back rode out, with his
sword *Galatine*
close at hand. Nine days after the burial of the great Once and
Future King,
good Sir Gawain set out on his quest. His journey would take
him across the sea
to the lands from which Sir Lancelot hailed—that man who with
the fair Queen
Guinevere had betrayed his king and thus instigated this deadly
war that had
killed many besides the king, and by Lancelot's sword were
killed Gawain's own

three sons:
The Fair Unknown Gingalain,
as well as Sir Florence,
and same was young Lovel slain;
and so Gawain hated that prince.

To Gaul, Gawain would take a different route than did his uncle:
due south the courteous knight would travel, as far and quick as
hardy Gringolet could carry him; a trustworthy man with a good
boat would he find to take both Gawain and Gringolet across the
water;
and on would go the knight and his mount to search for Merlin
the Magician,
Albion's only hope, God willing. Sir Gawain the Maidens'
Knight might have gone
east to Amesbury to visit his dear uncle's wife at her nunnery,
but in his mind
he had no time to spare, no matter his love for his aunt by
marriage. She
Gawain did not blame for her infidelity, for despite her flaws she
was virtuous
and kind and repentant; and her plight struck a chord in him that
reminded him of his
own mother. Aloud spoke he of his plans to sturdy Gringolet,
who understood his words and so did not need to be steered; with
an impeccable
sense instilled in him since birth, the horse carried Gawain fast,
hooves thundering against the worn traveling road and kicking
up behind them
                    dust clouds.
        They passed merchants and messengers,
        villagers and farmers and their children,
        and though they were all to Gawain strangers,
        he greeted them each as his well-wishing brethren.

But despite the knight's courteous demeanor, his mind and heart were in great turmoil. Alone he was in the world but for his steadfast steed,
for all his blood he once loved were deceased: his mother Morgause, Queen of
Orkney, beheaded for infidelity but her lover spared; his first wife the Lady Ragnelle,
who bore him Gingalain and died; his strong brothers four all died by the sword—
Agravaine, Gaheris, Gareth, and the traitor Mordred who slew Arthur; and finally
his children. And Gawain was so overcome with grief that he bade Gringolet to stop at the
roadside. He dismounted and wept and prayed on his knees for all their souls, until
at last he mastered his emotions and resumed his journey. Gringolet he mounted,
and urged him on along the southward road until they came at last to the beginnings
of the true adventure, where the road was pounded to dust that strangled the weeds
growing along either side, and during the rainy months turned to a strip of marshland;
but now the road was soft and imprinted with the marks of many, two and four-
footed alike, and the air was serene and cool against Gawain's face, and the trees
whispered
gently amongst themselves as though
to say, "Soft! soft! There goes a man
with a wearied face and eyes of woe,
yet one with a purpose, a plan!"

Indeed, as Gawain rode out from the castle he had begun to formulate a
tactic of parley with Merlin when he had freed him from his sleeping cell—
for as the magician would be indebted to him, it would be ungracious,
at least, to reject the knight's proposal entirely; so Gawain was contented in that
he would be heard when at last he had fulfilled his quest. His plan, which
grew more zealous and formidable as Gringolet walked many miles,
was this: Merlin would graciously thank Sir Gawain for rescuing him
from his slumber, and upon hearing the news of his good friend's death
might accept it readily, for he was wise and a prophet. They would then
speak of consequences, and Gawain would carefully maneuver their colloquy
toward the Saxon invaders who oft visited south Britain, and were each time
defeated by his uncle's stern hand; yet now there was no hand to shield
Camelot from these foes—no man alone could ward off the Saxons or
else wage war against them; and that was where Gawain would try to

   flatter:
 "My lord Merlin, you are professed
 to wield awesome power;
 and with unrivalled knowledge blest.
 We are in dire need this hour!"

Of course strong-headed Gawain was so caught up in his musings on the solving
of Camelot's imminent danger that it never quite occurred to him
that he had no means of revealing Merlin's tree, for it was rumored
to be hidden from the eyes of all but she who cast the enchantment;
but the thought came suddenly to him when he laid down to sleep that night.
He worried over this dreadful revelation, and tossed and turned on
his bedroll under the stars; so tormented he was that he abandoned all
pretense of sleep and instead meditated on the matter, and then prayed for yet
another answer. Neither of these yielded result, but still Sir Gawain could not
give up his quest. When the sun peeked over the edge of the world, the knight
saddled his steed and set out once again without breaking his fast,
marking south as his direction. He thought desperately on the subject,
utilizing every last ounce of his intelligence to solve this staggering problem.
And then at last he had it: if only she who cast the spell rendered could

    see him,
   then good Gawain's only choice
   was to discover the harlot who
   captured Merlin with her voice
   and convert her to his view.

His satisfaction, however, lasted only a moment or two, for then he realized

that though he had heard allegations of a certain woman named Vivien, who

was claimed to have been the enchantress, he had heard little tell about her

except that she hailed from the kingdom of Cornwall. But if Gawain turned toward

that place then the path would take him west whereas he needed to go south and east.

Besides, there was no guarantee that Vivien would be there still.

But if he were to find someone who might know of this woman's whereabouts,

then it was all too likely that this person would live in her homeland on the southwest

end of the Great Isle. Circumstance and need decided for him: Sir Gawain steered

his companion Gringolet away from their path and turned due west, in the

direction of the Cornish kingdom. Many days would be added to the knight's

adventure, any of which could be the dawn of battle with the wild invaders—

this fear hurried Gawain, and it was only when Gringolet grew weary that they halted

for water or for a night at an accommodating monastery along the way, where he slept

       restless.

      All the while this courteous knight
      thought of what to Vivien would he say,
      and whether listen she to his plight
      would, or his hopes and pleas betray.

"Good morning, madam," said Sir Gawain aloud, for he was unpracticed in the ways one spoke to evil seductresses and so wanted to be sure of his

words long beforehand, "my gracious lady, may Mary reward you, in good faith

I find myself in great need of your service. Of your prowess in magic

I have heard many a time, and it is this that I seek in this time of urgency."

Thusly the good man intended to woo this wily woman, and when he at last won

her favor he would contrive to convince the vixen Vivien to accompany him

to the forest he sought, and there she would reveal Merlin so that he was freed;

and Gawain realized then that this plan would be a game of strategy and tact

which would his wit's tongue push to the limit. His words need be chosen with extra care,

for now he dealt with sorcerers two—and worse still, these magicians did

one another despise, surely, and Gawain did not wish to have them duel when time

was so short, especially not if Merlin were to end up on the losing side again.

And good Gringolet knew of his master's anxiety in the matter, and he took

> great pains
> to stride swift and smooth
> over the land, and he took care
> to behave as a horse very couth;
> in this regard he was rare.

So it came to be that quite soon the pair had arrived in that kingdom

called Cornwall, where reigned the aged cuckold King Mark in his high
Tintagel Castle that overlooked the sea. Now Sir Gawain knew that this
king had been an enemy to his late uncle, and it was rumored that he had
under his control a number of sorcerers—how many the knight knew not,
nor whether there was any truth to that declaration—for though King Mark
was oft blind of his wife Isolde's affair with his sister's son Tristan, it did not
stop him from having himself a paramour, who most claimed to be Vivien.
Now this game was complicated still more, for another player, the king, had entered.
It was a delicate situation indeed, and Gawain found that his masterful tongue
usually reserved to speak eloquently to the maidens of the Isle of Britain
would be hard-pressed to content all parties involved: for the King of
Cornwall surely would not want to lose such a stunning woman from his side,
nor might she wish to assist him in discovering Merlin in his tree, and still yet the
> wizard
> may aggravate his cause
> by refusing to intervene
> in an affair with flaws,
> or else fate contravene.

Despite Sir Gawain's misgivings his plan was determined. A herald he sent to ask the king of Cornwall for an audience, and he was brought inside the castle

to await his answer; and in the meanwhile he was given refreshment and his

weary body washed by the hands of a gentle servant. But even as the knight

sipped at his honeyed drink he did not relax, for the game had finally begun.

It was a long while later that a messenger returned bearing apologies, for the king

would be unable to see him that day. Gawain, ever courteous, replied that he would

wait, but in truth these tidings made him much more anxious than he was before.

He resolved, however, to wait as long as it took—and besides, he was not confined

to pine for his audience in his guest chambers; so Gawain took to wandering the halls

hoping to meet with the Lady Vivien, or else to hear tell of her whereabouts and

whether she was present at the castle at all, or if she had gone to live in another place.

He came to find that the busy servants were more than willing to pause in their duties

to speak with him when asked; and of whatever subject he brought up, as long as

it was

about the fortress's inhabitants,

these servants knew all on the matter,

particularly if it were scandalous;

so Sir Gawain did about her chatter.

"The Lady Vivien!" they would cry, some appalled and some enthralled.

So in this manner Gawain learned much about the woman he sought:

indeed, Vivien was living at the castle as he thought, but rarely did she see

the light of day, let alone visitors—the only one she spoke to was her king,

and that was because she was his concubine; what she did whilst locked away

in her tower no one quite knew, but rumors were rampant, most of which

Gawain would not bear to repeat to any ear lent. She was a beauty,

but she was a terrible one—children would whisper stories of her wickedness to their

younger siblings. But, some would say, a secret figure often stole away from the

castle in the dark to gather spell ingredients in the wood outside the city walls—

this was widely believed to be Vivien, and any empty rabbit traps were oft

claimed to have been her doing; for she used rabbits in her spell work.

Sir Gawain had then politely inquired in which tower Vivien resided, and

as soon as he had his answer excused himself. That night, he resolved, he would

    her seek.

  Perhaps, thought he, she would
  before his audience with her king list
  to him, and thus, in all likelihood,
  to go with him she would insist.

To the west tower he embarked, following the spiraling stair as far as it went, which was to the very top, whereupon he happened across a locked door with

a serpentine handle; he knocked thrice on the wood and waited for a response.

It came quite immediately—a voice like honey, muffled though it was: "Who comes

hither a-knocking on my door, I who am no one to warrant visitation?" This Gawain

thought a strange thing to say, for if this woman were indeed the sorceress Vivien

then she would be worthy—of that he was most certain. He answered thusly,

"I am here to ask of you one question now: who you are I should like to know;

and whether you are the one I seek I shall inquire more of you, and if you are not

I should have more still to ask, for she I must find. So I shall seek your mercy and ask

you now, in good faith, who may you be, my lady?" On the other side of the door

for a long moment there was silence, but then came again the voice, this time nearer:

"I am she who should have the king married, but bidden I was by him a time ago to Camelot

go, to use my wit and my beauty to ensnare the other; but unable was I my quest to

> fulfill
> in that way, so another I beguiled
> and followed, and learned much;
> but my king believed me defiled,
> and locked me here in his clutch."

To the knight this was alarming news indeed, for surely King Mark would not allow this woman out of his sights to accompany Gawain to the forest, and the lady

in question could not free herself, or already would she have done so; but before

he made any plans further it was imperative to procure more information about the

current situation, so spoke he, "Madam, may Mary reward you! It seems that you

are indeed the one whom I seek. In fairness, I would fain free you from this

tall prison, where lovely maidens belong not, but first I must know more of this.

How is it one such as you cannot leave, and do you suffer here, and how might I

gain the wherewithal to rescue you? Let Gawain be your servant and Christ be your

Savior." And the lady began to weep, whether for joy or for despair the knight knew not.

"My dear sir!" cried she after a moment. "First I should like to know who you are,

and why have you come here, and what with me you should do once you've freed me!

For I cannot blindly trust you, stranger, who could be commissioned by my king

to ensnare me in treason and have me thusly beheaded!" And good Gawain granted,

"Madam,
Sir Gawain is my name,
and here I have come for you.
In truth, your help is my aim,
so this shall be your rescue!"

And with that, the lady in him trusted, and she told him all that he needed to know:

that she was unable to escape because the window was too high
and the door enchanted;
that one meal a day was she given, and it was of bread, cheese,
and an occasional
strip of bacon, so always was she hungry; and that her king came
only twice a week,
as time allowed, bringing with him two silent servants who
would clean her humble home,
though she tried her best to keep it in goodly condition. Gawain
knew that even
had this woman been one most foul and evil that he would rescue
her, for no lady
deserved to live in such squalor and misery; so the pair began to
devise a plan:
Sir Gawain would his audience with the Cornish king keep, and
convince him
to meet with Gawain alone; and once that object he had
achieved, the
knight would King Mark subdue, and take from him the magic-
imbued key
round his neck. This he would bear back to Vivien's tower and
free her, and they
in disguise would flee on the back of Gringolet. Preparations
were to be made
mostly by Gawain, for he had the wherewithal to pack provisions
and disguise

    obtain;
  all this the knight promised,
  and she him bade farewell.
  Of his own cunning Gawain wist,
  and thought he would excel.

The king Gawain did not see that night nor the next day, but he
had plenty

time to prepare his belongings for a quick escape and to see that his steed

was well cared for; he stopped a young servant and asked that while he was

attending his audience that his bags be packed and Gringolet rigged, only because

he wanted to leave as quickly as was possible; and the servant readily agreed,

detecting nothing but sincerity in the knight—for Gawain was indeed truthful.

On the next morning Gawain was informed that the king would that day see him,

so he borrowed one squire and dressed in his polished riding gear, intending both to impress

the king and to set out immediately after his deed, which would verily be construed

as a mad act, and one that would certainly be rewarded with death should he be

caught, especially with a sorceress at his side. But of this he had thought

carefully through the evening, and prayed throughout the night, and had at last

formed one plan that would certainly afford him privacy with the king.

Sooth, his idea left him but a few moments to snatch his prize and steal away,

> and less
> to return to Vivien's tower in secret
> and then whisk her invisibly to his horse.
> He prayed that this he did not regret,
> and hoped he was taking the right course.

When at last he was ready, Gawain was led to the throne room, where awaited the king his presence. His arrival was heralded, and his admittance

into the room granted, and this he saw as he entered: a grand room, indeed,

wherein streamed golden sunlight from the open windows, the rays' warmth

being soaked into the tapestries bearing the Cornish king's sigil, that hung

from arched ceiling to polished floor; the throne sat upon a dais overlooking

the fore of the room, and upon that was seated old King Mark, back straight

but for his neck, which was bent forward, and his skin sagged from his

face, a mark of true age; and surrounding the king were his advisors, who stood

poised and attentive; and at the king's side was a smaller chair, empty of

his wife Isolde. All this Sir Gawain noticed in a moment, though he did not

look for long, for he was striding across the room and kneeling on the lowest step

of the dais, as was proper of a knight before royalty. And the king spoke

without preamble: "Sir knight, I know you from King Arthur's Round

                Table.
        Tell me, what is it that brings
        you here, and your name, sir,
        and why you come in all your lacings,
        and whether you come to curry favor."

Sir Gawain, an ever courteous knight, answered thusly: "Your kingship,

66

I am the last prince of Orkney, and perhaps the last of my uncle's table
round, if Sir Lancelot still lives for my uncle's swift departure from his trail;
I am called the Maidens' Knight, and I am the one who wears this
girdle green after keeping my head from the Green Knight; upon my shield is the crimson pentangle, though I do not carry it now, and I am the last of my blood." And he would have gone on to list
all that he was, but King Mark interrupted, "Enough! I know now
your name is Sir Gawain. So, good sir, what brings you here to me?"
Gawain responded, "May God bless you, your majesty, but if I may
speak my mind and heart…" Impatient Mark answered, "Yes! by God, speak!"
So Sir Gawain spoke. "Camelot is left defenseless after that awful
Battle at Camlann; whereas I survived, my brothers in arms were all killed,
and for this I grieve; but I must beg your assistance in this serious matter, for the
Saxon
invaders will surely push
their armies here, and kill
indiscriminately, and ambush
your people, and their blood spill."

Despite the knight's passionate words, the king of Cornwall appeared
unmoved as stone. Said he, "So you, sir knight, suggest that I send to Camelot

my own warriors to give you the wherewithal to win against the
wicked Saxons.

I refuse! Defending your home leaves mine unprotected, good
sir, and I should
rather my kingdom fall fighting than by the folly of sending
away those men
who would this place guard." And in response Gawain
exclaimed, "May God
reward you, but will you not ponder the matter? Perhaps you and
I might alone
discuss such a thing further and in deeper contemplation, your
highness?"
King Mark shook his hoary head of hair, and held up a hand to
silence him.
"Nay, sir knight, for when I heard of your arrival here I had
already guessed
at your intention, and thought deeply on the matter long before
this audience.
I again refuse." So it was that Sir Gawain's strategy was made
impotent, and
he quickly racked his wits for another method that might his
promise fulfill.
"In truth, your majesty, I must request again that we might
together speak of this
                    alone,
          for I know of an alternative,
          one so simple, but it is perchance
          to you in nature rather sensitive;
          so I should like to know your stance."

The Cornish king did mull over this, and after a moment's
contemplation
sent away his advisors, who slunk out silent and obedient. Once
they were

gone, King Mark stood, and from beneath his silken tunic produced a key

on a leather strap. "Sir Gawain," said he, "this is the thing you seek from me,

not any parley or aid, though perhaps once you thought of it you wanted for it;

nonetheless I cannot endanger my own kingdom for another, and I have no

wish to conquer your king's domain now, though once I did. You arrived

intending to take from me my enchantress, I ken. Yet I know of her what

you do not, good sir, so I shall caution you against freeing her, lest you are

determined to regret this path taken." And at once Gawain felt quite contrite,

for though his strength was far greater than an old man's, his wit was no match,

as he had mistakenly believed. The knight begged forgiveness for his vainness,

and the king willingly granted it, for he had once been young and foolish.

"But ere your journey," said King Mark, "might I inquire how it is that you

> survived
> the great Battle of Camlann,
> whereas your brothers are dead,
> as is, so you say, your clan.
> Didst someone die in your stead?"

And so the knight had no choice but to recount his woes to the ruler,

and thusly he confided in the royal cuckold: "Kindly king of Cornwall,

I must confess that it was not my intention to live whereas my kinsmen died;

to that battle I rode fully prepared for death, my spirit commended to God;

yet earlier than the fight was I defeated, alas! I was not thrashed by a Saxon, no,

for if he had injured me 'twould have been to the death; but through none other's

fault than my own I found myself lying on the hard ground." Sir Gawain then

hung his head, too ashamed to go on; and King Mark, ever impatient, bade him

continue, despite the knight's disinclination; accordingly, Gawain told on:

"Eager as I was to fight at my uncle's side, and sure as I was to wax in strength

as neared noontime, but whether it was by fate or by divine will that I live

I know not—for I did no battle that day but was defaulted a day before it.

My patrol of the camp had come about on the eve of battle, for one cannot the Saxons

trust to the revered rules of war. They would sooner slit their own throats than

    obey
  the laws of a civilized country.
  Barbarians, they are, the Saxons;
  and as such they force their entry
  so that we must die or take action."

"Good sir," said King Mark, "but what was it that prevented your might?"

And Gawain answered, "Nothing but my own foolishness, your majesty!

It is as I said: on the eve of battle I patrolled our camp, ready to sound the alarm
at a moment's notice, should anything prove amiss; but a foe I did not meet.
'Twas my foot that met a tree's root, and down I went and received a sharp
blow to the head as well as a weak ankle for my troubles. Unable was I
to battle, despite my dearest wishes; and so I survived Camlann."
And the knight
appeared so ashamed that the cuckold king did take pity on him;
"Here is thy prize, good Gawain," said he. "Take Vivien as you will, but beware,
for she is cunning in her craft, and sure to curse you at the first."
With many thanks and grateful kisses and bows, Gawain accepted the magic key
and went on his way unhurried and unmolested. That was not to say that he
did not hear the king's advice—he was certainly wary of the sorceress, as men
should be. But the lady Vivien was essential to his plan, and he was determined to

        restore
    his troth and his honor, and to protect
    his dear uncle's bloodline and land;
    Gawain bethought Vivien not a suspect
    of evil, but one who with him would stand.

He returned to the west tower to claim the sorceress as his guide;
up the spiral stair Sir Gawain slogged, until at last he had reached the top
of the tall tower. Into the lock he entered his key, and turned it thrice right.
The knight pushed open the door, and there in the center of the

room

stood the sorceress Vivien, her chin held high despite the raggedness of

her appearance—she was quite proud, and did not rush into his arms nor weep

at her salvation. As she had told him the evening before, her abode was bare

but for the most basic commodities: a chamber pot in one corner and a straw mat in the other, and against one wall was a roughly-hewn table

upon which sat a stout pitcher; there were four windows in this single room,

one for each of the cardinal directions, but they were too high and barred besides.

And even through her dirty visage Sir Gawain could see her cold beauty,

just as one might peer through a clouded window at the blooming forest beyond;

and yet chivalrous Sir Gawain found himself quite unaffected by her, for he had a

mission

to complete; and no wily woman

no matter her form nor complexion

would distract him nor awaken stamen,

for he was bound for abstention.

The vixen Vivien regarded him with consternation, and said,

"Dear knight! What disguise do you bring for our escape? If you do

remember, you had thus given your oath to free and protect me from this cuckolded king." And Gawain only smiled and bowed to her,

and replied, "My dear lady! I will fulfill my promises, but we need not

any disguise, for I have convinced your Cornish king to willingly this key
give to me so that you are freed; and we shall go on our way unhindered
to the forest of Broceliande." She seemed impressed and intrigued by him,
and went gladly with Gawain: arm in arm they descended the great stair,
and to the courtyard they went that they may leave the kingdom.
There Gawain discovered Gringolet prepared and stamping impatiently under
his baggage, and also another horse—this one a lovely mare white as
sea salt, laden with supplies for the surprised sorceress. No farewell party
did they receive, but they mounted their horses and rode off without ceremony.

> Eastward
>> they rode, not without frequent pause
>> so that Vivien might her legs stretch,
>> for she had been cooped up sans cause
>> and she complained as she were a wretch.

Sir Gawain was impatient to reach their destination,
for the worry of the Saxons' arrival constantly at his mind
made him ever more nervous; but a gentleman was he, and Vivien
a lady despite her paganism, which Gawain bethought a disgusting
tradition—but of that he said nothing, though he was sure Vivien
knew at least some of his thoughts, for the knight had need of her
powers, namely of her Sight. His plan's end relied on Merlin's release,
and he was determined to see his wish come to fruition, God

willing,
so that his uncle's lands be kept within his domain, and
Gawain's honor
be restored that he might his shame forget, and with Merlin's
counsel
and magic the great island be kept free of villainous Saxon
influence;
only Vivien could help him to complete the first and most
difficult of
his quest. As this he mused over, he did not contemplate that
perhaps
the sorceress had ideas of her own, and these she perfected as
they neared the
                    border
            of Cornwall; for once she
            that boundary passed, the witch
            would no longer controlled be,
            she thought with her lips atwitch.

Once the knight and his companion had stopped for the night
to camp under the stars, for they were some miles from a
monastery
and too tired to ride through the dark on weary steeds, the
sorceress
her scheme put into motion: while he slept by the fire, snoring
softly,
she threw off her blanket and set about quietly packing her
things,
intending to steal off into the forest alone. Her mare quietly
obeyed,
but good Gringolet was awake, and so he brayed a loud warning
to his master,
who thus woke with a start and brandished his knife, intending to
frighten

what bandit had troubled his camp, but he saw only Vivien as she
leapt onto her horse and hurried away, hair flying behind her fleeing form.
In hardly a moment an enraged Gawain smothered the low fire and mounted Gringolet,
and they raced after the sorceress; so flew Gringolet's hooves that behind them
leaves were tossed up, and they quickly were able to spy the white haunches
of the traitor's mare glowing ethereally in the moonlight, and Gawain at her
        bellowed,
     "Thou villainous vixen, Vivien! I freed
     you from the west tower your prison,
     and though of you have I great need
     your blood shall paint my blade crimson!"

But Vivien to him gave no heed, and she spurred her mare onward
though she flagged in speed; and Gringolet the mighty warhorse
came astride of her, and Gawain unsheathed his sword *Galatine*,
intending to strike Vivien a blow; but forgetting that she was skilled in magic,
he was taken by surprise when she, with a single hissed word,
knocked him from Gringolet's back and landed him amongst the leaves
on the cold hard ground; and ever faithful Gringolet halted and turned back
for his senseless master. Vivien rode on and disappeared into the distance.
Gawain returned to consciousness after a long moment, and though his head
ached monstrously he knew that he had lost; and he wept

miserably, for that

sorceress had been his only hope in finding the wizard Merlin, who was

crucial to his ambition. And alas that his anger had gotten the best of him,

for if Vivien's magic had not checked him he would have dealt her death by

        his sword,

    and he would have been in worse position

    than was he now. For her he could search,

    though that task was not an easy one—

    so Gawain realized as his stomach gave a lurch.

Though Sir Gawain had expected her to be grateful to him for his kind act,

he should have kept the Cornish king's words at the fore of his mind—

that Vivien was not as she seemed at the first—and known the wily woman

would him betray. He knew that he could not follow her now, for the trail

was too dark to distinguish a path, and Gringolet was weary of travel; so

Sir Gawain knelt where he was and cleared his face of tears as best he could,

and prayed that he be given guidance: "Holy Mother, please forgive me!

I gave my trust too easily to a pagan and then was too impassioned to think clearly,

which has cost me my chance at redeeming myself and freeing the wizard,

and now the Christian kingdom of Camelot is sure to fall to these Saxon invaders.

My weakness has sullied good faith; I have doomed us all.

Mother Mary, may
what shall come be, but I pray that what does come to be is
salvation granted
by God's grace!" And with that he crossed himself, and the
weary knight
stood and grasped Gringolet's reins, and they trudged back to
their camp
                    to sleep
            away the last of the night;
            and Gawain dreamed of wars,
            his tears shining in moonlight
            as he lay fireless under the stars.

When Sir Gawain awoke the next morning, the birds chirping
gaily
amongst the green leaves of the trees, and the warming sunlight
kissing
him like greeting an old friend, and the wind whispering him a
good day,
his heavy heart was lifted, and Gawain rejoiced; for he knew a
divine sign
when he was gifted it, and that fleeting image which had woken
him was surely
an answer to his prayer. So he leapt up and saddled Gringolet his
steed,
and off they went with new purpose. The knight broke his fast as
they rode,
eating from the supply of salted meat given him by the cooks of
Tintagel Castle.
Gawain told Gringolet as they rode that all was not lost, as he
had thought
only the night before: Mother Mary had granted him a vision of
Vivien
and where she would be hiding. According to his dream, the

witch would

withdraw to the forest of Broceliande, the last place Gawain would for her

have searched, and with a hermit in penitence she would hide; though this man

would fain like her to leave him be. So Gawain would find Vivien, and

> compel
> her to help him find Merlin's tree;
> for though she was not bound by word,
> and neither was she a woman trusty,
> he would make his reason heard.

Gawain would not allow her to escape when he her found again;

for now he knew that King Mark was not a fool to keep her locked away.

She was a wily woman, and a sorceress no less, cunning in her craft;

he would not be confounded again, nor would he underestimate the witch.

So Gawain rode Gringolet hard and fast, following his original course

due south and east. Indeed, if he had known it, the pair were hounding Vivien,

who saw their speedy progress in her crystal, which spurred her on as though fire

licked her heels; it was this pursuance that persuaded the woman to flee to Gaul,

where she was certain to lose him—and where she was given strength, for the magic

that bound Merlin to his prison also tied his magic to hers; though Merlin could not

make use of it, deathly sleeping as he was. So it was that the knight and the witch raced

to the sea on the east coast, that deep dark gulf chilling the skin like a wraith's touch
even in high summer; Vivien reached the shore first, and brought her mare to a halt
at the edge of the inky water, where it lapped hungrily at the crunching pebbles; a
storm brewed
on the far horizon; the wind snatched
her hair and whipped her face, relentless.
Not a boat was in sight, but unmatched
was she in the power she did possess.

As good Gawain arrived on galloping Gringolet, he beheld a sight
most astonishing: the vixen Vivien, astride her horse and arms flung wide,
hair flying fiercely about her head, screamed shrilly across the water,
calling forth a bridge of thick white fog, curling and condensing
before her and stretching out into the darkness. And then she spurred
into motion and passed over the mist as it were made of sound stone;
and though Gawain was a brave man he pulled his horse short of it, wary—
and rightly so, for as Vivien flew over it the bridge dispersed, white wisps
snaking over the surface of the great watery chasm so that there seemed no passage.
Yet he would not forfeit so close to his prize, and nudged his ride aside
so that they might look for some boatman who would sail them despite
the oncoming storm, or else find some abandoned vessel they

might use.

Lo and behold! Less than a league along the beach, licked by the
lapping waves,

was a respectable craft with oars and all, and no one in sight to
claim it.

The knight

said a short prayer, crossed himself, and pushed the boat

out with little effort—it slid smoothly into the ocean,

and he leapt into it; and Gringolet chuffed a note

at his abandonment, but Gawain to him did motion—

For the noble knight had no intention of leaving behind his
sturdy steed,

his loyal companion. The vessel was in favorable condition, and
large enough

for them both, should Gringolet stand at the stern, long face
looking solemnly

out toward their destination. Gawain took up the oars and began
his arduous task;

through the night he rowed, relentless despite his burden—
though his strength

waned, he was a man of great fortitude. Even the thunder could
not deter him,

nor wind nor stinging rain! So it was that he rowed past the great
storm,

battling the cold, heavy waves that buffeted his small boat and
tried to turn them back;

and he at last arrived on the shore of Gaul, much to Gawain and
Gringolet's relief.

As they stumbled onto the wet sand the sun peeked out and bid
them welcome,

and Gawain spared a moment to thank his Lord and the revered
Mother

whilst Gringolet went in search of grass to eat. Though his body

ached and groaned
from his arduous work and too little rest, Gawain knew that
Vivien could not be
very far, for in his dream vision he saw her with a hermit in the
forest, and there,

        surely,
      would she be. So the knight mounted his steed,
      and though Gringolet still hungered he knew
      that it was time to go; he obeyed with speed
      and gentle grace to find and give Vivien her due.

South and east Gawain rode, pausing only to give his hardy
horse a rest
and to eat a little dried meat. He frequently peered up at the sky
to glean location
and to gauge time's passing. After a few hours' travel and having
met no strangers,
Gawain came to see the forest of Broceliande in the distance, and
with hope invigorated,
he spurred Gringolet into motion. Gawain felt stronger with each
passing moment,
as noon was nigh; and as his strength increased so did his spirits;
and so he was confident
that he would persuade Vivien to free Merlin, for Mother Mary
had granted him
this knowledge of the witch's whereabouts, and he was sure to
win, for God stood by him.
They had not long traversed the beginning of the thick trees
when good Gawain
his surroundings recognized: for it was precisely as it had been
in his dream!
Soon he would cross the hermit and his visitor—and just at the
moment he thought this,
so opened up the trees into a clearing, where stood together the

pair he sought.

"Ho!" shouted he, and they turned. At the sight of the hermit's visage Gawain's tongue stilled
for shock, until he cried softly, "Could it be? Is it you, Lancelot du Lac?" To which the
        hermit,
      responded thusly, quite dismayed:
      "Indeed 'tis I, Lancelot, Sir! Were it so
      that we never met again, for I have this maid
      promised to deal her pursuer a fatal blow!"

"And shall you keep your word?" Gawain answered. "Will you smite me as you have
my brothers and sons? Though you your oath to King Arthur betrayed,
will you keep your word to a wily woman, a sorceress who would as soon help you
as hinder you? Fie on this dog!" So the embittered knight stirred up Lancelot's blood
and ignited the fires of nobility in his heart again, which had gone to embers
with chastity—for Sir Lancelot became a repentant after he had fled to his motherland
in shame. Sir Gawain continued passionately in his tirade, "We are evenly matched now,
as the sun reaches his peak. Unless you be afraid, or weak, retrieve your sword,
and we shall duel here and now. He who hurts the other to the death shall win his head!"
And Lancelot threw back his cloak to reveal that underneath he wore his cursed blade *Arondight*,
for it reminded him of his sins—but it would serve him in battle, still. Said he,
"I accept your challenge, Sir Gawain!" So the men drew their

weapons, and Gawain dismounted
his weary warhorse; in the very center of the clearing they faced off and prepared
their deadly duel. This Vivien watched with interest, though she was certain that Lancelot

> would win;
>> but whatever the outcome of the fight,
>> the witch was sure to be free,
>> for her magic verily grew in might
>> the nearer was she to Merlin's tree.

In truth, no one but she knew that Merlin's prison was located in that clearing
where the once brothers in arms dueled; to any eye but hers it appeared to be a tall oak
just the same as the rest, whereas she saw within the strong trunk the sleeping form
of ancient Merlin, curled like a babe near the roots of the tree; and none but she
heard the leaves whispering, "Fool! fool! fool!" Vivien watched enthralled
as the battle between brethren began with an almighty clash of sparking swords:
and the duelers danced round the other, slashing and parrying with skill ingrained in them
since their years as squires. Neither spoke, for to do so was a waste of strength,
and a distraction to the self, besides; and even had Gawain spoken to Lancelot,
or Lancelot spoken to Gawain, his opponent would not have bothered to listen.
Good *Galatine* and accursed *Arondight* sang their hatred for them, sharp voices ringing
out into the forest, a cry of warning to keep away. Relentless and

fierce fought

the old friends, neither winning nor losing; for they were evenly matched yet

as the sun reached its pinnacle. But slowly and surely the sun began to sink as they

 battled,

 and Gawain's strength began to wane,

 whereas Lancelot seemed the stronger.

 Soon Sir Gawain started to struggle and strain,

 and could not raise his sword any longer.

And lo, the battle was ended, for when Gawain could not block Lancelot's strike,

he was hurt, and so fell. Lancelot over him stood, at first victorious and then appalled,

and he went to Sir Gawain's side with a cry, "Alas!" Yet Gawain, not dead but dying

from the mortal wound in his head, took Lancelot's hand and said, "Alas, indeed!

So ends my dear uncle's bloodline, and now must the whole of Albion fall to those

Saxons. Did we not once battle together? Lancelot, my friend, we are but men!

Therefore I repent of my bitterness toward you; you are forgiven in my sinful eyes."

And so Gawain's last breath left his body. In the next moment Lancelot took up his sword

and ran at the vixen Vivien, impaling her through the heart with such force

that she became pinned to the great oak behind her; for it was she that had caused

Lancelot to kill good Gawain. She died with hardly a flutter of her lashes, surprised

at the hermit's angry charge as she was. Then weeping the noble

hermit
put his deceased brother upon poor Gringolet's back, and carried him off
that he may be laid to rest. He did not look back, for he had no wish to see the horrible
pagan;
but he might have seen had he so done
the great tree to which Vivien was stuck
withered and shrank down into a tomb of stone,
his sword protruding skyward, ready to pluck.

The Hour of Their Need

Amy Wolf

Melliagraunce felt a jolt, like striking the ground in full armour. A two-beat rhythm started in his neck, chest, and groin.

"Did anyone bring the torch?"

A hissing, caught by a close-up barrier, to come back hot on his lips. His breath.

"Bunny, did you hear the wireless last night? When Jack Warner says 'di-da-di-da'—"

"Oh Uncle!"

Sensation. Burning down his body. Pressing his bladder; splaying fingers, which grazed a scaly surface.

"If only the Frogs had held Dunkirk, we wouldn't be huddled underground like moles!"

"Really, Bertram, moles don't huddle."

A clicking, as of a vault being opened, but Melliagraunce realized it was only his eyelids.

"So dull in the country, isn't it, Auntie? I do miss the shops and cinema, and dancing at the Savoy with soldiers."

"Dancing!" The man's voice. *"No one danced in the Somme, I can tell you that."*

Melliagraunce heard the words, but only along the edges. White pinpricks in darkness became wide horizontal bands.

"—hard enough in the blackout, but with no petrol to be had—"

The bands resolved into welcome solidity, circling the length of his body. He was completely encased in stone.

"Mummy, may we hear 'It's That Man Again' on Thursday?"

"We'll see, dear. Help me with the tea things now."

Melliagraunce half-tried to inspect his vertical coffin. His fingers, newly sensitive, ached as they scraped across limestone. He brought his hands up to his face. The long tapered fingers shook slightly. They were his mother's hands.

"Be honourable in all things," she had told him. "To a true knight, like your father, death is preferable to shame."

"Yes, Mother," he had said, believing it.

"No no, Betty, none for the pot. We've two ounces to last a week."

Food rationing. Melliagraunce nodded. Naughty old Adolph.

"But how wonderful to have chicken, and eggs too! In London, one simply can't find them." The younger female voice.

"Damned Channel bombing," said the man. *"Shipping a mess."*

Melliagraunce gripped his head. He didn't feel quite himself. Still, he thought: I'm alive.

A shiver of heat shook his stomach, seeping into his death wound. The two-beat rhythm pulsed its code: alive alive alive.

"Oh God," he said, and sank his forehead onto the rock.

Sleep must have come, for he opened his eyes in a second awakening. Dim light streaked the white bands of stone.

Melliagraunce rested his back against rock. He was happy enough to wait there, until he could die again.

The ground rumbled. *Good*, he thought, *I won't have long to wait*.

It happened again, not violently, but in languid waves which were like a massage. A fissure cracked the length of the stone, admitting more dimmed light.

"No!" Melliagraunce shouted, placing his hands on parting rock. New fissures, jagged as lightning, wrinkled and aged the stone. A moment of silence, then thunder, and Melliagraunce stood over six rock petals at the far end of a cave. He saw tables, chairs, four bunks, and enough tinned biscuits to last out a blitz.

Melliagraunce looked down, feeling stiffer than a boy in first armour. He wore knee-high, black leather flying boots; a smart blue uniform stitched with gold wings; and a red silk polka-dot scarf.

He touched his face—still his; same aquiline nose and underfed cheeks—but his hair no longer hid him: it was short and shrouded by a cap.

"Balls!" he yelled to the chamber, throwing himself against shards. The stone ignored his touch. It would not take him back. Melliagraunce cried the tears of a man who knows that no one is listening. If life—daily life—were unfair, what of that granted against his will?

Report to Biggin Hill station, someone said. *150 Squad at readiness*. It was his own mind.

"I won't!" Melliagraunce shouted, and sprinted from the cave into daylight. He blinked, pulling his cap down over his face. It was dazzling, this light, born of summer in a cloudless sky, like that of his own country, Dumnonia. He saw a red-bricked house one quarter-league off, as big as his grey stone manor; and the men in the fields, with their wide-brimmed hats and steady gait—they gave him a sense of timelessness.

The pressure on his bladder was killing now; he unzipped his trousers, relieving himself by the side of a well.

"Hullo! Have you been shot down?" An echo came over the water and he hastily zipped up.

He stared as a blond girl ran toward him, in a uniform of her own: school sweater, strict black tie, and socks that traveled to the knee.

"Where's your plane then?"

He continued to stare.

"Oh, you weren't flying! You've no Mae West or parachute!" She pouted with such elegance that Melliagraunce nearly smiled. "Why are you in our fields then? The nearest base is twenty miles off."

Melliagraunce didn't know what to say, until it was said for him. "Bad show! Went for a Burton in a ropey kite and had to hit the silk."

The girl giggled. "You sound like my brother Colin. He's a Hurricane pilot, you know."

"Bah! Hurribugs are a packet! Spits are it—even Jerry thinks so."

"Colin says the same thing about Spitfires."

Melliagraunce tried to smile, but his lips got stuck on his teeth. The bastards! They'd taken him from his rest, and now they were taking his voice. It was the last thing that was his and he wouldn't let them.

"What's your name?" The girl, motioning primly, led him out of the sun.

Melligraunce fought the expected response. "Melliagraunce," he said.

"That's rather queer."

"I was named after a king's son…" Melliagraunce knew he shouldn't be saying this—he should be talking of Oxford and rowing and flight school at Cranwell—but he pushed these false memories aside. "He turned out a bad man—the King of England had to punish him."

"Such a lot of kings!" The girl didn't seem that interested. "My name's Betty. Betty Mayhew. I've got a cousin, Bunny; and my Mum, Helen, and my Dad, Bertram Mayhew. He used to be a banker."

Melliagraunce shook his head. If she'd been trained to beware Fifth Columnists, the lesson hadn't taken. "What is this place? Where I've pranged, I mean." He cursed his tainted tongue.

"Oh, somewhere in southeast England."

"Hells bells!" So she knew enough to keep that quiet.

"What squad are you? Colin's in 32, at Biggin. I do wish I were with him. Mummy can be so awful strict."

Melliagraunce readied his "Glorious 150's" speech. He looked at Betty. She had given him a bit of truth; he supposed he should give some back.

"I'm not in any squad at all. I'm a Knight of the Round Table and I've been dead a long time."

Betty stared at him. "You look well enough."

"Well, I'm not. I'm the deadest corpse you'll ever see."

"Why?"

Melliagraunce sighed. Children could be so direct. "Because I've been through it once. I 'did my bit,' as you say, and my world still ended. That's the worst thing, you know—not giving up, because that's easy—but giving your all and having it still be meaningless. I can't do it again. I won't." Tears fell onto his stitched gold wings.

Betty seemed flustered. "I've never seen a man cry before."

"I know, pip pip and that's a good chap and 'Go it, R.A.F.'" He wiped his eyes with the polka-dot scarf. "Sorry. Where I come from, men could cry and be warriors too. Not that it mattered. Tears couldn't save any of them."

"Sir Knight," said Betty, gravely, "I think you should talk to my Dad. He was a warrior once, and he might be able to help you."

"No—" Melliagraunce called, but Betty trotted off toward the red-brick house, her feet as fleet as a pony's.

"Balls!" he yelled, and ran back to the well. He cast off the things that weren't his: cap, tunic, scarf. He watched them disappear underwater. A specialty, of sorts.

Melliagraunce fled through fields of wheat, ignored by men who were harvesting. He tore through a gate into the woods, his hard boots blistering his feet.

The woods. He had always felt safe there, his soft green boots padding between birches. There had been no feeling of danger—no bad men or thieves, for Arthur had driven them out—only parties of knights, and his brother, Agraveine, reading to him of adventure. Melliagraunce had loved the woods, as a retreat from his sun-drenched life.

"You there! Halt! Let's see your Identity Card!"

90

Melliagraunce stopped on a short dirt road blockaded by an ancient Rolls. Before him were three Home Guards, armbands official over denim, tin hats shadowing gray.

He tried to think his way out of it. "Say now, chaps, I've pranged nearby, and afraid the meat discs got lost. Rather fight Jerry than Dad's Army."

The Guard who'd hailed him drew out a pistol. He had a steady hand.

"We've no reports of any incident. What's your squad?"

"150 Phantoms, sir!"

"Never heard of 'em. Let's have a name."

"Knight, sir."

"What Knight? Come on now, you a Tommy, or a Jerry?"

"I'm Tom Knight, sir." Melliagraunce liked his invention.

The other two Guards looked grave, hoisting rifles older than they were. "Better come with us," said the leader, pointing his pistol and cocking it.

Melliagraunce didn't move. He knew what a gun could do; that it shouldn't be faced without armour. Grandfather and his pistol advanced. Melliagraunce guessed they'd both seen action—in Mr. Mayhew's Somme.

"All right, Dad, keep your hair on. Adolf's still back in the Reich."

The prison where they took him was small: a camouflaged shack in a nearby town, patrolled by Army brown jobs.

Melliagraunce glanced at a second cell catty-cornered from his. *This is livable*, he thought, slurping his portion of beans. He'd refuse to fight and be sent to a camp, like the Germans who'd fled Hitler for England. Tyranny—the enemy—was nothing if not democratic.

"You will excuse me for disturbing you."

Melliagraunce rose from his bunk. In the other cell stood a dark-haired man, his gray uniform spotless and pinned with an

Iron Cross.

"One half of you is R.A.F., yes?"

Melliagraunce looked down at his trousers.

"Hauptmann Peter Hartmann, *Jagdgeschwader* 12. I tell you this since you are a pilot, and have honor." His English was as polished as his boots.

Melliagraunce nodded toward the Cross. "You must be a great ace."

"Fifty-two kills. Forty in the Battle of Britain."

Melliagraunce whistled. Hartmann was the equal of a Lancelot.

"Whom do I have the honor of addressing?"

The German's manners pleased Melliagraunce. He bowed. "Officer Pilot Tom Knight."

"Then you *are* an officer. I'm glad. To be interned with a sergeant would be a disgrace."

Melliagraunce understood. This man lived by the Code. "How did you come to be here? With such a record, I mean."

"Ha, my glorious career!" Hartmann linked black-gloved hands over chipped-paint steel bars. "I am forced to bale out over Sussex. To the surprise of a Mr. Bowes, I went through the roof of his privy. 'Excuse me, sir,' I said, 'I seem to have come from the shit into the shit.'"

Melliagraunce laughed. The sound surprised him.

"Pilot Officer, my presence here is, shall we say, expected. And yours?"

His directness reminded Melliagraunce of Betty. "I suppose one could say I'm an objector."

"Ah." Hartmann's face clouded. "You shouldn't be, Pilot Officer. Hitler will come. The invasion has been planned for a month. Of course, with *Der Dicke* in charge—"

"Who?"

"Goering, the corpulent fool. He's losing the war, telling Hitler we can defeat you in four days; that there are no Spitfires left—"

"Why follow then?"

"Honor, Pilot Officer! I love my country, not the Reich. I love to fly, not listen to speeches."

"Yes." Melliagraunce knew. The Code. Once, it had meant something.

"What good am I?" Hartmann asked him, coming closer to the bars.

"I'm sorry, old chap, I don't follow—" Melliagraunce hid behind British reserve.

"Without wings, I'm as good as dead! Without flight, I'm less than a man! The feeling of speed, that nothing can harm you behind metal—"

Melliagraunce saw himself on the jousting field, his greaved legs guiding his charger; the world sliding by as leisurely as the Thames, though he hurtled at full-speed.

"I know what it is to be grounded."

"Knight, Thomas!" a Sergeant bawled, banging into the prison. "Ye're outta here, mate. They come for ya from Biggin."

Melliagraunce didn't move as his cell door opened. The Sergeant's pig eyes narrowed, and he saw he had no choice.

"Pilot Officer."

Melliagraunce stopped before Hartmann's cell.

"I wish you to have this." Something clicked into Melliagraunce's palm—the smooth-edged Iron Cross. "Wear it, when you go up. That way, a part of me can still fly free."

The Sergeant shadowed Melliagraunce as he stepped back into daylight.

"Officer Knight." An R.A.F. man waited for him—a real chiefy type. "Bit of a muddle with the Whitechester Guard. Air Marshal Dowding took care of it. He said to give you this."

He handed over a brown-paper package, fastened crossways with string. Melliagraunce burst it open.

Beneath the paper was a toy: a wood model Spitfire.

Melliagraunce woke to a perfect day for flying: blue sky, no wind, with just a wisp of cloud. He rose and walked through his safe place—the woods—hungry, but afraid to leave.

15 August 1940. Tom Knight knew the date. This was to be the real *Adlertag*, a Luftwaffe flight of eagles. Melliagraunce wished he knew more of the day, but his other self stayed silent.

It was all very Code.

Like the R.A.F., the fools, who trusted him to report. They shouldn't trust a restarted heart. It never beat the same.

Melliagraunce sat on a rock in a clearing. Above him came a buzzing. *Stukas. Junkers Ju 87 dive-bombers. Vulnerable to attack from the rear.*

"Hey!" Melliagraunce shouted, as they wheeled line astern to the east. "I'm here! I'm right here!"

The planes droned heedlessly on.

There were many planes in the sky that day: Ju 88's, Me 110's—they came to bomb everyone but him. Melliagraunce, from his rock, traced an invisible battle: screams of engines; bursts of flame and white vapor trails, a dragon's exhalations. By evening, it was over.

So much for the Big Day, the one they'd brought him back for. When he was younger—say fifteen—he'd have been first up in the sky. Now he'd be the first to laugh at that boy.

Melliagraunce got up. He didn't mean to. There was pressure inside his head; a beetle's buzz in his ears.

He ran. Over to a mound of leaves, where he pulled out the toy Spitfire. His long white fingers shook as he dashed it to the ground.

Spitfire. The toy was gone, but the fighter was there: green camouflage over a steel-gray body; "bulls-eye" emblem behind the wing, crowded by white initials, "S-M-K."

Melliagraunce stared at the plane. It seemed small—just twenty-nine feet. It was sleek, he had to admit—those oval wings, delicately rounded, unmarred by their Browning gun ports. Still, he hated it.

"I'm not going!" Melliagraunce shouted, but he was: he seized a parachute and vest from the wing, mounting the plane from the left. A few steps, some sliding, and he strapped himself into his "office."

A brown leather helmet hung from the stick. Melliagraunce put it on; plugged in the R/T and oxygen. Sliding down goggles with one hand was as natural as shutting a helm.

"Balls!" he yelled, and tried not to press the starter switch. His bastard finger did it for him: the three-bladed propeller turned.

Melliagraunce released his hand-brake. He zigzagged over the clearing, pushing his throttle forward. The Merlin engine answered with a defiant lion's roar.

Take-off, and ascension—Hartmann's dream, not his.

Melliagraunce looked below him, seeing trees and fields streak past. England was still so green.

Tom Knight resumed control, flaps and undercarriage—up; bullet-proof canopy—down. Fine, Melliagraunce thought, this chap can go to crashland.

His harness pinched at his death wound. He gave the altimeter a glance: five-thousand feet and climbing. He hauled back on the stick, slanting his nose to the sky. Ten thousand feet. Fifteen thousand. His hand turned up the oxy, and he felt it hiss in his mask. Twenty thousand feet, heading straight for the sun at 370 miles-per-hour.

Its glare was dazzling, on this still-light summer night; coming out of it, from above, was a *staffel* of nine Stukas, hemmed in by two fighters each.

Beware of the Hun in the sun.

All that metal seemed confused to find a lonely foe. The fighters— Me 109's—finally swooped, but were stopped by a whirlwind of Hurricanes. Now Melliagraunce felt confused: one

95

minute, he was friendless; the next, witness to a half-dozen dogfights.

A Stuka loomed large in his windscreen. Melliagraunce tried to slow, but Tom Knight wouldn't let him: *"If you fly straight for five seconds, you'll never fly again."* Obeying, he shook off the bomber with a half-roll, sliding under fierce black crosses, and wheel spats that curled like claws.

Melliagraunce came so close he could see the rear gunner firing at him. He switched on his reflector sight and gave him a four-second burst. One of his tracers hit home, reconstructing the Stuka: it became a flaming sun.

Confirmed kill, thought Melliagraunce. Wouldn't they be pleased?

A Hurricane chappy flew by and saluted. They couldn't talk on the R/T—each squad had a different wavelength. Which is why Melliagraunce tensed when a high, pure voice rang through his earphones.

"Sapper control, Red Leader calling. All a/c airborne."

"Red Leader, vector 90. Bandits, 20 plus, at Angels 7. Buster." An older, gravelly voice, unmistakably Scots.

"There they are, Sapper! Bogies, twelve o'clock high— *Tallyho!*"

Melliagraunce looked up. Silhouetted by sunset were Me 110's, chased by angry Hurricanes and forming a "circle of death."

Melliagraunce joined the circle, hoping to be hit, but instead, he squeezed off a burst. The slow fighter in front of him was no *Zerstorer*: black smoke clouded his windshield—-when it cleared, there was one less 110.

Melliagraunce saw a squad of Spits head right up the middle of the circle. Me 110's broke and headed east, dogged by his squad—and him. Very few Jerries made it to Dover; still fewer crossed the ditch.

"Melly, old chap! Glad to have you!" A voice, youthful and

familiar.

That was it for Melliagraunce. Out came the R/T lead. He pushed on his stick and went into a dive, beneath the bellies of his squad-mates. Negative G's blacked him out: when he came to, he saw he had company—a yellow-nosed 109.

Invert! Invert! Tom Knight yelled, but Melliagraunce couldn't obey: his Merlin's carb had fouled, and the 109—fuel-injected—was master of the air.

Merlin, thought Melliagraunce, *you should have stayed in your stone, like me.*

The 109 was on him, letting loose with double cannon. It was like the pounding of horses' hooves; the crash of lance against plate.

Send me back, Melliagraunce asked, as shells struck by the pair, exploding his front-mounted gas tank. Flames tore through the cockpit; over hands, legs, face. The dashboard dripped on his fingers and he heard himself scream through his mask.

Not like this, Melliagraunce thought. He reached for the hood but it stuck. *I'm a knight*, his own voice told him; *a Knight of the Round Table*. His charred hands slid back the hood and threw off his Sutton straps. He got his shoulders clear of the Spit; the slipstream took care of the rest of him.

Isn't this odd? he thought, *I'm an unwinged thing in the sky.* He couldn't see—his eyes had seared shut—but the sensation of falling was fine. He started to sing "A Nightingale Sang in Berkeley Square." After a while they told him It don't mean a thing if you don't pull that ring and he did, his harness wrenching his body. This falling was so much more pleasant.

"Balls," said Melliagraunce, as he plopped into the Channel. He released his chute and blew through a tube, inflating his bulky Mae West.

Everything seemed to be burning. His face burned in the sun, the one that came out at night.

"Black as the stone!" he yelled, and felt a great satisfaction. It would be nice to stay here forever, caressed by the black churning water. Then he remembered he didn't like water; water had never been his friend.

Melliagraunce's teeth chattered. He heard a pounding from the shore. Horses, bearing metal men who ran at metal foes.

"No!" Melliagraunce shouted. It wasn't time for the end. Mordred and Arthur sought terms: steel had been raised to slay a snake, not to signal a war.

The two hosts fought by Camelot, in sight of her gold-topped towers. Dragon banners flew from them, but the heart of the beast had died.

I am sorry my son, said his father, *it is Lancelot whom I must support. No sir, that is betrayal!* but then Uros was banished to Benwick, while *he* pledged his sword to the Table. Why? For honor, dear brother, said Agraveine, at rest on his candle-lit bier; for honor, dear son, said his mother; and for honor he'd gone forth to Camlann, to fight on her crowded plain.

"No!" he yelled, as an ax smote his helm, hurtling him from his mount. His red-plated foe reined in, and Melliagraunce drew out a broadsword.

The twist of a wrist, an airborne ax. Red Knights did not fight to Code. Melliagraunce fell on his back, an inch of steel in his stomach.

The Red Knight took his horse. Melliagraunce slipped off his helm. Wherever he looked there were bodies, stained black by the curtain of twilight. A hundred thousand—his fellows among them—who would never rise from Camlann.

Melliagraunce heard a sound. It was strange to hear it, on this field of corpses. He sat up, wrenching out steel. Arthur dealt Mordred his death stroke, receiving his own through the brain pan. It would not be long now.

Melliagraunce shooed off a vulture. He watched as two knights rushed to the King, dabbing his bloodied head. One of them died of his wounds, but the other went off with Excalibur.

Twice, he hid the weapon, and reported his lies to Arthur.

This miscreant fell too. Melliagraunce rose to his knees. The sword. He had to reach the sword. He could see its red-tinged steel, twenty paces away, propped enticingly against a tree. He stood, clutching his wound, and swayed past Arthur like a drunkard.

Snaking runes and sea-smoothed stones burned the steel of his gauntlet. Melliagraunce dragged the sword on the ground, down to the River Cam. With an effort that pumped out blood like a well, he threw Excalibur in.

An arm rose above water. White fingers seized the blade, brandished it thrice, then settled back with a ripple, sliding the sword from view.

Melliagraunce nearly swooned. A black-creped barge, arrived from Glastonbury, moored smoothly onto the grass. In her hull she bore three Queens—one of them Morgan le Fey. With great lamentation, they lifted the King, covered his body, and left.

Melliagraunce coughed up blood. So that was it then. Excalibur: lost forever. The King: in the hands of his sister, she who had borne him Mordred. Fame was infamy after all.

Cold, he thought, hitting the ground, as creeping rock engulfed him. The tomb was so black, and cold.

Freezing. Melliagraunce struck out with his hands, skin in strips at his wrist, but he only succeeded in splashing himself.

"Help! Help!" he yelled, knowing that no one would hear on this mined and bulleted sea.

He went under. It should have been hard, with his bosomy Mae West, but in fact, it was very easy. Limpid and relaxed, he floated to the bottom, and saw a woman in white approaching. She didn't swim, but walked, her pale hair fanning behind her; her skin white as her eyes, which were flecked with tinges of blue.

She stared at him and from her smile he caught a reflection of pity. He must have looked a mess.

99

She put up her arm and showed him something: leathery, belted—a scabbard. She fastened it about his waist; straightened, and kissed him once on the lips.

Melliagraunce could feel her warmth as he floated back to the surface. The night air seemed mild on his face.

In the darkness, he heard a thrumming.

"That's one of ours, ain't it?"

"Can't be sure."

Rough voices, trying to drown him. "Hey there mate, you a Tommy or a Jerry?"

Melliagraunce called on Tom Knight. He always knew just what to say.

"Jesus fucking Christ, pull me out, you bastards!"

"He's one of ours," said a seaman, and hauled him over the side.

"Pilot Officer Knight?"

An R.A.F. man stared down at Melliagraunce, with the air of knowing his secrets. *Intelligence.*

"Yes?" Melliagraunce stared up from his hospital bed.

So much for his pleasant stay. He'd had relative peace for a month, but word got around: this chap had more lives than a cat.

"I've brought you a uniform, sir. The Air Chief requests your presence."

Requests or demands? Melliagraunce thought, shrugging into a tunic.

He kept his talk to "Yes" and "No" on the lorry ride from London. Eighteen miles later, he and his friend crossed a highway, stopping at a patched-up place: Biggin Hill sector station.

"A miracle, this," said Intelligence, as they legged it over a runway. "Just two weeks past: shelters hit; Ops Room and planes on fire. Old Adolf's done us a favor—"

"By bombing London to bits?"

"Know your onions," Intelligence nodded. "Most of them still alive do."

They crossed the airfield boundary to a cemetery thronged with civvies. Melliagraunce looked down. Gravestones formed neat rows, as if standing at a last attention. *How many there are!* he thought. *Such a lot of deaths.*

An R.A.F. chaplain coughed and unclasped a miniature Bible. Melliagraunce thought of his own chapel, candle-branched and smoky.

"'If I take the wings of the morning, and dwell in the uttermost parts of the sea; even there shall Thy hand lead me.' Even there—"

Melliagraunce's mind wandered. He focused on coffins poised by their graves like swimmers waiting to plunge.

"Just as Crusaders and knights of olde—"

The coffins creaked in their harness.

"—these brave boys in blue, with their planes as armour; guns as lance; and the honor of Britain their shield—"

Melliagraunce heard "Go to it!" when the chaplain mentioned 'knights.' Jaws tightened around him and someone said, "We can take it."

A man approached Melliagraunce, stiff in braided blue. "Sir Hugh Dowding, Air Chief Marshal. I trust you're feeling well?"

Melliagraunce said nothing, remembering Dowding's gift.

"I didn't ask you here, Knight. Your friend did—a girl."

Melliagraunce scanned the crowd. In the midst of black, he saw Betty, dwarfed by a horrible hat. He stared at Dowding's thin face. "Colin?"

"Third coffin from my left. Not everyone shares your good fortune."

Melliagraunce couldn't be sure, but he thought he saw Dowding glance at his scabbard. "I'd hardly call it good—" he said, but his words were drowned by a buzzing—of two Dornier 17's.

The bombers dove at full-throttle, "Flying Pencils" slim in the sky.

"Take cover!" Dowding yelled, over the rattle of ten machine guns. Melliagraunce hit the ground. Feet stampeded around him, heavy boots and women's heels. The earth erupted with geysers—dirt and grass and debris—unloosed by errant bullets.

Betty. Melliagraunce raised his head, and everything seemed to slow, as it had at the bottom of the Channel. He saw her, stockinged feet flying, rolling into an open grave. Colin's. She teetered for a moment on the edge, then was gone.

"Jesus." Melliagraunce's tears mixed with dirt. He couldn't allow this to happen. Brothers might lie in newly dug graves— boys, no more than 18—but this new crop, the children, should not have to lie there as well.

Knights. Of olde. They could still inspire a people. His world was dead—mist—but the Legend had somehow survived.

"It meant something," he said, and that was all he heard: not ack-ack, not shelling, not bombers. What he did at Camlann had meant something.

"I say, everyone, All Clear." Dowding, on his feet, served as human siren.

Melliagraunce flew past him to get to Colin's grave. He dangled over the edge, balancing on his stomach, and pulled Betty back to the surface.

"Thank you, Sir Knight," she said, brushing her frock clear of dirt. "I expect you're a regular Lancelot."

The dispersal hut of 150 Squad was deep in Biggin's North Camp. Melliagraunce entered at 0400. to find eleven men seated by a stove. Some read paperback thrillers; others listened to "Tuxedo Junction." They were a motley crew, this lot—in uniforms, flight jackets, or pyjamas—but the illusion created was perfect. They looked just like R.A.F. pilots.

"Hallo! It's Melliagraunce!" A fair-haired youth stood up; he of the high, pure voice.

"Galahad. Call me Hal. This is Gareth, or Garth; Gaharis—Harry; Ector—Rory; Tristram—Sam; Percival—Percy; Lamorak—Lanny; Bedivere—Dickie; Lucan—Luke; Accolon—Ack Ack; and Bors—Boris. We all have silly nicknames as well."

Melliagraunce held in his laughter. Galahad was still such a prig.

"Melly, we're glad you've come." Red-haired Gareth rose, his Scots brogue thick as ever.

"Pukka of you, old man." Lamorak, next to Galahad, extended a bandaged hand.

"Every pilot counts," said Accolon, turning away rather quickly. He must have caught sight of the scabbard, which he'd once stolen from Arthur.

"Isn't it hard to keep up this fiction?" Melliagraunce walked to a makeshift table and poured some lukewarm tea.

"Not really," Gawaine—Sapper Control—spoke from the back of the room. "New men come in all the time, some with a few hours' training, so *we* seem right as rain. We're from '13 Group,' you see; our Spits are 'hot off Beaverbrook's line.' The rest, Dowding takes care of."

"Who is he?" asked Melliagraunce, balancing his tea.

"He needs pilots is all we know."

Melliagraunce nodded and bowed to Bedivere, the miscreant from Camlann.

"Pay attention, sprog." Lucan took Percival aside. The grizzled vet—no more than 20—tried to advise the new lad. "Don't follow a 109 down; another one'll get you if you do."

"Always maintain the height advantage," said Gaharis, demonstrating with his hands.

Melliagraunce smiled. "This squad. Is it any good?"

"Good! Come on now!" came the chorus.

"I'll have you know, Melly, we've the highest kill ratio

going, and we've flown five sorties a day. For a month!" Bedivere sounded indignant.

"Shhh!"

A duty corporeal came in, scattering the men. Melliagraunce took up paper and pen and pretended to write home.

Daybreak. The corporeal removed blackout shutters, flooding the hut with sunlight. Melliagraunce went to a window. He had forgotten that England was lovely in summer.

10.00 A.M. The telephone bell sounded. Melliagraunce noticed a change in his squad: Accolon started to tremble; Lucan had to put down his cup.

"Yes sir. I understand sir. Right away." The corporeal stared at the phone, finally hanging it up. "Breakfast will be right over."

He was greeted with a barrage of cushions.

11.00 A.M. The gramophone squeaked out "Don't You Ever Cry" as Churchill exhorted from the wireless. Melliagraunce looked at the knights. They were shaky compared to Winnie. Every time they went up, they risked a second death.

11.05. "Yes sir. Yes sir." The corporeal clicked on a microphone, activating the Tannoy. "Phantom Squadron, scramble—phantom squadron, scramble." His voice sounded quite calm.

Melliagraunce ran with the others and seized a kit from the corner. In seconds, he was outside, ignoring a loud silver bell.

"This way, ace." Ector pointed to the tarmac, where Spits were dispersed in blast pens. Melliagraunce, sprinting past him, realized he had no plane.

"Over here sir! Over here!" Melliagraunce followed a young man's voice until it led him to a three-person ground crew. "We've taken the liberty, sir. We've been waiting."

The armourer, hands still greasy, led him to a roaring Spit. Beneath the cockpit was the painted word "DEFIANT"; on the side, familiar white letters, "S-M-K."

"'Sir Melliagraunce, Knight,'" said Melliagraunce. He swung

into his seat, and the rigger took over—fixing his straps; clipping his mask; connecting the R/T and oxy. "Sorry about the wait," said Melliagraunce, shouting through his mask to be heard.

He gave his crew the thumbs up. They yanked a battery cable from the Spit's nose; freed *The Defiant* from her chock block. Melliagraunce gunned the throttle, grass flattening beneath his slipstream. He took off not too badly, he thought, for only his second time.

Planes rose from every direction, narrowly escaping collision. The whistle of Spits grew louder as his squad formed up into three-man vics, with Galahad in the lead.

Galahad's voice—clear as always—crackled on the R/T. "Phantom Red Leader, calling Sapper. Airborne. What height?"

Gawaine answered from the ground. "Angels 20. Five-hundred bandits over the coast. Vector 180."

"Five-hundred! That's the whole bloody Luftwaffe!" Tristram sounded personally offended.

Galahad ignored him. "Check in, Red Section."

"Red Two," said Percival.

"Red Three," said Melliagraunce, holding steady at Galahad's wing. As the four vics swung to the south, he formed part of a metal diamond.

Percival started to whistle "It Don't Mean A Thing (If It Ain't Got That Swing)."

"Put a sock in it," said Bedivere.

"Bandits approaching Canterbury, Red Leader. Let's gain some height!"

"Message received, Sapper. Listening out."

Galahad arced up sharply, almost standing on his tail, and Melliagraunce did the same. As his head pressed back, he tensed. Fighting to die was one thing, but fighting to live seemed so much more complicated.

"I say, it's a lovely view." Percival, his first time up, thought he was a tourist on holiday.

Melliagraunce looked in his rear-view mirror. He saw a tiny Canterbury Cathedral, twin spires outspread, like hands begging not to be bombed.

From above came the telltale drone.

"Bogies, twelve o'clock high!" Ector yelled.

Galahad throttled to maximum speed. "All right, lads. *Tallyho!*"

Melliagraunce followed him up, squinting against the glare.

Black dots grew larger, becoming familiar shapes, and he realized that each German bomber had an escort of five 109's.

Beware the Hun in the...

"Fatty's put up the whole fucking lot!" Gaharis, young as Percival, enjoyed his R.A.F. cover.

"Cut the chatter!" Galahad ordered. *"Line astern!"*

Melliagraunce stayed with him as the 109's peeled down. Galahad dropped his nose, leading the squad in a steep climbing turn. The Germans now buzzed below them.

"Stupid bastards!" Gareth yelled.

Melliagraunce saw explosive shells coming from a 109's wings. He went to switch on his gunsight, and discovered he'd already done it. Tom Knight was looking out for him.

To Tom, the sky was a cinema, black flak and white contrails. To Melliagraunce, it was a miracle, filled with British planes. Old Dowding ought to be king.

Melliagraunce hauled back on his stick, trying to keep up with Galahad. But swastikas—on yellow-gray tails—forced him into a roll.

Damn, Melliagraunce thought. *I'll never make a proper wingman.* He kicked his rudder and turned to the right, searching around for prey. A Do 17 filled his windscreen, its fighters harassed by Hurricanes.

Done this before, he told himself, and thumbed his firing button. Smoke poured from the bomber's port engine, followed by a sheet of flame. The place it had filled in the sky was empty.

"Good show!" Percival broke radio silence. "That's one Flying Pencil erased!"

Melliagraunce tried to smile, but his helmet was drenched with sweat. The kill had been too easy.

He craned his neck to the right. Percival took on a *staffel* of Heinkels, directing them back to France.

"Hey!" Melliagraunce had seen something else: a 109's yellow nose. "Percival—Percy—your tail!"

Percival looked back, featureless, headgear acting as helm.

The 109 played Mordred, using cannon instead of a spear.

"DON'T DIVE!" Melliagraunce screamed, a phantom smell—his own burnt flesh—nearly making him sick.

Too late. Melliagraunce trailed both planes down, knowing which had the advantage. He gave the German a burst, but smoke clouded his windshield; when it cleared, he saw Percival's Spit, a meteor shower of pieces.

"Damn!" Melliagraunce pounded his control stick. He hadn't known Percival well, but both were sworn to the Table. He wouldn't let the German get away with it.

The 109 saw him coming, and made a series of snaking turns. Not smart, Melliagraunce thought, to turn in front of a Spitfire. He let the German have 1200 rounds, the recoil shaking his shoulders.

Old Yellow Nose snuck behind him and the air lit up with tracer. Melliagraunce rolled on his back, straining against his straps. He caught a strange view of Canterbury—Cathedral touching his head—before bringing the Spit around.

109. There he was, the bastard, arse exposed, trying to go into a half-roll.

"Now!" Melliagraunce yelled to his guns, and he fired from 200 yards. The 109 sputtered and went belly up, a fish already fried.

Melliagraunce yelled over engine noise. "Hal, we lost Percy, but I got the bugger who chopped him. Where are—?"

A thud, like being brained by steel. Trailing black smoke and the strong smell of glycol. *"Where are you?!"* Melliagraunce shouted, craning his neck around. He spotted his attacker—a lone 109—who'd tailed him as he'd tailed Mordred.

Don't follow a 109 down...another one'll get you if you do."

Right, Melliagraunce thought, popping the hatch, tearing off his straps, and baling over the side. This was getting to be old hat.

He pulled his ripcord and felt the wrench as his canopy unfurled. All was fine, except for one thing. The 109, diving with him, getting ready to strafe.

Not Code, Melliagraunce thought; *not Code at all.* He wished this Jerry were Hartmann, an opponent one could respect; a true Knight Of the Air. Hartmann. Melliagraunce reached in his right trouser pocket, pulling out the Iron Cross. It had suffered a bit of a sea-change, but was none the worse for wear.

The German came closer; so close, Melliagraunce feared for his chute. He looked at the man in the cockpit: he was big and blond and clenched a cigar in his teeth.

The German pointed to the Cross and waved; Melliagraunce waved back, watching him climb out of sight.

He drifted down in a quiet sky, the September sun at its apex. He hoped that the AA and Home Guard wouldn't take him for a Jerry.

No sign on the ground of pitchforks or guns. Maybe his luck had changed. He kicked up dirt as he landed in a garden, between the cabbages and the sprouts.

Melliagraunce took off his harness. A man—dour-faced and ancient—came round with a hose in his hand.

"Excuse me sir," he said, "but this happens to be private property."

Melliagraunce went up two more times that day. At 3.00, he raced over London, playing skysweep to a band of Heinkels; at

6.00, he and his squad drove twenty 110's from Woolston.

Funny how a scabbard—and a toy or two—could scare the mighty Luftwaffe.

9 P.M. The Phantoms met at the WHITE HART in Brasted, all except Percival and Accolon. True to R.A.F. form, no mention was made of the fallen.

Melliagraunce raised his glass. *Here's to you Percy; and you, Ack Ack. Again, you served as The Few. No man could ask for better.*

"Shhh!" A Captain waved his cap for silence. From the wireless came the Report: "*185 enemy aircraft shot down…*"

Fours squads of Spits and Hurricanes doused one another with beer. Melliagraunce drained his glass. He'd added three to that score.

"It's all bosh, you know."

Melliagraunce turned to see Dowding, who led him to a quiet table. "In truth, they lost 56. No matter. Propaganda will make up the difference."

"You're a one-track man, aren't you?" Melliagraunce stared at Dowding's gold braid.

"When I tried to follow two tracks, I'm afraid it ended badly."

"You mean Mordred, I suppose." Melliagraunce, light-headed, decided to play his hunch.

"I mean Guinivere, son of my friend. I'm afraid you've confused me with Arthur."

"Ah." Melliagraunce understood, which only confused him more. "Where *is* he, Sir Hugh?"

"Look for the man with the walking stick. He leads the country still."

A queer way to talk about Winnie, thought Melliagraunce.

"Knight, let me tell you something." Dowding refused a drink. "In two days, Hitler will cancel this invasion. The Battle of Britain is over."

"Then you don't need us." Melliagraunce looked down. The thought of the stone seemed so cold.

"Not at present. But in future...one must be at constant readiness."

"Yes sir."

Dowding put out his hand, and Melliagraunce grasped it firmly. To be honored by the world's greatest knight was as good as a Victoria Cross.

It drizzled the morning of the 16th, when the Phantoms took off from Biggin. Only ten now, with Lucan and Gaheris battered. They all needed to rest.

"Check in, Red Section."

"Red Three," said Melliagraunce.

"Red Four," said Bedivere.

"Four? There is no Red Four!" Galahad sounded offended.

"Lighten up, man! It's not the Grail." Gawaine acted as his wingman.

"This is the last transmission of Phantom Squad. Angels 10. Listening out."

Melliagraunce banked away from the others, watching them slant toward cloud cover. He saw each man go through, green Spit merging with white, but none came out the other side.

Melliagraunce took the plunge. He raised his hood and ripped off his mask, exulting as the soft stuff touched his face. Hardness—and stone—had no place above the surface.

Before him was an island. An island on an island, fragrant and green, with a near-full Table of Knights.

In a short space of time, he'd look forward to seeing Lancelot there; and Arthur, with his walking stick...the sword to fit his scabbard.

Paste-Bones and Ragdolls

Thomas Olivieri

My name is Willard of Gullminshire, and I will not lie to you. I
believe in horses, taxes, and the solid earth—and I will not be
fooled. On a cool summer evening I was riding back from
Hedgerowton when a storm came and overtook me quite
unexpectedly. It had been a clear day and I had hoped to make it
home by morning. But I was not desirous of catching a cold and
so secured shelter under a large oak where an old man on foot
had already stopped and appeared to be sleeping soundly. He
seemed quite vulnerable but had the one quality that was the
downfall of all common thieves—abject poverty. I am no baron
but a simple small-time merchant, and one who fancies himself a
gentleman, and so I was in no position to reduce the wretch
further. I saw no scoundrel's profit in the plucked hen of a man
before me.

It was a trick of the half-light that made me comment—
aloud—on his gaunt and twisted figure: "What a sad pile of rags
and bones is he. He is so thin that one can practically see through
to his skeleton. Indeed, he has hardly more skin than a roasted
chicken. I imagine that a fairy-tale witch would refuse to buy
such bones as his thinking that they were paste."

I was scarcely done speaking when the old man began to stir.
As he did it was clear that he was as healthy as a man could be if
any man lived to his advanced age. He spoke no English in his
half-sleep, but went on mumbling and hocusing-pocusing like a
street magician; even more, his accent had an unwelcome
singsong quality, an odd lilt, that made me fear that he was a
confidence man or Welch. As he began to start and stretch I
unharnessed my horse and let him graze under the tree. I didn't
bother tying him up as he disliked the rain even more than I did.
The skies were darker than I had ever seen them. In a few

moments noon had been transformed to midnight and I was
thankful that the canopy of leaves above me let in only a little bit
of rain. All around the tree the runoff fell like the water from a
fountain. In the few moments in which I had my back turned,
Old Paste-Bones had sat up and was regarding me with those
confidence man's eyes. I could tell from his sad ragged look
that, though he was harmless, he would be poor company and I
eagerly awaited the rain to lift. I dearly missed my wife and
hoped that she was doing well without me.

"You have the air of a worried man about you." The old man
sounded groggy and I could hardly hear him over the sound of
the rain. "As if you were concerned with your wife's actions
while you are gone."

"Why," I said, "every man should have his mind on his wife
while he is away."

"Hmmm..." he said. He hmmmmmed a long while and he
spoke in a way that blended with the patter of rain drops... "and,
I might add, you have a look of a man who has failed to sell a
horse. It's surprising what one could learn from 'a sad pile of
rags and bones.'" The old man of course had made a lucky
guess, about the horse. Indeed I had heard of such deeds from
thieves and Welchmen. I wasn't in any position to argue and I
had no desire to play his game so I hmmmmed him as
thoughtfully as he did me. In fact I did him better. I hmmmmed
in as superior a manner as I could.

But he said nothing, made no reply at all, and being so not
spoken to by one such as he infuriated me, passed reason
perhaps. "I have no need for such a nonsensical conversation as
the one you have given me!" I have nothing to prove or hide.
My worrying or not worrying about my wife and my selling or
not selling of my horse are none of your concern! My Christian
name is Willard and I am not a fool!" I was shouting—partly
over the sound of the rain, partly because an old man is likely to
be hard of hearing, and partly because old men are very often

112

boys who need shouting at.

"I suppose that you already know me," the old man said. I have been famous for many long years in these parts since before the days of Merlin. I was famous before him and and more famous because of him, being, as I was, something of a mentor to him. Indeed when he set the kingdom ablaze with glory, I was a 'Bleys' already."

"Arrant nonsense!" I reminded him. "And next I suppose that you will swallow a live toad to show your invulnerability to poison!" I then gave Old Paste-Bones as forceful a screed as if he were a saucy school-boy and really I didn't—and to this day don't—think that he was much else.

He grinned at me like a backwards child.

What could he have said? "Why I don't believe in this Merlin any more than I do the witch who wouldn't buy your bones." I thought that I could feel a change in the air coming as I spoke and looked forward to better conversations with drunker people at the tavern up the road.

"Indeed she wouldn't: she isn't real and they're not for sale. And, anyway, there is still my inconvenient roasted chicken flesh hanging on them, however loosely. So you think the old stories are nonsense? I was there. I wrote them down as they happened, at least the ones dealing with my old apprentice…" His voice trailed off in the sound of the rain.

Sitting in silence with this man was as insufferable as speaking to him. Furthermore, I didn't want him to think that he had fooled me, so I began again: "Those are nonsense tales of wizards, and elephants, and lions—imaginary creatures no sensible man has ever seen!"

"But a sensible man simply uses his senses. What if I had proof? Something you see? After all Gawain's skull is kept on Skye…"

"So they say, but I have seen enough skulls of Saint John the Baptist to supply all of the building stones required in building a cathedral to Saint Credulity. While one skull may be Saint John's all of them cannot be. And I doubt any of them are."

"Hmmmm...you are right about that, but aren't the stories enough whether they happened or not?"

"No they must be real to be real! That fact is a fact! One must believe what one sees! One must not indulge in willful illusions or doubt one's senses."

I must have been looking down for a moment and when I looked up again he was holding a large harp (which previously must have been obscured by the tree-trunk), perhaps three feet tall and two and a half wide with carven knights and ladies painted in strong colors with gilded highlights, and began playing and chanting in the old manner:

> *The good king   called to tourney*
> *powerful knights   proven in warfare,*
> *and young squires   eager for the saddle,*
> *and eager to prove   their prowess in combat,*
> *to please a queen   and to pacify a crowd*
> *longing to see   the sight of blood*
> *and wanting to watch   the glory of the winners*
> *and the losers languish   as they lie on the field*
> *uncertain of the prospect   of a second chance.*
>
> *He sent out word   to villages and cities*
> *and so gathered about him   the strong and great.*
>
> *Each took a favor   from a favored woman:*
>
> *Sir Bors was first   who never boastful,*
> *carried in battle   a lady's kerchief*
> *that he might do   his sacred duty*
> *to please a king here   and so his King in Heaven.*

114

The second in the field   was fearsome Sir Kay,
who was fearless in combat,   and who carried a favor
to win glory   on the gore-strewn pitch.
Hail and brash   he boasted to his comrades.
He was a knight of courage   and kinsman to the king.

The last was the greatest   and was sung in legend—
the queen's protector   and lone consort
the Breton, Sir Lancelot,   Knight of the Lake,
who took her favor   and tied it to the hilt
of his long sword   hung by his loins.

Those names shook the knees   of stalwart knights,
And few men   would face them in battle.
All of them were young   and yet they were legends.

Not one   had deigned to notice
a little child   loafing about,
a dirt-stained girl,   who'd brought a doll
—twine-fastened refuse   of rag and bone—
to give to a knight   like a noblewoman's favor.
Those knights nearly   knocked her over
rushing passed   as they readied for battle.
Till she came to Gawain   leaning on a gate.
Though he didn't intend   to fight that day,
he donned his armor   and took her doll
for he couldn't neglect   the strictures of courtesy.

He didn't care   for cheering crowds,
the notice of kings,   the courting of ladies,
the clangor of swords,   or queenly notice.

And soon Bors was unhorsed   his shield broken,
as was fearsome Kay   who crumpled to the ground,

115

and Lancelot fell   by his friend's sword.
And a peasant girl   dined with great
at the king's court,   beside the queen

who heaved a sigh   and a sidelong glance
at her lone consort   The Knight of the Lake,
(her favored failure   whose fault brought a peasant)
and coldly regarded them   with queenly distain
as she pawed the doll   in her delicate hands.

When he was done chanting I had wanted to quibble with several points (not the least of which was the pronounced lack of his alleged apprentice), but a weariness overtook me and I fell asleep. I am usually better company but something had made me tired. When I awoke the next day I found the old man had stolen my horse, and, as I was no longer mounted, and it was a bright and sunny midday (a whole night must have passed—there wasn't a puddle on the road) I saw no reason to try and follow him. And as the hoof prints had washed away, I couldn't guess which way he went.

I could not say that he left me entirely in the lurch as I found in my pocket a strange coin with a tired young king on the face, and a hand arising from the sea holding a sword on the reverse. It was heavy and real gold, but I suspected it was foreign and so I traded it for a handful of copper pennies at the earliest opportunity.

Bel Nemeton

Jon Black

The dream was over. Tears streaked down his wizened face as he surveyed the landscape. Bodies lie strewn throughout the Camlann Valley, chill winds carrying the stench of smoke and blood into his acute nostrils. He had arrived too late, taking too long to escape the bewitching Nimue's imprisonment. The escape was a tale worthy of Arthur's best knights, but it didn't matter. He had failed in his duty.

In his mind, Myrddin saw how the battle had unfolded, as surely as if he witnessed it. Without the benefit of his counsel and his knowledge of tactics learned from the old Romans, Arthur and his men had simply charged, trusting that valor and strength of arms alone could carry the day against the rebellious Mordred and his Saxon allies. Arthur and his knights had won the battle…and destroyed themselves in the process. The king had lingered for several hours afterward, so Myrddin had been told. But the old man had not reached the Camlann in time to say goodbye.

Now, Brittan was without her king. The foe was vanquished, but there would be another wave of Saxons. As far as he could tell, there would *always* be another wave of Saxons.

"Myrddin."

He looked up, it was Cei.

"Is it done?" Myrddin asked, wiping the tears from his face.

Cei nodded gravely. Myrddin noticed the wound to his face. His cheek would always have a scar. It would match the one on his heart.

"What will you do now?"

Cei considered the question. "Stay here. Rally the others. Try to pick up the pieces. You?"

Myrddin, too, thought before answering. "Darkness descends upon this land and no man shall stop it. I shall walk the wide world searching for Arthur's spirit. And, if I do not find it, I shall simply go home."

"God be with you in your quest," Cei said.

"And the gods be with you in yours."

"Damn it," Vivian Cuinnsey swore at her computer. Once again the document she was preparing failed to format properly.

"Everything okay, Doc?" Grant, her graduate assistant, poked his head through the door.

"I'll get this. Eventually. It'll be fine."

That stretched the truth. Since becoming department chair last year, she had been immersed in a world of budgets, policies, and departmental politics that bordered on vendettas. Keeping a department full of idiosyncratic Celtic Language scholars running was a full time job. Unfortunately, her four classes, complete with rubrics, lesson plans, and grading meant Vivian already had a full-time job.

Now, she faced additional pressure from an impending meeting with an Irish-American CEO who, having embraced his roots, was considering making a sizable endowment to her department. The document which had frustrated Vivian all afternoon was part of her campaign to make the donation a reality.

Another half-hour resolved the formatting issue. Sending Grant home for the day, Vivian also prepared to leave. Checking email once more before closing her laptop, she was surprised by a message from Dr. Weldon Grassley, a venerable professor emeritus with her university's Department of Archeology. Well past retirement age, Grassley remained on the university's payroll and perpetually in the field at excavations throughout Central Asia.

"Dear Vivian, I would be interested in your thoughts on this."

An attached photo showed a stele, an upright stone plinth, bearing inscriptions in three alphabets. The top two were unrecognizable to her. The first was all thick shapes and dramatic lines. The second was full of thin lines and loops. The third was Latin.

She was unsure why Grassley sent the photo to her, though Vivian's interest was piqued. Greek inscriptions, courtesy of Alexander the Great, were sometimes found that far east. Latin was another matter entirely. A glance told her that, while the script was Latin, the language it recorded certainly wasn't. That was no surprise. The script of the far-reaching Romans was borrowed by many peoples for recording languages not previously written. Excluding the cumbersome Ogham script, that included her beloved Celts.

Unraveling the Latin script's phonetics, Vivian saw familiar patterns. They were patterns far better suited to the tongues of long ago Britain and Gaul than to the dusty caravan routes of Central Asia. The inscription appeared to be some form of Insular Celtic, the language family to which all living Celtic languages belonged. Grabbing pen and notepad, Vivian scanned the weathered letters again. She jotted a quick translation, using brackets to indicate words that were likely to be proper nouns and offsetting confusing or unclear sections with parenthesis.

The Great King [Tarkhun] (causes to be raised?) this monument. (Unclear) house of the Great Counselor [Mirdin] in his honor. (Unclear) Great Counselor to King [Tarkhun] for this (two-ten years?), formerly counselor to Great King [Irturus] of the sunset lands. With Great King [Tarkun's] blessings, [Mirdin] departs to the sunset lands to look upon (its?) green trees and endless water (one last time?).

The inscription was a potential bombshell. A career could be made, or broken, by those few lines in stone. But it might have implications far beyond that. A quick mental calculation told Vivian it was too early to call Uzbekistan. By the time she got home, made dinner, and settled in, it would be the perfect time to catch Grassley before he left for the dig site.

Leftovers put away and coffee in hand, she sat at her computer. Dart, Vivian's black cat, orbited her legs, occasionally staring up at her with his yellow eyes and big ears. She thought about the scrawny kitten he'd been when he first appeared on her doorstep, one ear inexplicably smudged with motor oil.

Initiating a video chat, Vivian was rewarded with the image of Dr. Grassley's birdlike features, mop of white hair, and thick spectacles. "Dr. Cuinnsey, I thought I might be hearing from you."

"Dr. Grassley, what have you dug up?"

"It is a puzzle, isn't it, my dear? We're excavating near a small structure the locals venerate as the tomb of a Sufi saint. But we've dated it to the Sixth Century, a couple centuries too old for a Sufi." Grassley paused and cleaned his glasses. "Were you able to translate the Roman script on the stele? Was it Celtic?"

"It was. And I was, most of it, anyway. I'm emailing the translation now. How did you know it was Celtic?"

"An educated guess. After making a phonetic transcription, I consulted the standard references and did some online research. Celtic was one of the few language families I couldn't rule out. I thought I'd see if you could shed any light on this little mystery."

"What are the other languages on the stele?" Vivian asked. "I didn't recognize either script."

"They are both in the Sogdian language. The first is the classical Sogdian script. The other is the slightly easier Manichean script. With the caveat that we understand rather less about Sogdian than Celtic, they give translations broadly matching yours."

That pleased Vivian. Of course, it didn't really answer any questions about the stele or its inscriptions.

"Sogdian is distantly related to modern Farsi," he continued, "The spelling of this word 'Mirdin' on the stele is equivalent to 'Lord of God' or 'Noble of God.' I imagine this translates conceptually as 'pious leader' or something like that, which sounds like a title. But notice that the word is already accompanied by the title 'Grand Vizier,' or what you translated as 'Great Counselor.' So, I am inclined to believe 'Mirdin' is a name, not a title."

Grassley flashed a mischievous smile. "Of course, 'Mirdin' would also be phonetically identical to the Celtic name of the individual commonly called Merlin, wouldn't it?"

"Careful, Grassley," Vivian shot back with hard-earned caution, "You're about to open one of the biggest can of worms in Celtic studies. The historicity of Merlin, or Myrddin in Celtic, is very controversial. Even the affirmative camp posits Myrddin is an amalgam of multiple figures stretching across centuries. Arguing for the existence a single individual analogous to the character from mythology is a good way to end a career."

"An intriguing point, given the reference to the 'Great King Irturus' and the 'sunset lands.'"

Thrilled by those same implications just hours ago, Vivian was suddenly in no mood to discuss them with the elderly archeologist. Again, Vivian cautioned Dr. Grassley about the rabbit hole he was circling.

"You can grasp the significance of uncovering Latin inscriptions in Uzbekistan," he told her. "To say nothing of ones used to transliterate Celtic. We're holding a press conference in Samarkand next week. I'd really like you to be here."

Vivian thought it over. "I'm going to follow this development very closely. But, at this point, I can't justify taking time off from my department based on one find, no matter how unusual."

"Regrettable. I always enjoy seeing you. But I understand. I will keep you informed of any developments."

"On more thing, Grassley."

"Yes?"

"Not a word about the whole Merlin thing. Not one word."

Her meeting with the CEO went well. If Vivian guessed right, and she usually did, a few more glad-handing sessions would secure the endowment. For now, it was on to preparing for next week's meeting with the board of regents.

She had tried to put Grassley's puzzle, with all its bizarre implications, out of her mind. Tried with only limited success. Vivian spent more hours than she cared to admit trying to date the inscription using telltale elements of its grammar and vocabulary. She reached a verdict of late Sixth Century. The right era, it had to be acknowledged, for a historical Myrddin.

Writing follow-up emails to the CEO and his staff, Vivian received another email from Dr. Grassley. "Excavated the structure today. Features are consistent with a dwelling not a tomb. Think you might be interested in the interior's more…unusual…aspects. Yours, G."

Many photos were attached.

The first showed a weathered stone building adorned with flowers, colorful scraps of cloth, and little bits of paper. This was the structure Grassley referenced during their conversation, Vivian concluded. Using the people in the photo to provide scale, the building must have been about ten feet wide, a little taller, and maybe twenty feet long.

The following photos showed interior decoration. The spirals and elaborate scrollwork certainly looked Celtic, but that could be coincidence. She knew Sarmatians and Circassians used similar motifs. Why not another steppe culture of the same era like the Sogdians?

The frescos were an entirely different matter. The enclosed structure and arid environment combined to create a perfect preservation climate. The vivid blues of the ocean and greens of endless forests, neither found within a one thousand miles of Uzbekistan, testified to that. And were those Red Deer and Otters? One picture could easily be the white cliffs of Dover. Another the pink cliffs of Brittany. Another fresco could only be Stonehenge. Its trilithons and bluestones, accurately but artistically rendered, rose above Salisbury plain.

It all bespoke a man suffering terminal homesickness in a faraway land.

Finally, a stylized portrait of a king, painted in the traditional Celtic fashion. Young, handsome, almost saintly. Clutching a sword in his hands. Vivian sounded out the Ogham inscription on its blade, "Caledfwich." That name would become Caliburnus and, still later, Excalibur.

"Grant, send an email to the regents. We need to reschedule the meeting."

"Sure, Doc, why?"

"I'm going to Uzbekistan."

He had been to the end of the earth, literally. Myrddin found where the sun rose over another endless water. Unless, of course, the Greek sages in Alexandria were correct that men walked on a sphere and all waters eventually flowed together. At the end of the earth, he traded wisdom at the court of Sui Emperor, who was said to be immortal. He learned the secrets of the silk that flowed ever westward, eventually becoming worth is weight in gold.

He walked westward, following the path of silk, returning to the land where cities worthy of the Romans sprang from rainless wastes. Here were peaceful, honorable people. They paid heed to the spirit world, in such a multitude of forms that even Myrrdin found it overwhelming.

Some worshiped the God of Rome that was, somehow, also not the God of Rome. Others worshiped one God that was not the God of Rome. A third group worshiped no Gods and focused on releasing their souls from the cycle of rebirth. Others saw spirits in every rock, tree, and animal. It was among this group that Myrddin felt most comfortable, able to speak of things he had not spoken of since Britain.

It was not Camelot. Tarkun was not Arthur. But both were the closest he had found, so he stayed. He had mastered their strange tongue and curious right-to-left scripts. He offered his services to Tarkun just as he had to Arthur.

It was the most grueling flight of Vivian's life. First to London, then Dubai, then finally Samarkand. The city's name itself, she learned from her inflight reading, was Sogdian in origin, "Town of stone fortifications." She had pushed off most of her departmental commitments for a week. More importantly, Dart was in Grant's care. After all, what were graduate assistants for?

Spending nearly a full day in the air, Vivian reviewed what little was known about the Sogdians. Even the names and dates of their kings were incomplete. Sogdia had been a thriving and affluent trading civilization along the Silk Road. Its peaceable people were ethnically and religiously diverse. Animists, Buddhists, Nestorian Christians, and Zoroastrians had rubbed shoulders in a climate of tolerance and intellectual exchange.

She also reviewed material infinitely more familiar to her. Almost every word written about Myrddin, whether as a figure of history or mythology, was controversial. Even the simple question of whether Arthur's beloved counselor and wizard came from Wales or Brittany provoked academic feuds and bar brawls alike. Vivian was grateful her Manx heritage allowed her to remain safely neutral in such feuds.

There were many legends about the fate of Merlin or, rather, Myrddin. Imprisoned in a tree. Buried in Broceliande Forest. Ascending the World Tree from Bel Nemeton and transcending earthly concerns. Those were just three of the more common tales. Even allegorically, none of them seemed to suggest Myrddin wandered thousands of miles into Asia's heart.

She resolved to stay gun-shy when discussing Myrddin with others. In the privacy of her own head, however, Vivian realized she was become less so.

From the air, Samarkand appeared to be a place apart; a separate creation by some god whose first love was desolation. A few unremarkable glass and steel skyscrapers gave lonely testimony to the outside world's existence. With its turquoise-capped mosques and gracefully arched structures of stone and baked clay, the rest of Samarkand looked as it must have in the days of the Silk Road. Beyond, rocky desert stretched unbroken in all directions.

Clearing passport control, Vivian was greeted by Dr. Grassley's welcoming grin. His gangly arms wrapped her in an affectionate hug before introducing his colleagues from the excavation's partner institutions. Dr. Laziza Abdulin, from Samarkand State University, was a petite woman in her late-twenties Dressed in a tasteful pantsuit and matching hijab, she radiated energy. She was quiet, with the eyes of someone who misses little and leaves much unsaid. Dr. Adrian Price, from the School of African and Oriental Studies in London, was near Vivian's age and maintained an air of detached calculation.

Nothing had prepared Vivian for Samarkand's streets. Bumper to bumper, the motley assortment of European sports cars, four-wheel drives, aging Ladas, ancient buses, and donkey carts had one thing in common. They were all going nowhere fast. Only the flocks of mopeds and bicycles, darting like hummingbirds amidst elephants, moved.

After checking-in to her hotel, one those lonely modern buildings glimpsed from the air, the archeologists treated Vivian to dinner in the city's old quarter. One thing could certainly be said for the Uzbeks, they knew how to cat. Platters of spiced minced lamb, roasted beef, hot flatbread, and rice with apricots and nuts left her feeling fit to burst. As the quartet ate, they discussed the press conference scheduled for the following morning. The three archeologist dropped hints of some big announcement but all of them, even Grassley, were coy about specifics.

They also talked about the dig itself. While a certain amount of theft and smuggling was to be expected at excavations in remote parts of the world, the problem as this site was endemic. The archeologists suspected a mole somewhere on the dig team.

Detecting a faint musical lilt in his otherwise flawless

Oxbridge accent, Vivian inquired about Dr. Price's origins. The archeologist, it turned out, was Welsh and from an old Swansea family. Occasionally speaking with him in his native tongue, Vivian felt she softened his prim exterior just a bit.

Before separating for the evening, Grassley caught her alone. "I have something for you, my dear."

"You're going to let me in on the surprise you keep hinting about?"

Grassley laughed, "Even better." Reaching into his pocket, he pulled out a small bracelet of delicately worked bronze. "We found this in the structure," he beamed. "The preliminary processing and necessary paperwork is all done. When you get home, I'm sure my colleagues in the archeology department will find it a worthy addition to our collection. Until then, consider it a gift."

Back at her hotel, Vivian examined the bracelet. She was no archeologist, but the scrollwork appeared be a combination of Celtic and Roman styles. Although it was most unprofessional, she slipped it onto her wrist. It fit perfectly.

By his reckoning, Myrddin had seen nearly 100 turnings of the year. It was a potent number in any culture. He thought briefly of the clever counting system he learned from the sages of the Deccan Plateau. In his mind, he saw the "1" slide into place in a new column, followed by two of those ingenious placeholder digits which carried meaning but no value.

Even had all the stories whispered by Britons about Myrddin's origins been true, he could not have much time left. True, there was no Arthur to go back to. No Camelot. But he still yearned to hear the laughing waves and smell the fragrant pines one more time. His bones cried out to slumber in their native soul.

Home was calling him. Myrddin resolved to go.

Next morning at the press conference, Vivian was greeted immediately by Dr. Grassley who took obvious pleasure escorting her to a first row seat. At the front of the room, a raised platform with three empty chairs indicated where Drs. Grassley, Abdulin, and Price would sit. Vivian was more intrigued by the small table in front of the chairs. A black sheet covered the tabletop, concealing a lumpy form beneath.

Vivian was pleased that the conference room was full. She spotted many of her colleagues from around the world, specialists in the languages, history, or archeology of the Celts. Though she wouldn't recognize them, she knew their counterparts specializing in Central Asia were here as well. More surprisingly, there were plenty of journalists present.

Seated between the academics and the journalists were several questionable looking individuals she couldn't recognize. "Who are they?"

"Vultures," Grassley responded. "Treasure hunters," he clarified, "You get used to their type working out here." The archeologist identified some of the more infamous ones for her. "That's Mikhail Levich," he pointed at an avuncular man wearing a finely tailored suit. "He was with the KGB in Uzbekistan back when it was part of the Soviet Union. He still has a lot of influence." Next, Grassley indicated a man in a cowboy hat. "That's Jake Booker. He owned a company that made a lot of money prospecting for oil and gas. Then he went into treasure hunting." Finally, he gestured to a small man in an extravagant uniform. "That's Gumanizov. He's a general in the Uzbek army but his real racket is smuggling arms and drugs. Maybe antiquities, too."

The press conference began with Dr. Grassley summarizing the stele, and the excavation of the dwelling. The archeologists provided translations of the stele's three inscriptions, thanking Vivian for providing the Celtic translation.

Grassley acknowledged the possible connection between the word "Mirdin" on the stele and the Celtic name "Myrddin." It was from the latter, he pointed out, the name "Merlin" was derived. Though not endorsing any hypothesis, the team noted the frescos could certainly argue for a Western European connection. Without mentioning the possibility that Mirdin was, in some sense, the figure known as Merlin, Grassley and his team left the question hanging heavily in the air.

So far, Vivian thought it a deft performance. While the excitement the team generated would be great for publicity and funding, they stopped just shy of saying anything that could get them academically drawn and quartered.

"In the days after excavating the dwelling," Grassley continued, "We uncovered another tablet dealing with Mirdin and his departure homeward from Sogdia. This tablet adds that, when Mirdin left, he took with him what the tablet refers to as 'his great treasure.' It also includes a detailed description of the area where Mirdin planned to build his tomb. In theory, the tomb's location could be pinpointed by matching the tablet's description with known landmarks. So far, we have been unable to make such a connection."

Together, Grassley, Abdulin, and Price yanked the black cloth off the display table. It revealed an unassuming tablet of baked clay, not much larger than a paperback. Flashes from a hundred cameras and phones went off at once.

What Grassley and his team were calling the Treasure Tablet also contained tripartite inscriptions in Sogdian, Manichean, and Celtic written with Roman script. Clearly, this was the surprise Grassley had teased her with last night. She couldn't imagine why he hadn't invited her to examine the Celtic. Was he more jealous and territorial than she realized?

After the team presented the Treasure Tablet, they opened the conference for questions. The room erupted in bedlam.

Vivian cringed as the journalists seized upon the Merlin angle. Many were incredulous but a few seemed far too credulous, instead. The treasure hunters, in contrast, were pragmatism. Where is the treasure? How do you get there? Do you know what kind of treasure? Grassley politely rebuffed such questions, repeated they just didn't know yet. If the hunters persisted, Dr. Abdulin's baleful stare silenced them.

The academics were the worst. Like circling sharks, each was determined to be the one responsible for discrediting the archeologists' claims. Even with limited information, the other scholars confidently proclaimed that the frescoes must be of the Aral Sea, or the team had dated the site incorrectly, or their translations were erroneous.

Vivian was not immune. Not having examined the Treasure Tablet, she asked some pointed questions about why the team assumed the tablet was Insular Celtic rather the extinct Continental Celtic. She also emphasized the risks of reading too much into transliterations of proper nouns. Vivian kept to herself the fact that she has spent much of the past week doing precisely that.

As a linguist droned on about a minor point of Sogdian grammar, Vivian's attention drifted. It came roaring back with the cacophony of doors crashing open and sounds of gunfire and screaming filling the conference room.

A dozen men in olive-colored fatigues marched into the room. Their uniforms lacked names or insignias. Bandanas concealed their faces. With guns leveled and firing, they first secured the main door and then rushed towards the display table.

Her head was down but her eyes and ears were open. The screams, she noted, were screams of fear, not pain. Scanning the room she saw few actual injuries. The gunfire seemed intended to frighten rather than kill. Vivian began paying careful attention to events unfolding around her.

She watched in fascination as a treasure hunter, "Booker" she thought Grassley called him, calmly stuck a cowboy boot in front of the lead gunman. As he stumbled and slowed, the other gunmen piled up behind him and struggled to keep their footing.

Vivian kicked off her heels, the better to run with, and dashed madly toward the display table. Before the gunmen fully recovered from their collision, she grabbed the Treasure Tablet. Sprinting through a side door, Vivian's peripheral vision saw the assailants following her.

In the lobby, Vivian crouched behind a potted plant, trying to remain unseen. A hand pressed upon her shoulder. It was the cowboy treasure hunter, an index finger pressed tightly against his lips. Face-to-face, she took a good look at Jake Booker. A mane of silver hair framed a craggy face and pale blue eyes. A trim, athletic frame testified that treasure hunting kept him in good shape.

He motioned for Vivian to follow. On impulse, she resolved to trust him, for now. They were almost outside before the gunmen spotted them and gave chase.

Rushing across the street and weaving through the heavy, creeping traffic of one of Samarkand's busiest roads, the cowboy led them into a vacant construction site. The steel skeleton of a large building stood unfinished and abandoned in the summer heat. As they ran under the metal frame, the cowboy rounded on their pursuers. Landing a solid uppercut on one, he grappled with the other. He wasn't losing the brawl but didn't seem able to gain the upper hand, either.

As the fight continued, a third figure clad in olive drab arrived. Drawing his submachinegun, he ignored Vivian and pointed it toward the melee. Amid the chaos, he was unable to get a clear shot at the cowboy. Irritated by the gunman's complete disregard for her presence, Vivian noted a length of pipe on the ground.

The treasure hunter finally incapacitated his two opponents. Looking back, his eyes traveled to the third gunman, unconscious on the ground, and then to the pipe in Vivian's hands. He looked at her quizzically.

"What, you're the only one who can rough up a goon?"

"I didn't say anything." He dusted off his hat.

"Jake Booker," he extended his hand.

"Dr. Vivian Cuinnsey," she said, shaking the hand.

Exiting through the opposite side of the construction site, a black sedan roared to a stop in front of them. Its doors flew open as more gunmen got out. "Why don't you step into my office?" Vivian cringed at the slight melodic trill of the voice from inside the sedan.

Dr. Price's smile appeared courteous. The smile of the gunmen next to him, less so.

"The Treasure Tablet, please?" asked the Welshman.

With no real alternative, Vivian took the heavy clay piece from her purse and handed it over. As the car made its way through Samarkand's streets, the guard kept his weapon trained on her. She tried not to think about whether the safety was on. If the answer was no, given the state of Samarkand's roads, the results could be messy.

"I don't get it," she told their captor, "You're a principle investigator on the team that discovered the tablet. You'd have access to it any time you want. Why go through all of this?"

"I have my reasons."

"It's the treasure, isn't it? You think it's real."

Price said nothing.

Something else clicked into place for Vivian. "You're the one behind the thefts, aren't you? You're the mole."

"As it turns out, mercenaries aren't cheap. I needed a way to fund today's activities. Regrettably, your actions have complicated matters." Price held up a hand and the sedan came to a stop. Exiting the vehicle, he added, "I can't have the two of you connecting me to this. My associates are going to take you for a long ride into the desert."

They rode on in silence until they reached the edge of Samarkand. In what she assumed was Uzbek, Jake spoke to the gunmen. They broke into broad grins. A few moments later, the sedan made a U-turn and headed back into the city.

"What did you say them?" Vivian asked.

"Seven little words I've found extremely useful. 'Whatever he's paying you, I'll double it.'"

"Oh, and what if the person cutting the paycheck is female?"

For a moment, he looked a bit sheepish.

By the time they returned to the site of the press conference, Dr. Price had vanished from the city. Vivian checked on the other archeologists. Dr. Grassley had some nasty bruises from a hard fall during the attack, but nothing permanent. Dr. Abdulin was in state of shock which, after being informed that Dr. Price was behind it, turned to stony rage.

When Vivian found the cowboy again, he was speaking with the authorities. As that conversation concluded, he turned to her. "They know about Dr. Price now. They'll do everything they can. But, honestly, I wouldn't expect much. Anyone that planned all of this would have his exit from the county planed as well."

"You speak Uzbek?"

"I try to pick up the language anywhere I do business. It shows respect for local partners. And it's a way to watch your ass by being aware of what, and who, is being talked about."

"Jake, I don't want to be rude, but what's your angle in all of this?"

"Fair question," he replied. "I listened to your questions during the press conference. And you had the cajones to grab the tablet and run for it. If I were a betting man, and I am, I'd say you're the one who can find whatever that tablet leads to. Given recent events, I figure you might in the market for a partner."

"That's not a bad idea. But I'm an academic. Even if I do find anything, there are professional standards I have to follow. I can't just let you sell off pieces to the highest bidder. I don't see what's in this for you."

Jake smiled, "Let me worry about that. If I can't find a way to make money off this which doesn't involve selling your precious artifacts, I don't deserve to."

She though that over, "Okay. Tentatively, yes."

They shook on it.

That evening, they sat down with the other archeologists. Vivian was unsurprised to learn it had been Dr. Price who objected so vociferously to giving her access to the Treasure Tablet before the press conference. The archeologists were initially wary of Jake's presence but, after some whispering, acknowledged his involvement was probably a lesser evil then allowing Dr. Price to loot Myrddin's tomb or whatever else he had in mind.

"Dr. Grassley and I have already been considering how to proceed," Dr. Abdulin said. "The world's largest collection of Sogdian manuscripts is in Berlin, gathered from expeditions during the early twentieth century."

"It seems to us," Grassley picked up where his colleague left off, "If anyplace has information that duplicates the Treasure Tablet or provides other useful insights, it's there."

The archeologists had found an abstract of the Berlin collection, itself published in the 1920s, summarizing each manuscript and providing a master index of key terms and proper nouns appearing within the collection.

Scanning the index, Vivian found that the word "Mirdin," transliterated exactly as in the stele, occurred in three manuscripts. According to the abstract, Manuscript Six was a religious document, Manuscript 17 chronicled events in the kingdom, and Manuscript 24, potentially the motherlode, recorded Mirdin's life and travels. The abstract indicated each manuscript was trilingual. Vivian hoped this included the now familiar Latin-scripted Celtic.

"I don't suppose the full text or images of the manuscripts are available online?" Vivian knew the answer to question before she asked it.

Dr. Grassley smiled apologetically, "My dear, you of all people know how little money most institutions have for digitization. And these manuscripts have to be near the bottom of a very long list of priorities."

Jake looked at Vivian, "So, I guess you and I are going to Berlin."

Returning to the land between the two rivers, Myrddin again marveled at the ruins of humanity's oldest cities. Sheltering from the summer heat, he ate and drank in the shadow of a great temple, its series of ever-smaller stories stacked atop one another. As wind whistled through the vacant streets, the weight of time pressed down heavily. These stones had been abandoned for millennia.

He had been traveling for six weeks. Though the bulk of the journey still remained ahead, Myrddin swore sometimes he could already smell the sea, the morning mist, the plants and flowers of home.

He missed the smiling faces of Sogdia but had only one real regret. Among all his treasure, he had forgotten to pack the bracelet. It was nothing, really. Just a little bronze trinket. Still, it had been Nimue's. It was all he had to remember her. Momentarily, he considered returning for the bracelet. But, once more, he caught the scent of the sea.

Home was calling. And reminding him he had little time left.

Getting an early flight out of Samarkand was no problem. Changing their tickets in Dubai proved to be another matter entirely. Air travel's newest global hub was incredibly busy and, apparently, filled to capacity.

Jake had a long conversation with the ticket agent. Though Vivian didn't understand Arabic, the treasure hunter's tone sounded like equal parts pleading and threatening. In the end, he secured them same-day tickets to Frankfurt and, from there, Berlin.

"How many languages do you speak?" Vivian wanted to know.

"Enough." Jake replied.

They touched down on an unseasonably cool day. Their taxi

traveled downtown through Berlin's wide, tree-lined boulevards. On each side, they were flanked by the city's distinct architectural hodgepodge. Bold experiments in modernism rose alongside stately old imperial edifices from the days of the Hohenzollerns. The Ethnological Museum of Berlin, formerly the Royal Museum for Ethnography, was one of the latter.

The pair were met by the museum's assistant curator. After introductions, she escorted them through dimly-lit tunnels to a research room in the institution's expansive subbasement. Then she disappeared into deep storage, pulling one manuscript box at a time for Vivian and Jake to examine.

The manuscript in Box Six recorded a religious debate at the court of the Sogdian king. The participants were the enigmatic Mirdin and the head of Sogdia's Nestorian Church. As the abstract indicated, the name was transliterated precisely as on the stele. Calling the manuscript revolutionary was an understatement. In expounding his polytheism, Mirdin referenced deities which, even transliterated, were clearly Bel, Brighid, Curnnunos, and Lugh. More than that, it discussed spirituality as it related to the Great King Irturus. It referenced Irturus' court at Calmalod or Camalot, the fragment was inconsistent in its transliteration.

Now Vivian was comfortable connecting Mirdin with Myrddin. A historical Merlin, the possibility of whose existence she had refuted just days earlier, now stared her in the face.

After Box Six, the manuscript in Box 17 was an anticlimax. The Celtic segment only rehashed information from the stela and Treasure Tablet. Mirdin was a great counselor. He had departed Sogdia as an old man, with his treasure, to die in the land of his birth. But the manuscript lacked the Treasure Tablet's descriptive language about Mirdin's destination.

The manuscript had a mystery, however. The segment written in Roman-scripted Celtic was much smaller than the Sogdian part. Vivian thought it very unlikely former contained all the information in the latter. Perhaps the untranslated bits contained useful information. She emailed a photo to Dr. Grassley. If there was anything useful in the Sogdian, he and Dr. Abdulin would find it.

Before fetching the manuscript in Box 24 from storage, the

curator was apologetic. "If memory serves, that box was heavily damaged in the war."

She didn't exaggerate. The surviving manuscript fragments were blackened beyond recognition. Vivian wandered what use there was in keeping them. Beyond frustration, something else troubled her. "When you told us about Box 24, you said 'If memory served,'" she quizzed the curator. "I doubt Sogdian inscriptions from a century-old excavation fly off the shelves. Someone's requested these records recently, haven't they?"

"Yes."

"Who?"

"Dr. Cuinnsey, you know that would be a violation of patron confidentiality."

Vivian figured German civil servants willing to accept a bribe were rare as hen's teeth. Jake got lucky. A one hundred Euro outlay from him confirmed what they both suspected, Dr. Adrian Price had examined the collection only a few months ago.

Returning to their hotel, Vivian was shocked to be confronted by two Polizei investigators. "Jake Booker, Vivian Cuinnsey, you are wanted for questioning on suspicion of smuggling and violating the Antiquities Act. You will please come with us to police headquarters."

Discretely, Vivian slipped the bracelet off her wrist and into her purse.

Getting back to their room around dawn, she realized things could have been much worse. Jake's company kept a good European law firm on retainer in Brussels. Fortunately, Dr. Grassley had completed all the required paperwork for the bracelet. Otherwise, she would have been in serious legal and professional hot water. As it was, the Polizei had been very thorough.

"You know who's behind this, don't you?" Vivian asked.

"Uh-huh. Price. Obviously, he's figured out we didn't bite it in Uzbekistan. Even if the authorities didn't find anything sufficient to detain us or charge us, he probably figured it would eat up time and intimidate us."

"The real question," she reflected, "is whether he knew we were going to Berlin to examine the Sogdian manuscripts or if it was just an educated guess."

"Actually, I think the real question is where we go from here. I'm not feeling intimidated. How about you?"

Vivian shook her head. "But what's our next move? Dr. Grassley already responded to my email. There's nothing else useful in Manuscript 17. He also says that other collections of Sogdian manuscripts are scattered all over the world. Without the Treasure Tablet, Myrddin's trail is cold. How do we pick it up again?"

Jake scratched his head. "So." He paused, "I have a vague memory from my time at Oxford of hearing about a Victorian monograph that claimed, after Camelot, Merlin traveled the world and was actually behind a lot of legends about wandering sages."

"Your time at Oxford?"

"Yeah, I did the whole Rhodes Scholar thing. I'm a pragmatist. I attended the state university near where I grew up, majoring in petroleum geology and minoring in business. That didn't mean I wasn't curious about life's bigger questions. After establishing myself a bit, I applied for Rhodes and spent a couple years studying history at Oxford before getting back to the oil patch.

"I genuinely don't know what to say to that. But what about a monograph?"

Jake searched online. With a satisfied chuckle, he motioned for Vivian to look at his tablet. "Here it is, Herbert Price," Jake said. He located a chapter about Price in an anthology of unusual and unconventional Victorians. Together, they absorbed the text.

Herbert Price, who studied at Oxford in the 1880s and briefly lectured there, had also been a Welsh nationalist and an eccentric. He became obsessed with the idea of a historical Merlin who traveled the world. When his obsession began interfering with his lectures, Price was asked to leave Oxford.

The only child of a prominent Swansea physician, Price used family money to fund his efforts tracking down alleged accounts of Merlin's travels. In 1899, he self-published a monograph summarizing his findings.

Eventually dismissed as a crank and having exhausted the family fortune, Price returned to Wales and died in poverty and obscurity.

Earlier in life, Price was friends with Sir James Frazer. Much of the data Price collected allegedly found its way into Frazer's *Golden Bough,* one of cultural anthropology's foundational texts. The two men ultimately broke over increasingly heated disagreements regarding whether kernels of truth existed at the heart of Arthurian mythology.

Among his many eccentricities, Price argued passionately for the Welsh origins of Merlin, becoming enraged and even ending friendships when presented with other positions.

"We should get our hands on his manuscript," Jake said, "maybe there's something we can use."

Vivian shook her head, "You're not seeing it, are you?"

"What?"

"Price. Herbert Price. Adrian Price."

Jake slapped his palm against his forehead, a gesture from a thousand cartoons brought to life.

The biography of Dr. Adrian Price on his university's website confirmed Vivian's suspicion. "He is the great-grandson," it read, "of noted scholar Herbert Price."

Unsurprisingly, Herbert Price's obscure monograph was not available online. A call to Oxford's Bodleian library secured a promise to scan and email the document as quickly as possible. As they waited, Vivian and Jake grabbed a few hours of badly needed sleep.

Before drifting to sleep, she looked over at Jake's bed, "The whole roughneck bumpkin thing you play up, it's not really you. Why stick with it?"

Jake laughed. "A lot of times it pays to be underestimated."

The next morning, the scanned document was waiting for them. Over coffee, they read.

The monograph was written in the thick, ponderous, and grandiloquent style she associated with Victorian academic prose. Even that, however, couldn't obscure the undercurrent of feverish obsession running throughout the text. As Jake had recalled, Price hypothesized that Merlin traveled widely throughout the known world after Camelot's fall. The monograph used the Anglicized "Merlin" rather than the Celtic "Myrddin." Drawing on a variety of obscure and questionable sources, he attempted to piece together a chronology of Merlin's wanderings.

Price believed that Merlin first traveled to Gaul, alleging he met the ancestors of Charlemagne. He then traveled to the lands of the Gothic tribes before turning south to Rome.

From Rome, Merlin sailed to Alexandria where, Price claimed, evidence showed he spent a full year among its scholars and sages. Braving a crossing of the Sahara, he reached the city states of the Niger River. Price speculated about links between Merlin's arrival and certain stories of Anansi, the West African trickster god. Making his way past the headwaters of the Niger, Merlin went to Axum in present day Ethiopia.

He crossed the Red Sea into Yemen and wandered up the Arabian coast, through Irem, Mecca, Judea, and into Constantinople. Price tied Merlin to pre-Islamic Arabian legends of a wizardly battle among the pillars of Irem. He also cited obscure folklore suggesting Merlin carved the true story of the Grail Quest into the wall of a cave which had belonged to Joseph of Arimathea.

In Constantinople, Price linked Merlin to records of an audience between the Orthodox Patriarch and an unnamed "wise man of the pagan west." Thence, Merlin went southeast, through Mesopotamia, to the mouths of the Tigris and Euphrates. He sailed the Monsoon winds to India. Traveling through jungles and mountains, Merlin reached Sui China and the Pacific. Price claimed the Sui Emperor's court records showed Merlin eventually turned back westward, traveling the Silk Road.

The body of the monograph concluded with an acknowledgement there were no further records Price could confidently connect with Merlin. He hypothesized that, somewhere between China and Constantinople, Merlin either settled down or passed away.

The monograph was extensively end-noted, including full transcriptions of many of the sources Price used to piece together Merlin's alleged travels. Vivian was annoyed that, in accordance with the scholarly conventions of his day, Price rendered most of these in their original language.

Following the endnotes was a single appendix. It appeared to be an early draft of the monograph's conclusion. In this version,

Price noted two accounts, each from about 30 years after the Sui Empire records, fitting the pattern of earlier Merlin stories. These accounts, one from Constantinople and the other from the Merovingians, led him to speculate Merlin had indeed settled along the Silk Road before returning to Western Europe toward the end of his life. Clearly, Price later developed enough skepticism to exclude this idea from the main body of the monograph—but not enough skepticism to expunge it altogether.

"What do you think?" Jake asked. "I think he sounds crazier than an oilfield rat."

"No question the man was obsessed." Vivian sighed. Part of her still rebelled at what she was about to say, "But Myrddin, or someone so like him as to make no difference, was in Central Asia. So, I think we have to treat anything in the monograph as at least possible. The question is, what does that give us?"

Ticking them off on his fingers, Jake listed the modern equivalents of locations where the monograph hinted at leads to follow, "France, Turkey, Egypt, West Africa, Israel, and China. Of those, Israel is the only record Merlin supposedly created himself."

"That's a good point. And, if he did record write full story of the Grail Quest in Joseph of Arimathea's cave, it might have some hints about Merlin's origins. Even if it doesn't, it's not a bad silver medal."

Dawn at his back, Myrridin gazed across the Bosporus. On the far side, Constantinople spread as far as his still keen eyes could see. He was more than halfway home. The slowly approaching coracle would carry him across the strait and into Europa.

Briefly, his eyes traveled south to the old pilgrim and trader's road. His thoughts flickered to the hollowed ram's horn he still carried. Twenty years ago, he had followed that road. He remembered it as if it was yesterday.

After Axum, where he sat with the priests in their churches hewn from living rock, he sailed across a great channel to the land once known as Sheba. It was there Myrddin developed his fondness for the invigorating brew made from black beans. Traveling north with the caravans, he journeyed through Irem of the Pillars, where he dueled their chief wizard, through the City of the Black Stone of 1,000 Gods, and on into Judea…

Riding his donkey into the hills north of Judea, into the heart of old Arimathea, it occurred to Myrddin that the herdsman he hired as a guide was at least half crazy.

At last, the herdsman brought his own animal to a stop. With his crook, he pointed to the top of a steep slope. Small caves dotted its upper reaches. A feint trail led to one cave, testament to a small but steady stream of pilgrims over half a millennia.

"Remember what I told you," the herdsman said. "Do you have the horn?"

Myrddin raised the hollow ram's horn, a *shofar* in the local tongue. The guide nodded approvingly.

Carefully, Myrddin followed the trail. Outside the pilgrimage cave, he turned around and took a deep breath. He blew the shofar. From the herdsman, he learned it was expected of all pilgrims visiting the cave, a gesture of respect for the man known as Joseph of Arimathea. The horn's deep sound bellowed through the empty valley. This pleased him. Since childhood, Myrddin loved making noise. His ritual obeisance completed, he stepped into the cave of Joseph of Arimathea's cave.

It was tiny, not much larger than a hut. At the far end, a single niche was carved into the rock. It held a replica of the Grail. Or a replica of someone's idea of the Grail. It wasn't close at all, Myrddin scoffed. Nevertheless, if the pilgrims were correct, the niche had cradled the True Grail during the few years between the crucifixion and Joseph's journey to England.

Myrddin wondered what had become of the Grail. What had become of Galahad, Peredur, and Bors? Did it matter? He supposed not. He contemplated the niche and what had once rested there. In hindsight, the completion of the Grail Quest had been both Camelot's high point and the beginning of the end. He wondered how the tale might have unfolded had the Grail never come to the Isles at all. Would Camelot and Arthur still stand? Would they have never been at all? Or would fate ensure the story remained unchanged?

Rousing himself from reverie, Myrddin noted the walls covered with carved inscriptions in Hebrew, Aramaic, and Greek. Some praised the virtues of the man whose cave this had been. Others quoted the book of the God of Rome about the last days of his Son. A few told of Joseph's other adventures, tales not previously known to Myrddin and worthy of a bard. Of course, Myrddin knew a few things of his own about the man from Arimathea and what befell the Grail upon Britain's shores. Drawing a chisel from his satchel, he took the time to add them. Never lacking in confidence, he added a few lines of his own tale as well.

Myrddin turned to the cave mouth. It was still many days journey to Constantinople. Before walking down the slope, he blew to shofar again. Delighted by the instrument's noise, he resolved to keep it.

The old minivan bounced along the road. As she drove, Dr. Ella Peretz explained the area's history to Vivian and Jake. Vivian wished she'd spend more time watching the road ahead and less time looking at them.

"Arimathea is a puzzle," Dr. Peretz was saying, "Other than Christian scripture, and sources referencing scripture, no record of such a place exists. My colleagues disagree, often vehemently, whether this is because the place is entirely fictive or it is the victim of a bad transliteration."

Dr. Peretz always pronounced "colleague" as "CO-league," a linguistic tick Vivian found incredible endearing. A decade ago, Peretz taught Near Eastern Languages at Vivian's university. After marrying, she and her husband returned to Israel where she taught at Tel Aviv University. It was a serendipitous connection. With almost no notice, sweet Dr. Peretz dropped everything to assist Vivian with her visit.

Back in Berlin, research confirmed that there was a cave linked with Joseph of Arimathea located in northern Israel. She hadn't found written accounts of the link prior to the eighteenth century. That wasn't great but had been enough for Vivian to call her former colleague.

"In the earliest Greek copies of the Book of Luke," Dr. Peretz continued, "'Arimathea was written with an 'h' sound at the beginning. Copies from same period written in Syriac call it 'Ramtha.' So, scholars have claimed locations as different as Ha-Ramathaim, Ramah, and Ramallah for Arimathea."

As the minivan threaded its way into a narrow canyon, their

host switched from linguistics to local history. In the First Century, the canyon hosted a small colony of Essenes. The Jewish monastics had occupied caves high above the canyon floor. As Vivian already knew, one of these caves was connected with Joseph of Arimathea. Dr. Peretz thought that link was more ancient than the eighteenth century.

"You know, there is an apocryphal tradition," she added, "that after the crucifixion, Joseph renounced his wealth and became an Essene."

"There's also an apocryphal tradition that he traveled to Britain," Vivian added.

"I know," Dr. Peretz responded, "But that seems less likely, doesn't it?" Vivian and Jake exchanged looks as their host continued, "I suppose both things could be true."

"Have you been to the cave?" Jake asked.

"I have not, but one of my colleagues has. He found it very interesting. There is writing in Hebrew, Aramaic, and Greek all over the walls. We've talked about going out and doing a proper survey."

Dr. Peretz parked the vehicle. A short but taxing climb up the ravine took them to the caves at the top of the cliff. A narrow but well-worn path led to the cave they sought.

Its inside was diminutive. A niche in the far wall might once have held an ossuary, icon, or the Cup of Christ. Now it was empty. The inscriptions mentioned by Herbert Price, and confirmed by Dr. Peretz, were nowhere to be seen. Instead, pockmarks covered the walls and the floor was littered with shards of stone.

"Someone's been with here with a sledgehammer," Jake said.

Dr. Peretz was in a state of shock. "Who could have done this?"

Vivian and Jake knew.

They rode in silence back to the city. Tel Aviv always seemed out of place. Too crisp. Too sanitized. Too modern. It was as if the entire city was somehow inoculated against the enormous antiquity surrounding it in all directions.

At their hotel, Vivian sat on the bed and let her built up rage and frustration burst forth. "This bastard has been one step ahead of us this entire way. He's got the Treasure Tablet. He's got whatever information was in the cave. He's probably got materials from Herbert Price that weren't in the monograph. What have we got? We've got some weak leads scattered across the globe that might contain something useful. If we can find them. Jake, there's no way we're going to win this."

Jake remained silent as she spoke. When Vivian finished, he sat beside her.

"Look, I'm not good at compliments, but you may be the smartest person I've met. There's more than one solution to any problem. Somewhere out there is information that's going to lead us to Merlin's tomb." He chuckled. "Merlin's tomb. I can't believe I'm actually saying that. Your job is to find that information. You're going to sit down and Sherlock Holmes this thing."

"What are you going to do?"

"I'm going to take a nap."

She stared at her laptop, lost in thought. Glancing up, she saw Jake's sleeping form. The artificial light from her screen accented the treasure hunter's age. He must be nearing sixty, in contrast to her nearing forty. Refocusing on the computer, she reflected on everything the two of them learned about Myrddin and everything that was known or speculated before.

On her notepad, Vivian listed Myrddin's reputed final resting places. From the stele to Price's monograph, the materials they had discovered all indicated he intended to be buried in the place of his birth. Almost every source agreed Myrddin was either Welsh or Breton. She hoped they were right. Bringing up online maps of Wales and France's Brittany Peninsula, she compared the alleged resting places with ancient and modern place-names. Finding something that had remained overlooked until now was a longshot, but it was a start.

Broceliande Forest was an early favorite. Its modern French equivalent, Paimpoint, was a distant cognate, and contained an alleged tomb of Merlin. A photo of that structure did not inspire confidence. The haphazard pile of small rocks seemed an unlikely monument to a man who had walked half the earth.

Maybe "Broceliande" didn't refer to the forest? In the Celtic of the Sixth Century, the word could be translated as "Region of the Horses." Perhaps a reference to the presence of horses, horse breeders, or a temple to Epona? It was plausible, but described so many places that only extensive research would narrow it down.

Bel Nemeton was "Sacred Grove of Bel," the Celtic Sun God. Not a very promising match for contemporary geography.

More obscure potential resting places yielded nothing more tangible.

Her attention wandering, Vivian gazed at her bracelet. She remained enchanted by its beauty and syncretic blend of Celtic and Roman designs. In her mind, an idea blossomed. Roman Culture was well established in Gaul by the Sixth Century, leading to many hybrids. Not just material hybrids, but linguistic ones as well.

What if Merlin's tomb had become obscured by such a hybrid, the original name of its location corrupted or fully translated over the intervening fourteen centuries?

She returned to her prime suspects, Bel Nemeton and Broceliande. In English it was "region of horses" and in French "pais de cheval," which she found only as a descriptions and not as specific place-names. Literally translated, "Sacred Grove of Bel" was even less encouraging.

Phonetically, Bel resembled "Val," French for valley. A very common component of place names, "Val" made a promising candidate for linguistic corruption. The hybrid Val Nemeton, meaning "Valley of Sacred Spaces," sounded appropriate. A search revealed place-names translating as "Sacred Valley" in Ireland, a bit far to be promising, as well as Nepal and Peru, not even worth considering. Looking at other words from Sixth Century Celtic with the same root as "nemeton," Val Nemeto would be the "Valley of Aloneness, Loneliness, or Solitude." Again, she returned to her maps.

There it was. La Valee Isolee, "the Isolated Valley." It was sufficiently close to the meaning of *Val Nemeto*. The remote spot on the Breton coast looked like a big, black X. But Vivian wanted confirmation, preferably something not dependent on millennium-old linguistic shifts.

Hours later, Jake woke. "Okay, Sherlock, that grin must mean you found something."

"La Valee Isolee in Brittany." She explained the linguistic reasoning behind her conclusion.

"Anything else?"

"Uh-huh. I can't believe Myrddin made the journey from Sogdia by himself, especially if he was carrying treasure. He must have had help. The region around Valee Isolee has a legend about a group of dark-skinned men arriving from the east. Written accounts of the legend date back to Charlemagne's time. That's two centuries after what we're looking for. Hopefully, it just took that long to write down."

"That's good," Jake nodded.

"It gets better. There region has some unique surnames. They're gibberish if you treat them as Celtic, Romance, or Germanic words. But they're phonetically similar to some Uzbek surnames that happen to have Sogdian origins." Vivian beamed, "We're going to France."

Arriving in Paris from Tel Aviv, they boarded a train for Brittany. Vivian was relieved there had been no encounters with Price or his minions. So far. As their train rolled through the hills and woodlands of Brittany, Vivian reviewed her notes. Jake was engrossed in his tablet.

"You won't believe this," he said.

"What?"

"So, according to the *Golden Bough,* not only does the village nearest to La Valee Isolee still preserve folk-memories of visitors arriving from the east, the event is commemorated in their annual Solstice festival. Or, at least it was when Frazer was writing in 1890."

"You have a copy of the *Golden Bough* on your tablet?"

"Doesn't everyone?"

"I found a potential problem with our plan," Vivian said.

"Which is?"

"Dozens of tombs, from Neolithic to Iron Age, have been identified in the valley. How are we going to figure out which one is the right one?"

Jake looked thoughtful, "I don't think that will be a problem. Myrddin doesn't seem like a guy who would travel the world without learning a few new things. If I was a gambling man, and

I am, I'd bet his tomb won't resemble anything else in the valley. Have you found any pictures?"

"Not of every tomb in the valley, but some."

Sharing Vivian's laptop, they examined her images. They knew it the moment they saw it. Jake was right, it didn't look anything else. It was an overhead image from a 2007 aerial survey by the University of Remmes. The structure's base was carved directly into the valley's rocky slope with tiers of concentric squares resting on top. Vivian was certain no regular Breton, Gaul, or Roman built this. The survey indicated the structure was unexcavated, or at least had been in 2007.

The train pulled into Quimper, the ancient town at the heart of old Brittany. Church bells sounded over the half-timbered buildings of the old town and footbridges crisscrossed the confluence of the three rivers that were Quimper's lifeblood. Though they were more than five miles from the ocean, Vivian thought as she caught the invigorating smell of the sea on the strong breeze. Eager to leave no trail Price could follow, they caught an intercity bus to Bocages, the village near the valley.

The past week had strengthened Vivian's faith in the power of serendipity. She was only half-surprised to realize they were arriving during the Summer Solstice festival Jake had discovered within the *Golden Bough*'s pages.

Bocages was postcard perfect. Aside from the bus station, municipal building, schoolhouse, and a service station, no building appeared to date from after the industrial revolution. They checked into a pension on its cobblestoned main street. Too late in the day to head to the valley, Vivian and Jake rested in their room before joining the festival.

The festival procession began with a marching band, leading the rest of the parade with arrangements of traditional Breton folk music. They were followed by members of Bocages' civic organizations and an open-topped limousine carrying its mayor, the local National Assembly representative, and their spouses. Trailing behind the limousine was a phalanx of morisques, the French equivalent of mummers and Morris dancers, clad in outrageous costumes adorned with garlands and ribbons.

After the morisques, four revelers donning oversized papier-mâché carnival masks paraded down the street. Their heads were the color of café au lait, with black hair, black eyes, and attired as per the traditional European images of Moors. This was what they had read about in the *Golden Bough*. But it was the fifth figure, sandwiched between the Moors, which commanded Vivian's attention. His papier-mâché mask was fair-skinned, with snow white hair and black lines suggesting wrinkles. He wore a robe and a white beard dangled from the mask's chin down to the cobblestones. As the five figures walked, their outsized heads bobbing comically, they tossed sweets and coins to children in the crowd.

Following this quintet was another wave of morisques. At the end came the père of the village's church. Swinging a silver censer that billowed pungent incense smoke, the priest was flanked by young acolytes. With this final note in the procession, it was as if the church, rather sheepishly, wanted to give a veneer of religious respectability to the festival's obvious pagan overtones.

After the procession passed, the festival became a street party. Wine, song, and food flowed freely. Rambunctious children ran through the chaos, tossing eggs, flour, and the occasional firecracker. As the hour grew late and the outdoor festivities were increasingly claimed by reckless youth, Vivian and Jake retired to a tavern adjacent to their pension.

At the bar, Vivian introduced herself to the proprietress. Anne-Marie was a sturdy woman whose good health had clearly endured into late middle age. Vivian smiled to learn that she bore one of the unique surnames discovered in her research. Physically, however, nothing distinguished her from other villagers she had seen. Anne-Marie seemed charmed by Vivian's not-quite-fluent Breton and enjoyed the opportunity to practice her own English. As the wine glasses emptied, both women found themselves switching haphazardly from one language to the other. Quickly scanning the tavern, she spotted Jake sitting in the corner, chatting animatedly with men from the village.

Eventually, Vivian asked the question she wanted to hear Anne-Marie answer. "So, what's with the figures with the big papier-mâché heads?"

"Well, my grandmere, she always insisted it was something that actually happened here in Bocages many centuries ago. But now, most people don't think that. They say it represents the Magi coming to adore the Christ Child, or the legend of Prester John, or some bit of lost pagan ritual."

Interesting explanations all, Vivian thought. Of course, if the procession was supposed to represent the Magi, why hold it during the Summer Solstice? Whether coincidence or garbled folk memory, the Prester John story held a kernel of truth. Sogdia, like the mythical Prester John's kingdom, had been filled with Nestorians. Vivian suspected Myrddin would be horrified that his arrival became linked with the monotheistic Nestorians.

Before retiring to her room, Vivian asked Anne-Marie if there were any taxis or cars for rent in the village. The older women informed her there were several young men in Bocages who could be hired as drivers, preferring such odd jobs to the tedium of steady work. On a napkin, she wrote down a couple of names and numbers for Vivian.

The next morning, Vivian made some calls. She secured the services of two surly twenty-somethings and their beat-up Citroën. The car, she realized, was as old as the young men in the front seat.

Vivian startled as the Citroën turned off the main road and onto a tiny path between two hedgerows. After a quarter mile, stopping the car, one young man produced a tire iron as the other drew a butcher knife.

"You're kidding me! Not again." She cursed.

Jake addressed the boys in rapid French. They didn't stop.

"You told them whatever he's paying, you'd double it?" Vivian asked.

"Not exactly."

She arched an eyebrow.

"Like someone suggested, I told them, 'Whatever he or she is paying you, I'll double it.'"

"They don't look impressed," Vivian commented and gave it a try. Unlike Jake's French, her Breton got results. The young men froze and seemed to reconsider their actions. Playing a hunch, she pressed the issue. In her experience, in small communities around the world, the threat of social sanction was a powerful motivator. "Anne-Marie gave me your names and numbers," Vivian said, invoking the colorful matriarch, "She'll be very disappointed if she finds out what you're doing."

An outlay of cash from Jake sealed the deal. As the boys turned-coat and spilled their guts, she translated for him.

"Price has most of Bocages' ne'er-do-wells on his payroll," she relayed. "This pair says there are two walkable passes through the hills into La Valee Isolee. Price is having them both watched. Otherwise, it's an actual climb to get into the valley. I don't know how we're going to get over the hills."

"We're not going over them. We're going to go under them."

Jake grinned as she looked at him quizzically.

"I'm a geologist, remember? These hills are part of a formation called the Armorican Massif, a band of sedimentary rock stretching from here to central France. It struck me that these hills must be shot through with caves."

"You found one?"

"Yeah. While you were talking to the bartender, I talked with some guys from the village. There's a cave called the Sentier d'Ermites, the Trail of Hermits, running all the way into the valley."

"Wonderful. How do we get there?"

"If we can get your new hooligan pals to give us a lift, we can hike there from the roadway in half an hour or so." Jake tossed her his canvass bag. "I brought some water, food, and two heavy-duty flashlights."

Back on the main road and another mile toward the sea, Vivian and Jake were let out where the blacktop crossed a small stream Along the waters, a footpath wound its way toward the hills.

As they walked, Jake shared what he learned about the cave's rich history. It been used as a base by the Resistance during World War Two. Local tradition also claimed a group of Templars took refuge there after their order was disbanded in the thirteenth century. Older folklore tied it pre-Christian mystery cults. And it was home Paleolithic cave paintings, like those at Lascaux a couple hundred miles away.

Vivian had pictured something larger. The tiny fissure Jake indicated was only a couple feet taller and wider than a person. At least they were alone. Price either didn't know about the cave or didn't expect them to know. Unless there were guards inside the cave or at the other end, she thought unpleasantly.

"Done much spelunking?" Jake inquired.

"Nope."

"Let me go first on this one."

Vivian marveled at the complete darkness. Even the powerful flashlights succeeded only in cutting slices out of the black. She imagined the experience from the perspective of someone carrying only an oil lamp, torch, or nothing it all. Small wonder caves once featured so prominently in humanity's rites and rituals.

Not far inside, they found the cave paintings. Evocative profiles of deer, wild horses, birds, and fish were rendered in pigments of black, brown, red, and white. Like the painters themselves, some of the animals pictured, aurochs, cave hyenas, and European bison, now inhabited only the past.

Further in, paintings gave way to petroglyphs. Mother goddess imagery, warrior figures, concentric circles, and spirals were incised into the rock with great care. Vivian's training was insufficient to tell if they were Celtic in origin, dated from earlier in the Bronze Age, or both. She would definitely tell the Archeology Department about this place. Assuming she survived the next few hours.

Ducking dangling stalactites and sidestepping the looming stalagmites required constant attention. "You can always remember which is which," she fleetingly recalled her Seventh Grade science teacher saying, "because stalac*tites* must hold tight to avoid falling."

Darkness consumed her sense of time. It felt like they had been walking forever. This, too, yielded insight into the awe with which earlier peoples held caves. When Vivian finally spotted a pinprick of light ahead, it did feel a like Persephone returning to the sunlit lands.

He felt badly for the young men who accompanied him on the journey. True, they thought it an honor. But it was unlikely they would see their homes and families again. Of course, several of them had already found girls from the farming village. Myrddin was happy for them. He was more ambivalent that some of them had also found the God of Rome. Like him, the old ways were dying.

His tomb would be less than a bowshot from the village where was born. The stone huts, once filled with the laughter and songs of fishers and weavers, stood empty now. By appearances, they had been abandoned many years. Myrddin wondered what became of his people. The newcomers from the farming village beyond the valley could not tell him.

Myrddin sat on the same turtle-shaped rock that had fascinated him as boy. So many days he had played on and around it. Now, he sat on it as he watched the construction of his tomb. He wondered if some of his magic had found its way into the rock.

The men from the new village were good natured but often regarded him strangely as they worked on his tomb. Certainly, they had never seen one like it. He wondered if the world had ever seen one like it. That was not his problem. His problem was figuring out how to safeguard his treasure.

La Valee Isolee was a place apart. Geography and climate conspired to create a world utterly unlike the one on the other side of the hills. Initially, Vivian noticed the wind. The narrow valley, more accurately a box canyon opening onto the ocean, funneled the sea breezes into formidable gusts. She tucked her hair up under her ballcap.

The blues of sea and sky seemed deeper and more vivid than normal. The valley was awash with sunshine so potent it was almost tangible, like she was somehow closer to the sun. Compared with riotous fertility of the rest of Brittany, vegetation here was sparse. Stunted by the salty air and twisted by the wind, diminutive pines, little taller than she, reminded Vivian of bonsai trees. Clumps of resilient shrubs and hearty coastal grasses clung to a precarious existence in the windswept valley.

Patches of bare rock poked through the thin soil while stones from pebbles to boulders lie strewn throughout the valley. Some stones clustered tightly together, forming shapes and outlines the eye eventually recognized as the work of human hands.

From a stony beach, the valley floor rose sharply to the end of the canyon. Vivian and Jake walked up the slope to where a wide ledge doubled-back towards the ocean and ended in a promontory jutting hundreds of feet above the waves. According to GPS coordinates from the University of Remmes survey, the structure she identified as Myrddin's tomb was at the end of that ledge, overlooking the ocean.

Approaching the edge, they found one of the strangest structures either of them had encountered. The ground level was carved directly into the Armorican limestone. On top were several faux-stories built from local stones. Each level diminished in size from the one below.

"It looks like a damn ziggurat," Jake said, mirroring her thoughts. The ground level, though, reminded her of the Ethiopia's carved churches.

"Yes, yes, it's very curious structure."

Vivian's blood ran cold, realizing it hadn't been Jake that spoke.

Turning around, she found Adrian Price stalking them from behind. He clenched a pistol firmly in one hand.

"Apparently, I am a slow learner. After Samarkand, I should have figured out the only way to take care of the two of you is to do it myself."

"Price, I still don't get it," Vivian admitted. "If you had played it straight, you would still get most of the glory from this. Why do you want to keep it to yourself so badly?"

"There's the principle of it all. By right of my decent from Herbert Price, this site is mine to do with as I wish. My ancestor also had some curious notions about what the tomb might contain and about what 'Merlin's Treasure' really meant. Just in case he was right, I need to examine it before anyone else."

"What kind of notions?"

Instead of answering, Price pointed the barrel of the gun towards the edge of the promontory. "We are going to take a walk now."

When Vivian and Jake were ten feet ahead, too far to rush him, Price followed.

As they marched, Vivian stepped in scree. As the loose stones scattered beneath her, she lost her footing. From the ground, she saw Jake regarding her with concern as Price watched with irritation. Standing, she hissed as she put weight on the foot.

"Sprained," she said between clenched teeth.

"In a few moments it won't matter anyway." With the muzzle of his gun, Price motioned for Jake to help her. One arm wrapped firmly around her, Jake helped Vivian hobble along. Every few steps she gasped from putting too much weight on the ankle.

"Unlike Uzbekistan, here I'm wary about leaving evidence. So, I'll let nature do the work for me. You'll both take a walk over the cliff. Even if they find your bodies, and that's a big 'if,' it's simply two more unfortunate accidents in the wilds of Brittany."

"Price?"

"Yes, Mr. Booker?" the archeologist looked amused, "I assume this is your last, desperate plea?"

"Nope. I just wanted you to know you're a son of a bitch."

Price appeared taken aback by Jake's trash-talk. As he was distracted, Vivian sprung atop a perfectly convex stone. Planting one foot against the solid rock, she kicked out with the other. Connecting firmly with Price's chest, the archeologist wheeled backward and over the promontory's edge. Falling toward the crashing waves, gun popping harmlessly into empty space, the wide-eyed surprise on his face was nearly comic.

Then Price was gone.

"What the hell was that?" Jake laughed, "I thought your ankle was busted!"

"Someone once told me that it can pay to be underestimated. I decided to test that advice."

"What do you think?"

"I'll have to thank him sometime."

They embraced, relieved to be alive. Taking a deep breath, their attention turned to the megalithic structure behind them.

Even as darkness gathered, Myrddin knew the sky was clear and it could not be long past noon. It was his light that was fading, not the sun's. The tomb was complete and his treasure safeguarded within. He was confident only those worthy of such riches would find them.

As he rested comfortably on his pallet, the world went black. From a distance, the songs of wind and wave still reached his ears. Myrddin wondered what would come next. Would he dream? Would he find Arthur? Nimue?

A stone slab about four feet tall and two feet wide blocked the structure's only entrance. Fourteen hundred years of sediment covered its bottom. Improvising tools, Vivian and Jake dug away the sediment before turning attention to the monolith. Using a pair of stout pine branches as levers, together they eventually moved the slab enough to enter the tomb.

Its interior consisted of a single chamber, about 30 feet to a side, with a high ceiling. Plaster covered the walls, another distinctly un-Celtic touch. Brittany was not Uzbekistan. The preservation climate here left only faint traces of once brilliant frescos. It was enough for Vivian to see obvious similarities with those near Samarkand.

At the center was a sarcophagus built from local stones and covered by a monolith much larger than the one that had blocked the entrance. This stone would not be moved easily. Perhaps that was just as well, Vivian thought. For now, at least, that seemed disrespectful to the final resting of place of a man as close to the Merlin of legend as to make no real difference.

In true Celtic fashion, the tomb swelled with grave goods. There were piles of bracelets, amulets, torcs, and similar creations. Most were bronze or iron, but Vivian saw some silver and gold, as well as inlays of tortoise shell, abalone, and semi-precious stones. There were smaller collections of amber and topaz as well as a pile of what appeared to be coffee beans. Next to the sarcophagus sat a fancy saddle of distinctly Central Asian appearance. A small statue of a Fu Dog rested next to one of Anubis. And was that really a shofar in one corner?

Scattered throughout the tomb were dozens of clay jars, sealed with resin that long ago became hard as concrete. They resembled Greek amphorae. Perhaps they contained grain, oil, and wine for Myrddin to use in the afterlife? Not very Celtic, but the man had traveled. They could also be canopic jars. But that raised unpleasant questions about who all those organs would belong to.

In the end, when Jake suggested it was impossible to make an omelet without breaking a few eggs, she offered only token protest. Breaking the top off a jar revealed half a dozen tightly rolled sheets of vellum within. The centuries had left them brittle. Carefully, Jake handed one to Vivian. "Okay, Doctor, if it breaks, it's on your head not mine."

"Gee, thanks."

Gingerly, she unrolled the parchment. The ink was badly faded but Vivian could still discern the seemingly random sequence of characters: numerals, Roman letters, characters from Sogdian and other scripts.

"Some kind of encryption?" Jake asked. Vivian nodded.

"What do think they are?" he asked.

"No way to know until they're decrypted," she replied. "Myrddin's life story? His wisdom? Magic scrolls? All three? Whatever they are, this is the real treasure."

On the flight back to America, Vivian dozed. She was pleased with how things were turning out. The French government had been very cooperative about their discovery. They agreed to a ten year moratorium on announcing the site's location. Vivian's university, along with a French institution, would share first rights to excavation, analysis, and discovery. Just translating and interpreting Myrddin's manuscripts could take ten years. His cypher, however, was falling faster than expected. In at least one way, the modern world outfoxed the cunning old sage. He assumed anyone trying to crack his cypher would be unfamiliar with decimal-based mathematics.

Jake's company would have the rights to a traveling museum exhibit and a high profile documentary. It would be a small fortune but a fortune nonetheless. Whatever was between the two of them remained undefined for now. Undefined but delightful.

In a few hours, she'd be curled up with Dart. The thought made her very happy. Next morning, she'd go into her office. The mountain of paperwork awaiting her did not make her happy. In fact, it almost made her wish she had jumped off that cliff in Brittany. Almost. After checking in at her office, Vivian would walk over to the Archeology Department and turn over the bracelet Dr. Grassley had given her. She smiled, observing its graceful form on her wrist.

Then again…

The Knight of the Ice Moon

Patricia S. Bowne

Now it came to pass that after the fall of Arthur, there sprung up self-styled 'kings' throughout the land, all at war one with the other and none strong enough to prevail. Yet one, Bilinas, proved mightier than his neighbors. In the second year of his reign in Selanto, after his victory over the blue men of the North Marches, King Bilinas bethought him of copying the late Arthur in grace as well as conquest, and declared a tourney for the Ice Moon. So all his noble knights journeyed to the castle in HighHollows, and much merriment was held from the day of first frost until the full moon thereafter.

King Bilinas bade every high family of Selanto and even the noblest of the blue men to his feasting, for he held it no shame that they had valiantly striven against him. So it came about that the King's ladies and knights, and the knights and ladies of all his allies and past enemies, sported and made merry in halls that had but lately hosted councils of war against him, and hands once raised against one another in battle now clasped in friendship.

On the night of the Ice Moon, when all the knights and ladies sat at table, the door of the hall flew open wide with a great noise though those at guard had seen nothing, and in rode a knight in full armor, with his visor down; but he carried neither sword nor lance nor shield. His gray war-horse was caparisoned in blue and white, and beside him on a white palfrey rode a veiled damsel clad richly in the same colors, carrying a lance and with an unsheathed sword upon her lap. To the center of the hall they rode, and there the knight halted and stood still and cold as one carved of marble.

"My Lord Knight," cried King Bilinas, "I charge you, tell us what brings you armored to our feast; for the jousting is past, and

155

it is time for good fellowship."

The knight neither moved nor spoke, but the damsel raised her head, and through her veil all saw her eyes dark and bright. "Oh King," she said, "this is my brother Sir Lionel, and there lives no nobler knight; but he bears a curse cast upon him, that he may neither speak nor show his face until he is deemed worthy to be one of your company."

At this the knights wondered mightily, and muttered among themselves. "Sir Lionel died at Arthur's side," said one, and another, "Nay, Lionel left the field at Lancelot's side, and lives to this day; 'tis so written," and a third, "Lionel set by his arms and took holy orders." Then King Bilinas hit his fist upon the table, and all fell silent.

"Surely he is a noble knight," said the King, "and if he indeed be Lionel, none would better grace our court. But he is come behind time, for the jousting is finished, and we will spend the waning of the Ice Moon in hunting and other merry sport. The which, you are most welcome to enjoy."

"That we may not," said the damsel, "for the curse laid upon my brother. And I tell you truly, if it be not lifted before the Ice Moon has grown old he will die, and the land will lose its most valiant knight, one who has brought victory to every cause he fought for."

Then up spoke Sir Euryphar, who was a good knight and true, though he is mocked in the tales for his great mouth and his appetite. "My liege," he said, "I will battle with this knight, if being overcome by me will aid his cause. It would be pitiful waste for a brave knight to suffer such a fate, and I could not settle to my victuals knowing that fellow was starving inside his helmet!"

"So will I," cried stern Sir Esox, and Sir Argyro of the Bright Armor, and Sir Opsanus the ugly, who sang so sweetly that not a damsel but forgot his face when he oped his mouth. And Sir Linophryne the Bearded, of whom many tales are told, but at this time they knew nothing of his secrets. All of King Bilinas's knights agreed that they would joust another day for the sake of the Knight of the Ice Moon. But King Bilinas would not have it so, for the hunts that had been arranged. So they agreed at length, that the knight and his damsel would accompany them in the hunts, and every day another of King Bilinas's knights would joust with him, and by how he bore himself against them all, they would judge whether he were worthy to be one of their number. And meanwhile they should have a pavilion of their own, into which none might enter or spy, so that the Knight of the Ice Moon might feed himself in spite of the curse set upon him.

The first day did they hunt gently with hawks, and merry was the company that rode out on that morn. The Knight of the Ice Moon and his sister rode out, with a white goshawk on her arm, and only the Queen's hawk flew higher and brought back more game. But all day the damsel did not raise her veil, nor did the knight speak a word, or take sup or drink.

That evening when they had returned to the castle, the damsel said to King Bilinas, "Now let my brother contend against one of your knights, my Lord, for he is weary of the day and would earn his rest."

Forth came Sir Euryphar, laughing gaily, and there on the greensward they battled. And the Knight of the Ice Moon ran his lance into Sir Euryphar's thigh and laid him on the green.

"Tush," cried Sir Euryphar, who made light of all but his stomach, "It is no great wound, but I will not hunt with you tomorrow. You have beaten me fairly, Sir Knight, and may you eat well tonight on the strength of it."

But the Queen's face grew grave, and she said, "This is a sad ending to a merry day, and how many more shall we have?"

The second day, they hunted with bows and had much sport. The Knight of the Ice Moon's sister bore her bow in hand, and she did great slaughter among the birds of the forest. But the knight never took up weapon or opened his helmet, and neither did he drink nor sup all day.

That evening the damsel said, "Now let my brother earn his rest upon one of your knights, for how many must he overcome before he is made one of them and freed from his burden?"

Up came grim Sir Esox with his green eyes, and they made great battle, until at last the Knight of the Ice Moon smote Sir Esox a blow upon the hand that cleft off two of his fingers.

"By my soul, you are the better man," said Sir Esox, and made light of his wound; but the Queen was sore troubled. "This is another sorry end to a merry day," she said. "Let this knight be made one of your company my lord, ere all be lamed."

King Bilinas might have heeded her, but that his knights were so taken with the sport that they would not hear of it. "What," they cried, "would Gawaine or Agravaine, or any of that company, step back for fear of a noble adversary?"

The Queen was not convinced. *And are not all those noble knights dead?* she thought to herself, yet held her peace.

So went on the King's hunting party, while the Ice Moon waned. Each day they hunted with the Knight of the Ice Moon and his sister; each evening another of King Bilinas's knights challenged the Knight of the Ice Moon and was overcome, though none were wounded sore and all made light of it. Still, each day one knight fewer rode out to the hunt, and their pleasure was the less when they bethought themselves of the wounded in the castle.

At last, when the Ice Moon was worn thin as a sickle of straw, King Bilinas and his Queen and her ladies rode to hunt with no companions but the Knight of the Ice Moon and his sister. They hunted with hawks, for that the most of them were ladies, and the King was sore vexed at it. That noontime as they ate his face was shadowed and his speech short, so little pleasure was there in his company.

The Queen rose and took her leave, and none dared follow

158

her; so she wandered further, a little into the peaceful forest. Then she heard a voice weeping, lamenting in words too soft to hear. She crept further, and what did she see but the Knight of the Ice Moon stretched full on the sward with his helmeted head in his sister's lap, and she bent over it weeping and grieving. *What has befallen him?* the Queen thought, and drew nearer. Then she stopped, for the sister spoke murmuring words again, and leaning forward she undid her brother's gauntlet and pulled it off. There lay the knight's hand, maimed of two fingers just as Sir Esox. Then the sister kissed and dressed the wound, weeping full sore, and put back his gauntlet. She undid his tassett and cuisse, moaning and weeping all the time, and there was a wound just the like as he had given Sir Euryphar. This likewise she dressed, and before the Queen's eyes she did search and clean wounds the likeness of all he had given in his jousts. The Queen wondered how the knight had come by these very wounds he had given, and how he had prevailed in battle, bearing them all.

At last the damsel had bound and dressed every wound, and reclothed the Knight of the Ice Moon in his armor. Yet she seemed no whit pleased and continued her lamenting as before. "Oh, my brother, my brother," she wept, "but another night and your doom will be lifted, but oh, the night! I cannot bear it!" And she covered her face and wept so sorely that the Queen would have run to her side, but that the sight of those wounds had cast such fear into her heart.

Then she saw the damsel take loose the knight's helmet and draw it off his head, which she then cradled in her lap, stroking and kissing it. The Queen's heart beat high to think of seeing this knight's face. She watched as closely as a cat watches a bird, and finally as the damsel stroked and caressed it, her sleeve fluttered aside, and the Queen saw that in her lap she cherished the staring head of a corpse, bloodless and agape.

As the Queen stood frozen to her soul, the damsel kissed the corpse again, and laid its head upon the sward. Then heavily she rose, as one weighed down by grief, and the Queen saw her take up the knight's sword. It seemed she scarce could raise it, yet with all her force she wrested it aloft, pointing to the sky. "Forgive me, brother! Tonight you shall earn your rest," she said, and brought it down on the head she had just cherished, so that half of the face was cleaved off and the skull split open. Twice and a third time she struck, each time sobbing as if the sword bit into her own flesh, and then she fell down upon the ground. Yet she did not lie insensible, but gathered the knight's helmet and put it back upon him, over his ruined head.

"Brother," she said, kneeling beside the knight's body, "tonight is your doom accomplished. What I have given you, you will give again."

As she spoke these words the knight stirred and sat up, though he said no word. He rose to his feet, and the damsel with him; he took his sword from her and cleaned it in the stream, and wiped it upon the grass, as like a living knight as might be. Then they walked back to the party, while the Queen stood in the forest like a statue of fear.

All that afternoon they hunted until the sun fell aslant beneath the branches, and then they returned to the castle. There stood all King Bilinas's knights, jesting among themselves and eager to see what sport the King would make with the Knight of the Ice Moon.

Then the Queen brought her palfrey next to her husband's, to speak with him unheard. "My Lord," the Queen said to him, her heart frozen in her breast, "I beg you, send this knight from among us. Set him a quest, my Lord; so have young knights ever proved themselves."

"What, shall I lay a new task upon him when the first is all but fulfilled?" said King Bilinas. "That were ill-done. Do you fear he will overcome me, wife?" He laughed.

"No man could overcome you in my heart," said the Queen.

"Yet I fear one of you will be injured, and for what folly? He is no canny thing, my Lord. I saw his face in the forest, and the fear of it lies in me still." The image of the knight's dead face, cleaved through with his own sword, rose in her throat.

"My word has been given," said King Bilinas, "and I will not fall from it, any more than our good king past. Be of good cheer, wife; I'll do him little harm, for he is a bold knight, however foul his face may be, and deserves honor."

Then up came the damsel. "King, now must my brother's task be finished, according to your word, that he may earn his rest."

"Gladly will I do so," said King Bilinas, "for never I saw such a noble knight, and happily will we welcome him among us." The other knights cheered and cried "Aye, aye!" But the Queen was filled with dread.

"Let a pavilion be set for each of you, then," she said, "that you may clean yourself of the day's heat and vexation, before this last contest."

"That was well spoken, wife. Let us make ready," said the King.

"My brother is ready," said the maiden.

The King laughed. "Your brother is a young man, and an eager one. Let him give grace to his elder; I would refresh me."

The Queen lighted from her palfrey with a heavy heart, for had she not gained but a quarter-hour's time before the deathly knight would give her husband again the wound that his sister had given him? She hastened to the pavilion set for the Knight of the Ice Moon, not knowing what she might do except she challenge him herself, and bear that dreadful wound.

The knight stood in his pavilion, still as stone, with his hands at his sides, and the Queen trembled as she stepped in.

"Sir Knight," she said, but he spake never a word.

"Will you hear me!" she said, but he moved not a breath.

"I challenge you!" she cried, but he raised not a finger.

Then fury overtook the Queen, and she grasped the knight's

hand to pull it upwards from his side. "Will you not strike me down?" she cried. But his hand hung heavy as a hand of lead, and she could not move it, though she tried until her heart failed her, and she fell on her knees before him.

"Oh, spare him," she cried, and tears started to her eyes. "You are dead, and will this bring your life back to you? But he lives, and can know joy and give comfort. Oh, let him live, I beg you!" But the knight neither moved nor spake.

Then the Queen undid his gauntlet, as she had seen his sister do in the forest. She took his maimed hand in hers, though she shuddered to see again the cut he had given to Sir Esox, and pressed her lips against it. It was colder than ice, colder than the moon, and the cold ran into her blood as if she would never be warm again. "Forgive us," she said. "Tonight is your doom accomplished. What I have given you, you will give again."

Then the knight moved. He pulled his hand back from her lips, and held it out for his gauntlet. She heard movement outside and started to her feet, cold as she was. Her steps were as heavy as if she carried a heart of stone within her bosom as she went out of the pavilion, unseen by any, to join those who watched the contest.

King Bilinas was not so easy to overcome as his knights had been. Lances were shattered, swords drawn. Many blows were given and received, and all the time the Queen watched with ice growing in her heart. At last King Bilinas dealt the Knight of the Ice Moon such a buffet upon his shoulder that the knight dropped his lance and fell from his steed.

"Do you yield?" cried the King, dismounting in his turn.

For answer, the knight seized King Bilinas's hand and drew off the gauntlet. He bowed his head over the hand and raised his visor, so that his cold lip touched it.

All those watching murmured in approval. "Brave in battle, noble in defeat!" cried Sir Opsanus. "Make him one of us, your Majesty!" And all cried with one voice for King Bilinas to make him knight of their company where he knelt, so that his curse might be lifted at last and they might look upon his face.

But another voice cried out, "Brother, what means this!" The knight's sister ran onto the field. "Brother," she cried, "was this the doom laid upon you? What I have given you, you must give again!"

Quick as a cat leaps after a bird, the Knight of the Ice Moon snatched up his sword and leapt at her. He raised the sword high and brought it down on the damsel's head, so that half of the face was cleaved off and the skull split open. A moment she stared at him from half a face, while all around stood as they were struck stone. Then twice and a third time he struck, and then they both fell down upon the ground. And when the knights gathered round and pulled off his helmet, they found that brother and sister were dead of the self-same wound.

"This was the curse laid upon him," said King Bilinas. "Burn the witch and scatter her ashes one from another, but let the knight be buried with honor and let the Ice Moon new and old be carved upon his stone, that he may lie under it safe from all such sorcery. For never did I raise sword against one so valiant, cursed though he may have been."

The Queen kept all these marvels in her heart. And it is said that all those gallant knights regained their strength, only that King Bilinas never raised sword again with the hand that the Knight of the Ice Moon had kissed.

Mordred, Beguiled

Claudia Quint

Kelmscott Manor, Oxfordshire, Summer, 1872

William served tea, and from the window, I spied Ned walking up the path to Kelmscott House with a canvas frame under his arm. Nodding heads of cosmos and coreopsis bent in the wind, and I knew we would all refrain from speaking of Ned's scandalous affair with his mistress. She had threatened to throw herself into the river, and her brother dragged her away and took her back to Greece. Meanwhile, it was left to me and William to pick up the pieces of Ned's broken heart, and his destroyed marriage.

From the window, my reflection overlayed Ned's figure. His drawn face and his long, trailing beard and his gaze turned inward upon affairs of romance and discretion.

Behind me, William dropped a sugar lump into his tea.

"Do you suppose he will finish the painting?" I asked, turning away from my reflection. I adjusted my cuffs, fiddled with my cravat. My tailor in London insisted I purchase these constraining clothes, as they were the acceptable fashion for gentlemen in any society worthy of mention, but increasingly I found my long lost suits of armor less rigid, and longed for those days of my warlord past.

Now, I sipped tea out of chipped cups, and when I caught my reflection in the murky liquid, I saw the face of my father. I saw Arthur, calling to me, from distant places I cannot reach.

"He will," William said, jarring me back to the present. "It is a masterwork."

"Providing he will not be distracted by matters of the heart."

"This retreat will be just the thing he needs to forget her. And when he finishes the painting, I imagine that will put paid to it. No more reminders of a love lorn past."

Indeed. William's paunch pressed the boundaries of his three-piece suit, the striped vest distended, his beard, chestnut and brushing his collar. He tapped his fingers on the edge of the cup as we waited for Ned to enter the door.

"As I understand it," William continued, "you were instrumental in suggesting the material to him."

I nodded. Well I recalled the lucid day, bees swarming on the hawthorne bush and Ned, withdrawn and hiding his affair poorly, besotted with his current muse and adrift in his career, unable to find his rightful place. He wanted so badly for distraction, yet could not stop his frenetic and restless heart and in the space of an afternoon. I had told him, in halting voice, that perhaps Merlin and Nimue might prove a dynamic subject, and after all, he had a patron in line wanting to pay for it.

Ned eagerly lost himself in the study. In some ways, I could see much of Merlin in Ned. Some men are built for that kind of obsessive love that finds them, disarms them, and then traps them. Only, Ned would recover.

Merlin, I still sought, and hoped to still find.

"Has he named the piece yet?"

"I believe he is calling it *The Beguiling of Merlin*."

I approved of the choice.

When at last Ned strode through the door we greeted him with open arms and cries of excitement, all of which hid a deep concern for Ned's well-being. His eyes retained their vivid glitter as we returned to the table and he set his canvas against the wall, and I poured tea for him still hot from the kettle.

From thence we'd planned our weekend retreat. Our pantry filled, divested of our responsibilities, we reacquainted ourselves with the trivial details of life, of family, of which William and Ned could easily fill the hours.

If they noticed I had no family to speak of, no issue, no wife or love to call my own, they did not speak of it, and I would not divulge. All through the centuries only Guinevere had held the light in my heart, and I watched her pass away from me as I had all the others. One by one, they were all consumed by inexorable march of time, and I watched as they aged, I watched the knights grow old and die, while I remained youthful, my hair still glossy black and untouched by a single white filament. Well I remembered how Lancelot had cursed me, and even Guinevere, turned bitter and silent at the end.

I had wanted so much more for us all, and in wanting, destroyed everything.

But William and Ned did not need to know it. I kept my tragedy well dressed and meticulous, I drowned it in cups of tea.

"Enough of this," William announced, slapping his hand on the table. "I think we should go directly to the wine, if we are lucky Dante shall find time to visit us, and drink to beauty, life, and happiness. What say you?"

"A damn fine idea," Ned said, but behind his enthusiasm, I sensed him swallowing memories of Maria. No use telling him all things pass—and I had centuries of context in which to acclimate to the state of my broken heart. When he looked upon me, he saw a young man of limited experience, who, while I was invited on these retreats on account of my amiability and charm, could only stand outside their adult experience of marriage and fatherhood and never give hint as to what, to who, I really was.

And ever must it be.

I let William and Ned talk. In their typical way, they avoided any conversation that might give rise to those deep and dark passions which ran like a torrent through Ned's work, his restless fire which William, so practical and hands-on, served as his complement to damper Ned's flames to a more sensible fire. I poured the wine and cleared the tea cups.

Our evening progressed. We played charades until our drunkenness reached a state of heightened bliss in which the sun poured, golden, through the windows and rendered us both silly and divine. William spoke of Jane in passing and thus they spoke of women, which was precisely the topic we strove to avoid but kept under the grip of Dionysus, not plunged into with foolhardiness and we asked ourselves—what was the greatest love the world had ever known?

"Tristan and Iseult," offered William, draining his cup. I refilled it and he wagged his finger at me, muttering, "you're the devil himself, Morty old chap," and smiled and kept pouring.

"You don't speak of love," Ned said, and despite draining many a cup he still kept the air of deep sobriety. Perhaps the shock of his personal affairs had proved too much for wine to assuage and instead, he focused on me with eyes turned to a falcon's stare, suspicious and narrowed and very decidedly un-Ned like.

"What is there to say?" I answered, and proceeded to withdraw my tin and roll my cigarette, heaping fragrant tobacco into the center.

Ned cleared his throat. "We have been spending weekend after weekend together, and through it all, it has occurred to me you say very little."

"I speak when conversation warrants it," but my smile became harder to pin in place, focusing on licking the edge of the paper to seal my cigarette.

"And there you are, ducking the subject at hand once more." Ned snapped in a flash of anger.

"Come now," William said, and repeated it in a voice pitched to soothe, "we are all friends here, are we not?"

"Then a friend might tell us, what is the greatest love story," and Ned returned to equanimity, as though the mood had never shifted or changed.

I lit the end of my cigarette, and breathed deeply the smoke until the end was lit and burning and decided, this once, to breach my own etiquette and speak of what should not be spoken.

"I say, the greatest love story is the one that remains untold,"

I said, licks of smoke unfurling from my nostrils. "I say the greatest love story is that of Mordred and Guinevere."

William burst out laughing.

"You mean Lancelot."

I smiled behind the veil of smoke and Ned neither laughed or smiled, he sat still and rigid in his seat. *The Beguiling of Merlin*, half-finished, watched us. I could see where Ned had painted himself into Merlin's figure, and where he had painted his mistress into Nimue. There, Ned's poor heart displayed for all to see. And in my own way, I admired that naked sensibility, the courage it must take to love so ardently, and so painfully, he felt compelled to declare it to the world in a painting.

"Do tell," Ned said.

"Well, if you recall, the old Arthurian myths underwent some tailoring, but you know, before de Troyes got his mitts on it, it was Medraut whom Guinevere loved in Arthur's absence, not Lancelot. And when a queen commands love, who are we but small men to deny her?"

I met Ned's eyes over the cup of wine and if it were possible, he paled. A rumble of distant thunder echoed over the darkening sky and clouds encroached on the horizon swallowing up the sun. *I could use a good rain*, I thought, lazily, followed by *you should change the subject, you should talk of something else, you should distract them*, but I did not, and since when had I ever done anything I should have?

"I had not heard that story," William said. "Seems hardly plausible."

"Imagine, if you will, a king who has devoted his life entire to the responsibilities of a kingship. There is little time for care, for nurturance, for love. It makes for a lonely marriage bed, does it not, Ned?"

Ned fidgeted. "What are you implying?"

"A man consumed by his vocation has a tendency to let everything around him atrophy. It was no different in his time.

He was a good king. The best of them. He was like the sun around which all we satellites revolved, and languished in darkness until his return."

I sighed to think of it.

"He spent too long away. Do you know what endless war does to a nation? The people become exhausted with the blood shed. And a woman like Guinevere, a queen like Guinevere—I don't think Arthur truly knew her. And what did he expect? Leaving Medraut alone with her."

William snorted. "Well nowadays, he's not Medraut, he's Mordred, and we all know he's quite evil and he killed Arthur at Camlann."

I waved him off, stubbing out my cigarette as the first lashing of rain came unloosed from the sky and cast a veil of blue tinged rain in the gloaming.

"Before Mordred, as you prefer, was an enemy, he was a friend. A confidant, dare I say it—a son," I seethed. "Beloved. With great hate comes great love. What would you know of it?" I snapped, leaning my aching head against the back of the chair. "What would you know of the tyranny of fathers over sons? And to leave that son alone, alone with such a beauty, such a goddess as Guinevere…" I made a fist of my hands, and unfurled them, remembering her. Guinevere always had a maddening iciness to her, and she knew when to thaw just enough to give glimpse to her volcanic passions beneath.

"I understand your infatuation with the Greek," I blurted and Ned's eyes widened. William frowned with consternation for, of all the things we had planned to do this weekend, *not* talk about Maria Zambaco was paramount. And here I was, drunk, confessional, and destroying it, as I do all things. "I understand what leads men to such extremes."

"You bastard," Ned said, and launched himself across the table. He delivered a punch and I fell backward in the chair, to the floor, into a puddle. The damn house was flooding again with the nonstop flow of rain and the river so near. I stared up at the ceiling and rolled to my feet, swaying as William restrained Ned. My cheek stung, a stripe of blood where the skin broke, but I didn't care. I sloshed through the flooding floor to the painting.

"Ned," I cried, and Ned still breathing fire and hot headed, realized we were up to an inch of water at our feet, and his canvas sitting in it.

I reached it first, hoisting it up with horror and Ned, sloshing to stand beside me until he snatched at it, gripped the other end and gave a shriek, releasing it and thrusting his hands into his hair.

"Ruined!" he cried.

"We can dry it," I insisted, face to face with the portrait of Merlin.

"The wood won't suffer it, it all goes to rot," Ned said, cursing. William consoled him and I thought this might be the thing to do it, to reduce Ned to quivering mess. William patted him on the shoulder, reassuring, whispering in his ear.

Ned broke away from William, gripped by some fever while I stood entranced, staring deeply into the portrait of Merlin's face. And it seemed to me then the floor entire spread out as a lake under my feet, growing deeper. That the sensitive eyes of the painted Merlin burned with layers of oil lacquered upon oil and entranced me, held me still. To look into his eyes—how had Ned captured the spirit of the mage, that last Druid, here in the oil and the canvas? And how long had I roamed, seeking him, calling him, begging him to come out of hiding and deliver Arthur once more? To bring my father back. But no amount of tears and regrets had resurrected either. Long had I yearned that in finding Merlin, I could resolve the past, and make up for all my trespasses.

It had been Merlin's eyes I stared into, when I saw him last, before he went into tree or stone, which, I could not know. Merlin's eyes fixed me in place, and commanded me to live forever, so I might watch everything dear to me wither. Retribution for the crime of patricide.

But I had not killed Arthur once, but twice. First, when I stole his lady's heart, and again, when I stabbed it through.

"Merlin," I spoke to the painting.

The face, half-formed from the canvas, seemed raised up, so if I but touched it, I could feel the ridge and lines of my old friend's face, hear again his wise counsel. My hands gripped the canvas frame tightly, until I thought I might splinter the wood itself.

"Is he gone mad?" William muttered. Ned and he thronged me at a distance with the water lapping at our heels, the lightning spearing the night sky before blackness swallowed it once more.

Merlin's eyes blinked, and I cried out. Was it the presence of fear hammering in my heart, or excitement? A chance to set the scales of justice aright. Had I not paid for my crimes?

"Oh Merlin, that you would reunite us all again and everything might be as it was before," I cried and it seemed then the rain was everywhere, the rain came from within the house itself and I could hear William, frantic, Ned retreating to higher ground and I was sinking.

William's fist gripped the back of my suit, yanking at me like the scruff of a puppy with the painting still fixed in my hands and I would not let go. William cried out for help, but I shrugged him off. I did not need help. Merlin was here, in the stone, in the wood, in the canvas and in the paint. He was everywhere, in all things, and Ned, great romantic fool that he was, opened a portal he had no business opening.

Bless you, Ned, I thought, and Merlin's face uplifted into a smile. His image lurched forward; his fingers punctured out from the canvas, real flesh, real matter, to seize me by the shoulders.

"Old friend!" I cried. "Take me to my father!"

Merlin nodded, half in and out of the painting, holding me tight in his embrace as we sank, down and down into the lake of

Kelmscott house until I felt the flood swallow me up, plunging my upturned face beneath the water, and heard the cries of horror from Ned and William, and heard the thunder shake the house.

Down and down we went, Merlin before me. In the depths of this glimmering lake, I saw the lights of Avalon, dimly shining at the bottom. I shivered with anticipation. I have done wrong in my life. I found myself swept up by violence and passions uncontrollable. What was my crime but a lapse in judgment, a failure to think things through, to act rashly, recklessly? I followed my heart and ignored my head.

Above me, the wavering faces of Ned and William looked through the refracting depths to watch my descent. Ned would go on to make his masterpieces, I was sure, and William, his books. They would remember this as a strange night's drunken revel, and determine I had merely run off.

They would forget the shafts of light gleaming beneath me. Forget the greatest love story never told, forget the ruined painting, and forget this expanding lake, in whose depths might be a lady, might be a forgotten sword.

Forget the perfumed scent of roses, of apple trees saturating the land, loosed from some forgotten isle.

I am content to be forgotten.

The Saga of Freydis Beastsbane

David Wiley

It was the final night of the Althing and all the judgments had
been passed and the punishments doled out, wares had been
bartered and shopped closed up, and the mead had long run low
and the goblets now contained more water than alcohol. A dozen
men sat around a blazing pyre, trading stories of their exploits
and heroic deeds in battle. One of them was little more than a
child, a lanky boy of thirteen who had just been given his
armband and sworn his oath to his liege-lord a day ago. Not one
of them took a second look at Freydis Thorisdottir unless they
had need of more meat or mead or both. Soon more than one of
them might look upon her with different needs in mind. She kept
her head down low, eyes averted as she had been taught, and
made sure that none of them wanted for their food and drink. She
hated the work of women, the subjection of a servant, but she
also loved to listen to their tales.

"And that was when I brought down my axe, driving it from
skull to navel," roared Bogi Bloodbeard. He reenacted the
gesture for the men gathered around him, pale mead sloshing
over the lip of his tankard. "My brother was avenged, assured of
being able to take his place among Odin's halls in Valhalla."

"Valhalla," they all whispered with reverence. It was every
man's dream to die bravely in battle that they may be judged
worthy to feast in the halls of Valhalla with the gods. The
women that Freydis was grouped with never mentioned it, nor
did the care to discuss it. Any time one of the men brought
Valhalla up they rolled their eyes and crooned over how big and
strong the men were and how Odin would be a fool to not invite
them all to Valhalla upon their valiant deaths. Freydis had also
learned, long ago, that both the men and the women were agreed
upon one thing: Freydis would do better to learn her place as a

woman, tending animals and crops and learning how to care for her future husband, instead of dreaming of glory and battle. Yet her soul sang when she dreamed of being a shieldmaiden, earning her stripes in battle alongside other warriors as they downed lines of their enemy. They all knew the tales of shieldmaidens—Brynhildr, Lagertha, Hervor, Thornbjǫrg, Princess Hed, Visna and Veborg—and agreed those worthy women would be with Odin in Valhalla. But they were resolute that Freydis would never become a shieldmaiden.

"You, ge' me s'more mead," one of the men slurred, pointing his tankard at Freydis. He took a swig of the remnants in his tankard and pale mead dripped down his matted beard. Freydis wove through the crowd. She circled toward the man, the proximity to the fire warmed her thighs. She leaned in and grabbed the mug from his hand. It slipped and Freydis shook the mead off her skin before picking it up off the ground. A yelp slipped from her lips as a sharp pain flared on her bottom. Freydis turned and swung. A different sort of pain throbbed on her hand and she walked away to fill the tankard from the barrel.

Another woman, Hilga, swept past her. Freydis had spent three years envying the woman for her rapidly-developing body while cursing her own sluggish development. But Freydis now rued the day her breasts had begun to bud. The men were insufferable and she could no longer pass among them invisible unless they were preoccupied with other tasks or if she was hidden beneath layers of furs. When they did notice her, it was not always to have her fetch them something. If only she had been born a boy none of that would matter and she could be there among them without the risk of someone trying to claim her maidenhead or angling to get her promised to them.

The sharp, piercing blast of a horn echoed in the air three times. Muscular bodies rushed past her, tankards of mead forgotten. Their hands help sharp steel weapons and wooden shields. Shouts of joy rumbled. This was her chance. Freydis rushed around the corner and slipped into the narrow pass between two farmsteads. She slid a bale of straw aside. Her hands gripped the hard wooden ring around the outside of her shield. She slipped her left arm through a set of leather straps and pulled them tight. The oak haft of her axe was barely longer than her forearm, but the crescent blade had been forged in the hottest of fires and the blacksmith promised it would cut through chainmail. Freydis rushed back out to join the men in defense of the village.

A sound unlike any other called to her from the woods. The fierce braying of a pack of hounds rang out. There had to be many of them, at least two dozen, but the warriors all kept charging to the left through the forest. Freydis looked down the left path, toward the faint glow of torches and the clamor of steel scraping against steel. A shrill scream signified Odin had called one of his warriors into Valhalla. Freydis took a step toward those screams and the din of battle. The hounds cried out again, drowning out the din.

She turned and ran toward the hounds, frigid blasts of wind biting her cheeks. She would not let her home fall under attack without mounting some sort of defense. The men were all too busy fighting off the other invaders to notice this second front of the attack. At least now they wouldn't be able to steal her kills. She would prove herself worthy of bearing this shield tonight. Dead leaves crunched underfoot with every stride. Sharp branches raked their claws along her cheeks and thighs whenever she passed too close. The braying was growing louder, closer. The sound of men's voices, of horses stamping, of metal clanking never followed. She pressed onward, determined to find the source. She broke through a thicket of branches and her feet tangled beneath her. She slid across the ground, blades of grass tickling her nose and cheek and forehead.

Her left arm throbbed from the impact of landing on the circular shield. Her right hand held nothing but a few blades of grass. Freydis scrambled to her feet and pulled the wolf fur mantle tighter around her shoulders. Her gaze scoured over the sea of browning grass and dried leaves for sign of her axe. She paced in a slow circle, watching near her feet. Leaves crackled and crunched with every step and long twig fingers grazed the fur mantle with each pass. She stopped, taking a step backward. She stared down and blinked but the darkness enveloped the ground. She cocked her head to one side and the pale gleam of moonlight reflected off cold steel. She bent down to retrieve her lost weapon. The rough wood felt good in her fingers and her lips pulled up in a light smile. Her gaze lifted to take in the clearing around her.

The dense branches parted overhead to allow a thick beam of moonlight to reflect off the silvery surface of a small river cutting through the clearing. Dozens of birch trees encircled the area, adorned with pink and white and yellow poppies in the midst of their final bloom. The lilac blossoms of harebells danced in the light breeze blowing through the quiet opening in the woods. Small evergreen leaves of mountain avens waved to and fro as the wind lighted upon their branches. It was the perfect place of tranquility to disappear into nature.

Apart from the giant monstrosity taking a deep drink from the flowing water. The axe fell from her hand again with a whispered curse.

The beast raised its green-scaled head to look at her. Its forked tongue flicked in the air and the braying of hounds resumed. Until that moment she hadn't realized the sound had stopped. Freydis bent down, keeping her eyes raised to watch the beast. Her hand patted along the ground, crunching leaves and pressing grass beneath her palm. She gripped the haft and popped back upright. The beast turned away and was vanishing back into the forest on the other side of the river. Freydis charged at the water and leapt with all her might, landing on the other bank with a meter to spare. A small yellow tail, tipped with hair like the golden mane of a lion, disappeared into the darkness between the trees. Whatever this beast was, Freydis was certain to become a shieldmaiden if she could kill it.

The braying filled her ears and her head throbbed from the endless repetition of the brassy tone. Freydis dodged trunks and leapt over streams. Red blotches peppered her face and her lungs burned with each ragged gasp for air. The forest around her swam in circles but still she pressed onward in pursuit of her prey. She embraced the ground as it raced toward her, her vision blurring and fading to white. A massive figure loped into her view as her eyes flickered shut. A green and scaly head like a snake. Front legs lined with brown fur and black hooves like a stag. A long and sleek body, golden with flecks of black throughout like a leopard. The powerful and lean back legs of a lion. It was her uncle's monster come back to life. Come to kill her while she lay prone.

Freydis pushed against the hard earth. Her arms quivered and quaked with every inch she rose. The ground greeted her with a dirt-filled kiss. She spat the rough clump of earth and rolled onto her back. Her chest heaved. The darkness of oblivion covered her eyes and she slept.

She woke to the rich aroma of brewing tea. The earthy scent of birch bark blended with the fragrant scent of fresh-picked poppy petals set her stomach to rumbling. Freydis groaned and propped herself up on one arm. The forest was exactly how she remembered, except for the hodgepodge-beast of her uncle's nightmares. Her pulse beat like a kettle drum and she shielded her eyes against a bright ray of sunlight. Struggling to her feet, she felt as much as heard her joints. She took a step forward and pain lanced through her shin. She held her breath and took another step. It was a little better.

By the time she reached the outskirts of her village the aches were a forgotten memory, yet the encounter with the strange beast was stamped upon her mind. She drew nearer to the boiling tea and the words of the women.

"Leave it to a bunch of cowards like the Heimdris to try and attack during the final night of the Althing," said a woman who was taller and more wrinkled than the rest.

"My brave Thorkel Breakspear drove off a dozen men alone and sent those renegades off with more than a mere clout on the ear," chimed in a plump woman whose hair was as pale blonde as Freydis' hair. "I'd wager half of them die today of the wounds he delivered."

"Aye," said a third, nearly as young as Freydis but far more developed in her curves and with a babe suckling on her breast. "According to you Thorkel Breakwind could challenge the gods with his bare hands and win. By sundown it'll be half a score of men he drove off and killed two dozen more." The other women laughed and the blonde woman's face reddened.

Their laughter cut off when they saw Freydis approaching. She did not need a looking-glass to know she must be a dreadful sight after spending the night in the woods. She smiled and grabbed a wooden mug, eager to put some tea in her empty stomach before her morning meal.

"Did the Heimdris capture you?" the young woman whispered.

Freydis ignored her for the moment and scooped some tea into her mug. It spread warmth through her bones as she took a deep quaff and then refilled the mug. Freydis looked up at the three women, smiling.

"No, I never saw the Heimdris last night. I chased a magnificent beast, the likes of which none here have ever seen."

"Oh," the older woman responded, and there seemed no more for her to say.

"This wouldn't be the same beast your uncle chased, would it?" the blonde asked.

The six set of eyes watching her were cold, distant—not even concerned. The stories of her uncle's exploits were still told around the campfires for a good laugh, even among the women. They called him Weindahl the Witless when she was not around, and sometimes even when they knew she could hear. Freydis quaffed the last of her second mug and walked away without another word. She could hear their giggles as she disappeared around the corner. She would show them. The next time that beast appeared, it would not escape her. Then she would be the one laughing.

A quick dousing of water was all she afforded herself before setting about her daily tasks. She spent her hour at the large loom in her father's house, working the delicate threads into the desired pattern. She cooked some eggs and cut some salted pork for her father's midmorning meal, sneaking in a few bites for herself. She churned butter until her shoulders burned and milked the cows until her fingers were numb. In short, she did everything but go to see the one person who might be able to understand her encounter. She was not prepared to face her gaze. Yet as the sun began to drop in the sky, it was her grandmother who came to her, instead,, as Freydis was washed her father's clothes in a wooden basin.

She heard the thump, thump, thump of her wooden stick long before she saw her. Freydis bit the inside of her cheek until it bled and scrubbed at a spot on her father's breeches. She could hear her grandmother behind her, but refused to look, knowing that she would see the woman's short, hunched frame making its way up the hill at a sluggish pace. She would be wearing her usual blue robes, peering up at Freydis with her one large violet eye.

Freydis scrubbed harder even though there was no spot nor stain to be seen. Long, spindly fingers clamped down on her shoulder and she dropped the breeches into the water. Droplets of water crashed against her face and the soap burned her eyes. There was no avoiding the discussion any longer.

She stood there in silence, her eye searching Freydis' face. White brows drew down in a furrowed arch and she clucked his tongue several times. Freydis stepped forward when the old woman tugged at her shoulder, taking one step for every tug and no more. The woman circled around her, grandmother's carved runestick beating a soft rhythm in the dirt and grass. She stood before her again and sighed. Freydis licked her lips and waited. She knew that grandmother would speak when she was ready, and Freydis knew better than to be the first to engage conversation with the ancient Seiðr.

"You have seen the beast," she said at last. Her voice rustled like crumpling paper. Freydis forced her mouth to remain closed. She always knew things that she shouldn't. That was what made her a good Seiðr.

"How did you know?" Freydis blurted out in spite of herself. She knew her grandmother wouldn't answer or, if she did, it would be in a way that would explain nothing. But maybe for once in her life she would give her a straight answer. Grandmother leaned in close to her. Her breath warmed Freydis' cheek and the stench of rotten onions made her nose crinkle. A crooked finger tapped her on the forehead and ran down the bridge of her nose.

"You have been marked by the beast," she said. Her finger pressed into Freydis' temple until she had to take a step back to keep her balance. She flashed a grin at her and she could see the holes in the gums where each of grandmother's teeth had once been. Freydis reached up and rubbed at the spot where the finger had been and looked around the yard for a looking-glass to see the mark. Her grandmother cackled and clucked her tongue, pulling a small onion out from beneath her robes. "You won't find the marking. It isn't visible to common eyes, but it be there as surely as it had been on your Uncle Weindahl's face."

Freydis could feel her eyes burn as she bit her lip. She was mad, as mad as her uncle had been. Her dreams of being a shieldmaiden were vanishing into the vortex of insanity. Her seventeenth nameday had only been a few nights ago. This was the year when she was supposed to find her place, to earn her keep among the Jarl's warriors and raiders. She had put off persistent demands of marriage for over two years because her father needed her, but that excuse wouldn't last forever. Now she would earn her place in the stocks at best. But most likely she would be banished, forced to forage and hunt on the outskirts of society just as Uncle Weindahl had been. Or, even worse, forced to marry an old and senile warrior and bear him an heir or two. Her grandmother watched her without saying a word.

She took a large bite out of the onion and waited for Freydis to plea, to exclaim, to strike out in anger.

She did none of those things.

"I'll get my things," Freydis whispered. She took two steps forward but a long arm reached out and grabbed her shoulder, holding her in an iron grip.

"There be things you should know, Freydis Thorisdottir. Before you be making your mind up to banish yourself."

Freydis blinked and stared at her. "What things?"

"Your uncle was not mad, for one. And you not be mad, either."

"How do you know? Can you see the beast?"

"No, grandchild. But my twin sister could. And there be no one whose words I believed more than hers. She was as sane as anyone from the time we shared a spot in our mother's belly to the day when I buried her in the cold earth. I know not much about this beast, but what I do know may be enough to at least convince you that you not be mad."

Freydis debated the truth behind her words. Her grandmother was bound by oath, as the local Seiðr, not to spread falsehoods to those under the Jarl's protection. Yet everyone knew she was more than willing to share half-truths that failed to turn out as the hearers interpreted. If what she was saying was true, and she could shed some light upon the beast's appearances, it could be worth hearing. She nodded to her grandmother and the old woman's cracked lips spread wide to show three remaining teeth. She took another bite of the onion before turning away, beckoning for Freydis to follow as she trodded down the path.

Freydis ducked her head as she passed through the open doorway to her hut. The smell of smoke and spices made Freydis sneeze three times \ and she pressed a finger to her left nostril, blowing out. She repeated the process for the other side.

The aroma still lingered but at least now she could breathe. Dried onions were strung from the ceiling in bunches. Clay pots and brass containers were spread throughout, most covered with lids and charcoal markings to identify them. At least she had been told by her grandmother that those markings somehow helped to tell a person what was hidden inside. It made sense to have some system for knowing where to find what you needed, but she had never been offered the chance to learn this foreign systems of symbols.

Her grandmother plopped down on a short stool, the wooden legs scraping across the dirt floor. Her runestaff clattered to the ground with a dull thud and Freydis seated herself across from grandmother. She suppressed a shudder as she looked into that violet eye and clenched a nearby table for support. She broke her gaze and studied the random lines marked on a jar over grandmother's left shoulder instead. Her grandmother clasped her wrists in a tight grip and started speaking.

"I have been given a sign from Odin and Freya," she said with a smile that sent goosepimples running up Freydis' arms. "The gods have shown me things that no other man nor woman may know. But they be choosing this moment to allow me to show you, as well as tell you, about your secret heritage." She released Freydis' left wrist and reached into a jar without looking at what it contained. A fine black powder trickled from her grandmother's hand and she threw it into the embers dying beside them. Sulfur filled her nostrils and a deep indigo smoke undulated as it rose from the ashes. The embers flared anew, the fire blazing orange and magenta and blue. Freydis shifted her stool back a bit but her grandmother held her right wrist firm. Her back throbbed from leaning forward so far, but at least her legs weren't going to roast.

"The beast you saw be older than our people, nearly as old as the oceans raging along the shores. It has almost always been, and always will be until the gods call it into one of the other realms or some valiant warrior slays it in single combat. For many eons it passed through the world unseen by mortal eyes. And then it met a man, a noble knight named Pellinore, and it began a new form of existence."

The swirling smoke curled in upon itself in front of Freydis. When she blinked, an image the beast stood there in the smoke. Its serpent head weaved back and forth in a hypnotic motion. Its lion tail flicked lightly and it brought one cloven hoof to its mouth. And then the smoke swirled beside it, forming a knight clad in shining metal from head to toe.

"From the moment his eyes met the beast, he was called upon to pursue it. It became his quest, and thus the beast became known as the Questing Beast. Few others in that time be worthy enough to witness the beast, and some tried to take up the hunt, but none be successful in capturing or killing the Questing Beast." Within the smoke the beast turned and loped along, running away from the knight. The man ran after it, never getting closer to the image. "Eventually the years caught up to Sir Pellinore, until he was no longer able to keep pace with his prized beast." The image of the knight slowed its pace and the beast vanished into the roiling smoke. "And so he settled at last and found a wife. They had two children. Of those children, one saw the Questing Beast. And so the pattern began.

"Every generation in the line of Pellinore begets one who will see the Questing Beast and will be compelled to pursue it until their death. The exact timing of the first appearance varies, but it commonly falls near the seventeenth nameday. It seems the pattern holds true to you, as it did to your uncle."

The smoke formed to show her uncle chasing after the beast with axe and spear. Freydis clenched her fist and shook her head. "No," she said, "I will not believe this. It is not my fate to chase this beast without end for the remainder of my life. My fate lies along another path."

Her grandmother cackled and her violet eye pierced through a hole in the smoke. "What path may that be?" she asked.

"I will be the one to kill the beast and, when I bring its carcass in to the Jarl he will see my uncle was not mad, nor am I. He will have no choice but to make me one of his shieldmaidens so I can venture out to do battle for his honor and join the other warriors on their seasonal raids."

"The beast cannot be beaten," her grandmother reminded her.

"Because a thing has not yet been done does not mean it cannot be done. I will be the one to break the curse of Pellinore." She rose from her stool and spun on her heels. The sulfuric stench clung to her clothes the whole way back home and the first thing she did was to scrub them clean.

Three days and nights passed without a sighting of the Questing Beast. Freydis horded dried meats and grains, stowing them away with her axe and shield in a small bundle she rigged to sling across her back. She was prepared for the hunt, even if it dragged on to take days. Every few hours she thought of another thing to take along, such as flint and tinder, which might prove to be useful. Each night she stood near the campfire, warding off roaming hands and lustful eyes while keeping her own gaze on the forest. She began to wonder if it had all been a dream as she lay on her straw bed, drifting off to sleep after the third night.

But it had been no dream and she knew it in the depths of her being. The following morning she woke and dressed, grabbing her axe to split some logs. She knelt down and reached her hand into her hidden cache. She stood and slung the axe over her shoulder, turning into the forest. She paused and bit her lip. Hounds were braying in the distance and getting closer. Freydis looked around but no one else seemed to hear the brassy howls ringing through the trees. A strong breeze prickled her skin and she shuddered. She crinkled her nose as a maiden passed by with a full bucket to slosh into the midden heap. Freydis bent down, grabbing her shield and bundle before it was too late. She rose back up and it was staring at her, no more than a stone's throw away. It watched her with eyes the size of rubies, their amber hue shining in the sunlight. Freydis smiled and took a step toward the Questing Beast. Then another. And then it turned and ran.

She rushed after it, the exhilaration of the chase lending strength to her legs. She leapt over fallen trunks of trees and crashed through bushes, always following the straightest course toward her prey. She raised her axe up high to throw it but thought better of the tactic. She would be unarmed if she threw it. If she missed, or if it provoked the beast to attack in a rage, she would be at a disadvantage. Better to use her brains to outwit the beast and her body to outlast it.

Every time she gained a stride or two on it the beast would find a way to regain its lead. Her lungs burned with every gasp for air. Her legs felt as heavy as a sack of grain and her strides grew shorter with each passing mile.

The beast never gained enough ground to completely disappear from sight and the baritone braying of the hounds kept her muscles moving long after her body needed to stop.

The sunlight transformed into an orange-pink hue as it cast the waning rays of the day upon the earth. Freydis plowed through a bush, the leaves rustling as her body forced the branches to part. Her foot sank into a small hole on the other side and she went crashing to the ground. A soft cloud of dirt swirled in the air around her. Her chest throbbed, although she could not tell if it was from the impact with the ground or from the exertion of running half the day. She could hear her labored breathing, the chirping of a few birds flying from tree to tree, and the chattering of a squirrel as it chased off a bird from its branch. She lay there, relishing the tranquil noises of the forest. And then it hit her: the braying was gone.

Freydis scrambled to her feet and her gaze searched north and south, east and west. The Questing Beast was nowhere to be found. It had slipped away during her momentary distraction and she was miles from the village with night descending. She stood there among the trees and watched for any sign of the Questing Beast but it was truly gone.

How long would it be before it returned again? It had been three days for this sighting and her day's pursuit had gained her nothing but achy limbs and a shortness of breath. It had convinced her that she was inadequately prepared to hunt and slay the beast that had been her family's curse for generations. So Freydis ignored the aches in her body and the fatigue rushing through her like a raging river and walked back toward the village.

Freydis ignored the looks of the women when she stumbled out from the woods. She could not hear the words of their gossip but she could imagine what they were whispering amongst each other. She didn't care. She needed to sleep, but before she could do that she needed to assure her mind that she was prepared for the next sighting of the Questing Beast. If it reappeared that night, she didn't want to suffer another fruitless chase. The dried meats she had consumed on her walk back would need to be replaced, and she needed something a ranged weapon. If the beast would not let her get close enough to hack at it, she needed some way to slow it down and injure it enough so that she could catch up to it. Which meant she needed a bow, and arrows.

There would be hundreds of bows and tens of thousands of arrows in the Jarl's Armory, but she could hardly use one of those. So she set out to find Bjorn the Blacksmith and see what he might be able to provide.

Freydis realized after a few moments that she was drawing too much attention with her current disheveled state. Her furs were in disarray and her face was coated in dirt and debris. Her arms and cheeks had scrapes that burned a bright red. Bits of leaves and twigs were tangled in her pale blonde hair. She was a mess and it was obvious to everyone that she had been out in the woods all night long. That would never do if she needed to resort to skulking about the village.

Freydis took a detour, cutting through scarcely-used paths and across under-tended farmland. She allowed her legs to carry her as far and as fast as they could to her father's homestead.

A little water splashed on her face and a quick change of clothes and furs improved her appearance enough to avoid unwanted attention. She snagged her saved pouch of coins from under the floorboard and rushed back across the village to Bjorn's shop. She could smell the burning coal and wood before she could hear the forge. The heavy clanking of metal striking metal pierced through the air loud enough to drown out even the greatest of sounds. A soft whoosh came next followed by an angry hiss as the hot metal was submerged in water. Bjorn turned and waved when he saw her approaching. Smiled as his gaze took in the bag in her hand.

"Wha' can ay do fer ye, Freydis Thorisdottir?" he said, his voice a deep rumble that reminded Freydis of rocks tumbling down a mountain.

"I need a bow. And arrows. I can pay good coin," she added, hoisting the bag. Bjorn closed one of his great green eyes and his forehead furrowed as he considered her request.

"Le's say ay can do et," he said as he stroked the stubble on his broad chin. "Ay can get ye un in, say, a fortni't and 'nother fortni't for fresh supply o' arrows."

Freydis' shoulders slumped and the hand holding the bag of coins dropped down below her waist. She forced the corners of her mouth to lift in a smile, saying, "I appreciate the offer, but I need it sooner than that."

"For un added twenty ay can do et en 'bout a fortni't plus three days." His smile was soft and his gaze flickered to the bag in her hand. But she couldn't wait that long. If the Questing Beast came tonight she needed to be ready to give it chase. She shook her head and pivoted on her heel, flashing Bjorn one last smile over her shoulder before departing. She needed to rest. When her head was clear again she could figure out how to secure what she needed for her hunt.

By the time Freydis had napped, ate, and completed the necessary tasks around her father's farm it was nearly dark. She had debated her options for the hours that she spent tending crops and animals and had come to a bad decision on what to do. There weren't any good decisions to be found, but she knew that this was probably the worst choice she could make. She would be punished if she was caught stealing from the Jarl's Armory. Possibly killed, maybe even exiled. But stealing from one of the men in the village could start a blood feud that would spread to her entire family, and waiting more than a fortnight for the blacksmith to craft her the necessary weapons was not an option. Stealing from the Jarl would only involve her if she was caught, and enough people had seen her state from the woods to believe she had gone mad. That would be her father's defense, the thing that would save him from being implicated by the Jarl as well.

Clouds rolled across the night sky, casting deep shadows over the village. Reed torches burned throughout the village, but their light was easily avoided and would help to blind anyone who happened to look as she moved. Freydis placed the toe of her foot down first with each step, easing the heel to the ground afterwards. One crunched leaf or snapped twig could spell disaster. She held her breath each time as she crossed the open space from building to building. She didn't notice she was doing it until her lungs burned halfway across.

Her sluggish pace was impractical. Stealth be damned, she was a shieldmaiden in her heart and not some frightened maiden to be bullied and intimidated. She moved with more speed, still taking enough care to avoid making any huge blunders. The Jarl's Armory came into view, a longer and wider black shadow than all the other dark buildings sticking up from the ground.

She slipped around the side and over to a small window. She had to shimmy a little, but she managed to hoist herself up and through the window without making too much noise to alert the guard stationed at the front.

The room around her was full of weapons and armor and other battle essentials. She blinked her eyes and tried to adjust to the dim light but everything looked identical. There was a tall and skinny black shape over to the right, a short and squat one straight ahead, an oblong form to the left. She could guess at what some of the things were, but without a light she would be as likely to cut her hand on a blade or knock something over as she was to find a bow and arrows. The rough stones of the wall jutted into her shoulders and back. Her legs ached from standing in one place. The musty smell of dust and cobwebs made her nose itch and she rubbed at it with her index finger. She blinked over and over, willing her eyes to adjust even the slightest bit. But the darkness had banished all light from the room. It was time to decide whether to chance searching in the pitch black or to go back home and try again another night.

She decided that she would just have to come back another night. The risk was too great. Yet even as her mind decided this, her feet remained rooted in place. Her legs refused to obey the command. A light breeze tickled the back of her neck. Her eyes watered as a cloud of dust was stirred into the air. Her nose twitched. She doubled over with a sneeze and cursed Loki, the trickster god, in her mind.

She pleaded with Odin and Thor to let no one notice the sound. But the door opened a crack and an orange beam of light pierced the darkness. Freydis dropped to the ground without further thought, embracing the cold, hard floor beneath her. Her lungs burned as she held her breath. Her heart threatened to burst from her chest and she was certain the guard at the door could hear it thumping.

Tiny legs tickled her cheek as an insect of some sort marched over her while she lay prone among the arms and armor. The light moved to and fro, sweeping over vast parts of the room, but at last it began to fade and the door pulled shut.

She had confirmed her decision during the long minutes of hiding: she would leave without the bow. Freydis had caught a glimpse of a bow and three brimming quivers of arrows during the search, but they were far enough away that she wouldn't risk maneuvering through the darkness. Her limbs ached as she rose, begging for her to stretch them out before placing more strain on them. She strode three steps toward the window and stood on her toes to get a good grip along the sides of the frame.

She hoisted herself up and then it came. The sound of thirty hounds braying cut through the silence in the air. Freydis swore and dropped back into the room.

She turned, her mind racing to recall where the bow had been and what to avoid to get there.

A single beam of moonlight burst through the cover of the clouds, shining a spotlight on her prize.

The gods wanted her to have the bow. To hunt the beast. If it was their will, she would fight this beast and earn her place, either as a shieldmaiden in the Jarl's service or at the halls of Valhalla as a Valkyrie.

Freydis moved past crates and scattered weapons, staving off the urge to cut a straight path toward the bow. She still needed caution, although she doubted anyone could hear her move over the incessant braying of the beast. As her hand closed around the bow, the smooth, hard wood gave her comfort. She slung a quiver over each shoulder and strung up the bow with haste. She prayed to all the gods as she moved back toward the window, asking for protection, for their blessings in battle, for the chance to prove herself this night against the Questing Beast. She slipped the quivers and bow out the window first and then followed, wriggling through and landing hard on the soft ground. She scooped up her stolen treasures, vowing to replace them should she survive and to purchase as many new arrows as necessary to recover any she lost. And then Freydis ran, not caring if anyone heard or saw her now. She ran through the twists and turns she knew so well in the village, heading toward her secret stash while hoping her chance to chase the beast did not vanish.

Freydis grabbed her axe and her shield, rearranging the quivers so that they cross-crossed over the shield to hold it in place. She slipped the axe through a loop in the belt around her waist and, without further delay, she charged toward the distant sound. Her arms pumped at her sides and her face burned in spite of the chill in the air. She dodged around trees and leapt over streams.

She made it to the clearing where she had first seen the Questing Beast and stopped in her tracks.

It was there, drinking deeply from the cool water. Black slits in its amber eyes seemed to be watching her even though the head was low to the ground. One stag-hoof stamped the ground and its forked tongue lapped up one last drink of water. Freydis nocked an arrow on the string and drew it back to full draw.

She closed one eyes as she lined up her shot. Its head raised and cocked to the side. She exhaled and released the string. The projectile cut through the air and skimmed over the shoulder of the Questing Beast. Red rivulets of blood trickled to the surface and the braying of hounds amplified tenfold. It turned and fled before Freydis could get off a second shot. She loosened the tension on the string and raced after it, bow in one hand and an arrow in the other.

She leapt from stone to stone along a rocky slope that the Questing Beast appeared to mount with ease. Her left foot caught a loose rock and her arms windmilled as she tried to keep her balance. Freydis tumbled down the hill, sending an army of small stones marching ahead of her. The wind escaped her lungs with a great whoosh and she moaned. She could feel the burning along her arms and knees where she scraped her skin in the tumble but she put the sensation to the back of her mind. She kipped back up and charged up the rocky slope once more. Her ankle wobbled when she landed on another loose rock, but this one did not come free. She reached the crest of the hill, certain her prey was long out of sight. But there it was, watching her at the bottom on the other side. Its scaly features seemed to smile at her in amusement and Freydis scoffed. She raised her bow, nocking an arrow. But the arrow had snapped in two during the fall. She tossed it aside and drew a new one from the quiver. She was alarmed to realize only two remained in her quiver. But there would be no time to go back and retrieve the ones that escaped during her fall. She pulled the string back to its full draw and lined up her shot. The Questing Beast reared up as her arrow raced toward it. Thunder rumbled overhead, drowning out the braying for a brief moment. She prayed to Thor that her shot would fly true. It pierced the ground beneath the Questing Beast. Freydis swore.

Freydis raced after the beast as it charged away from the hill. She held the final arrow in one hand and rubbed her thumb along the smooth shaft as she ran. Her body was focused on chasing the beast but her mind was diverted in prayer to all the gods she could think of. The thunder rumbled and lightning lit the sky. White flakes of snow stuck to her hair and the fur of her mantle as it fell to the ground.

Freydis ignored it and followed the beast into a small valley hidden between a pair of hills. The Questing Beast reared up on golden lion legs as it reached a dead end. It spun to face Freydis and she loosed her final arrow. Thunder crackled and the arrow sank deep into the shoulder of the beast. The braying of the hounds drowned out all other sounds. The snake head opened its mouth in a soundless hiss, its tongue flapping in the air like a banner waving in the wind. Freydis tossed the bow aside and slipped the quivers off her shoulders. She slipped her left arm into the shield, gripping the hard leather strap in her hand. She drew her axe as the beast charged toward her. She rooted her feet into the ground and raised her shield for protection. And then it was upon her.

It lashed out in a flurry of hooves and fangs. Freydis struck with her axe as the head snaked around her shield. The cold steel of her axe bit into its scaly skin and the braying became thirty howls of pain. The beast recoiled and Freydis advanced with shield held between them. It spun about and Freydis swung her axe but missed the lithe leopard body of the Questing Beast. Its lion feet bucked into the air and sharp claws bit into her shield. Splinters showered into Freydis' face and she closed her eyes to protect her vision.

The Questing Beast capitalized on this distraction and backed into Freydis. She fell hard to the ground. A jagged stone pressed into the small of her back and the Questing Beast bore its weight down upon her. She got her shield up in time to catch the hooves pounding down and the force of the blow numbed her left arm. It reared up again and brought the hooves down on the shield once more and she felt the wood and iron break under the attack. Another blow or two and it would be useless and her end would come from this beast.

Freydis rolled backwards—a difficult feat with a shield strapped to one arm and an axe gripped in her hand—as the beast reared up to land another blow upon her. Its hooves crashed down into the dirt where she had lain moments before. The beast brayed in rage and shook flakes of fresh snow from atop its head. Her chest heaved as she breathed and Freydis felt only numbness in her left arm. Yet she stood between the Questing Beast and the only exit from this valley.

Retreat never entered into her thoughts. She knew this would become the gravesite for one of them before the night was done and she had the favor of the gods on her side. Tonight she would slay the beast.

The snow swirled around them with renewed force. Thick, heavy flakes clung to Freydis as she stood across from the bane of her family. She thought of her uncle, beloved in spite of his eccentricities. He had been driven from their society, forced to become an outcast living on the fringes of the wilderness, because of this damnable beast. How many other descendants before him had suffered similar fates from their maddening pursuit of an elusive beast that no one else could see? She could end that curse here and now. She could free her family from its burden and earn the right to carry a shield into battle for her Jarl. She gritted her teeth and charged toward the Questing Beast. She raised her axe overhead and brought it crashing down on its flank as it spun and kicked. Her shield absorbed the brunt of its counter and it sent her reeling. The hilt of her axe was slick with crimson blood and the Questing Beast turned toward her with a limp in its step. Freydis smiled. She had gotten the better of the beast that round.

It did not wait for her to advance this time. The Questing Beast tromped forward as fast as its hobbled hindquarters would allow in the snow. Freydis hid behind her shield and raised her axe overhead to strike. The handle was slick with blood and the axe slid from her grip, falling to the ground behind her. Freydis braced herself for the impact and the Questing Beast slammed into her shield. Its injured leg made the beast lose its footing and it toppled over on top of Freydis. She let out a piercing scream as the bulk of the beast's weight came crashing down atop her shield arm. They were a tangle of limbs, each scrambling to break loose and get to their feet. Freydis struck with her axe again and again. The Questing Beast stamped hooves on her broken shield arm and snapped at her with fangs. They parted and got to their feet. The blood of shieldmaiden and beast pooled together beneath their feet, coloring the white snow crimson. Freydis' shield arm dangled at her side and the shield slid off of its own accord. She knew it would be months before it would mend enough to bear the weight of a shield again. But first she must survive the encounter and she knew now that survival might not be her fate. Snow swirled around them like fog. It was time to end this before they both found their grave here.

The Questing Beast lumbered toward her. Its hooves and paws kicked up snow with every step and Freydis stood, swaying slightly, with her axe gripped in her good hand. She knew it still held a slim advantage in spite of its own injuries. A head-to-head clash would end in her death, even if she managed to take it down with her. She needed to do something unexpected. She leapt aside as it struck with its hooves. Freydis swung her axe at its side but it scuttled away from the blow and countered with a swipe of its head. Freydis ducked beneath the blow and moved toward the beast but it skittered sideways, using its long serpentine neck to its advantage. She ducked and dodged each snap of the fangs, but it also avoided each of her strikes. They were at a standstill and she was losing too much blood to keep this up forever. Perhaps if she had berserker blood she may have gained an advantage, but true berserkers were few and far between.

Freydis rolled backward to avoid a swipe from its lion's claws. Her left shoulder throbbed to remind her of the earlier injuries and tears welled around the corners of her eyes. Her arm still hung limp at her side and she could no longer feel her right hand as it clutched the haft of the axe. She gave ground as the beast struck out again and again. The snow was slick beneath her feet and she knew one bad step could end this entire encounter. This needed to come to a conclusion in a hurry, in the manner of her choosing. She shifted aside as it struck again, sliding along to its side. Its head snaked back to strike at her and she leapt back. The axe left her hand, spiraling as it crossed the short distance between them. It sank between the ribs of the leopard body and blood spattered the air.

Freydis slammed her bad shoulder into the side of the Questing Beast. It lashed out with its fangs as it fell over but Freydis had already removed her axe from its side and raised it to catch its attack. She felt the cold steel bite into its open mouth. The beast toppled backwards and the head fell limp to the ground. Its limbs twitched and its tail flopped in the snow but it made no effort to rise again. They braying of hounds quieted to a chorus of whimpers. Freydis stood there in the cold, watching it as her body struggled to get enough oxygen. She moved toward the Questing Beast, a deep sigh escaping her lips. It was time to put the beast out of its misery. She stepped toward the beast and its amber eyes fixed its gaze upon her. The blade of her axe pierced its hide and the beast breathed its last breath.

Freydis woke next to a burning campfire. The numbing cold had fled from her limbs and the snow had ceased falling upon the ground. Half a dozen men slumbered around the fire as well and Freydis wondered if it had all been a fanciful dream. She tried to raise her left arm but it wouldn't respond. She looked over to see that someone had rigged up a sling for her arm. Her body had finally given in to exhaustion once she had struck the killing blow on the beast.

The Beast! She craned her neck and saw its corpse laying not far from the fire. Had the men been able to see the Questing Beast now that it was dead or would they believe she was making up tales like her uncle? A form stepped between her and the fire, casting shadows upon her prone form. He leaned down and she recognized the Jarl himself, a small smile on his weathered face. He reached out an arm and clasped a hand on her right shoulder and shook his head.

"All these years I thought it was a fanciful myth," he whispered. His hot breath tickled her ear and his breath carried the scent of mead and spice. "But it seems there may have been truth behind your uncle's tales, after all." A tear trickled down her cheek, unbidden and unwanted. Freydis nodded and the Jarl looked up at the corpse of the fallen beast. The tears were gone by the time he looked back down at her. "The Bragi will have quite the time weaving the tale of your exploits for all to hear. I expect you be asked to tell it more times than you care to while that shield arm of yours heals.

"Tomorrow we will hold a feast to celebrate the vanquishing of this beast and we shall hear the first official telling of The Saga of Freydis Beastsbane. In a few months, when your shoulder heals, our foes will quake when they hear that Freydis Beastsbane is taking part in the annual raids."

Freydis tried to respond but her mouth was dry and her lips refused to open. She stared up at her Jarl, unable to believe the turn of events. She nodded her head and the world above her spun. She closed her eyes to stop the spinning and drifted back into a deep sleep, knowing that when she woke her dreams would be coming true. She would become a shieldmaiden for her Jarl and, perhaps, someday other young girls would dream of the day they could become shieldmaidens like Freydis Beastsbane.

The Confession of Mrs. Fay

Christian Bone

Father Pritchard stretched. Some of the village women had just been talking to him about their new fundraising idea…for three hours. The parishioners at his last post were surely not as needy as those here in Little Emrys. Of course, his vocation was to guide his flock in every manner possible, but he would occasionally like his lunchtimes to himself. Speaking of which, he wondered if that shop around the corner still sold those cheese and ham baguettes; the mayonnaise was divine.

He idly looked around the church, still a stranger to him. It was fairly small, built with chalky grey stone that felt like sandpaper if touched. The walls were sturdy yet ancient, supported by wooden beams that formed *A* shapes as they met the low-arched ceiling. He thought about how the place must have soaked up so many conversations, heartfelt prayers and joyful singing; it was as silent as the graveyard outside now.

He gazed out of a rounded window. The rustic village outside sat beneath a colourless spring sky. The scene could have come from any century—except the twenty-first. Pritchard imagined the village as a petulant child, refusing to follow its mother when she walks away; sooner or later Little Emrys would have to catch up with the world. And possibly have its favourite toy confiscated for misbehaving.

But despite his respect for the church and the pleasant surroundings, it wasn't home yet. His mind had still to unpack everything.

His stomach moaned. The food wasn't bad though.

Just as he was about to leave, he heard the percussion of feet on the smooth stone floor. He kept his head down and made for the door. It was probably just a tourist, he told himself without conviction. He made the fatal mistake of glancing upwards and noticed a hunched old woman hobbling into the wooden confessional near the altar. He sighed. His dedication was certainly being tested today. Pritchard made his way back with the air of someone who knew that the events of their life had been taken out of their hands, which was, handily, what he believed.

He blinked as he entered the cramped space, the midday light replaced by gentle darkness. Through the mesh grille partition, he could make out the woman's features. She was *old*; a face made of crinkly skin, the texture of parchment, was framed by thin curls of pure white under a pink woolly hat. Despite her age he imagined she would have been quite attractive in her youth, many years ago. He realised he had seen her around the village—Mrs. Fay was her name. She lived in the old folks' home on Hector Hill. Pritchard had never met her before—she was not a church-goer—but neither had many of the villagers, or so Mrs. Gawain, a woman fond of unremitting gossiping, said.

After a few moments silence, she spoke.

"May I speak with you, Father? I need to talk to someone." She had a strong voice. It reminded Pritchard of a crackling log fire that had once flamed brightly but was now fading into embers. "I haven't long left for this world. Lord knows I've been here long enough." He saw the light dim in her eyes, something he had seen in many individuals of advanced age. "I was once so…strong."

"Age catches us all eventually, Mrs. Fay."

"Mmm, but I did my best to hold it off."

To his shame, Pritchard had been expecting a batty, nonsensical woman to 'confess' to the heinous sin of once forgetting to feed her cat. Mrs. Fay seemed so wise.

"I tried everything to prevent it. But, in the end, even my spells failed."

The words sunk in.

"…Sorry?"

She didn't hear him; her unfocused eyes told him she was temporarily in another time. "I was once the best sorceress in the land, but most of it's faded now." She said the last point like another woman of her years would talk of a hip replacement.

Pritchard made to speak but nothing came out. Poor woman, he thought. Something similar happened to his elderly aunt after she watched *Harry Potter*.

Mrs. Fay continued. "I suppose what one usually does in this situation is confess their sins, but we would both be here a while if I did that." Her reverie showed no signs of waning. "My sieges on the kingdom, for example, they led to some *nasty* things."

Pritchard sat quietly. He was beginning to suspect Mrs. Fay had a rather black sense of humour.

"It wasn't just me though. We were all like that back then. But I'm the one who gets all the bad press while my brother is labelled a great hero. He was an imbecile—awful at making tables, couldn't get them square. Never saw past the end of his nose either, that grail thing he was after all that time was only—"

She stopped, she had been getting quite irate and her chest was rising heavily. As she caught her breath, her eyes grew big and sad.

"I have to be honest with you, Father," her voice was weaker. "I'm not really here under any religious guidance. This new-fangled faith of yours wasn't really around in my day. Things have just been playing on my mind."

They certainly have, thought Pritchard.

"What's really got me down over the last few hundred years—" He thought he would let that one pass "—is my poor boy. I was never really what you'd call a devoted mother. I had ambitions for him, though. Wanted him to be…"

"A doctor?"

"No, the king. I had it all planned; it would have been glorious." She gave a heavy sigh. "I pushed him too hard. He…left me, long ago."

There was a pause.

"I'd just like to be forgiven."

Pritchard contemplated the old woman. Even though her head was muddled, her son wasn't fantasy. Her eyes, full of deep regret, gave it away. Noticing things like that was one of the skills Pritchard had acquired, being a priest. And from reading lots of detective fiction.

Suddenly a loud, heavy coughing interrupted the quiet that had filled the little space. It was Mrs. Fay.

Pritchard leapt up and removed the wheezing old woman from the confessional, managing to guide her to the nearest pew. After a few moments, she had calmed down.

"Haven't got long," she said through gulping breaths.

"Don't say that, Mrs. Fay. How can you be so sure?"

"I know about these things." Her eyes closed slowly. "You will begin to like the village, Father. Just listen…"

Pritchard heard a soothing young voice peal behind him.

"Hello?"

He was a young man, fresh from his teens, with a slim, handsome face and long blonde hair. Pritchard rarely saw anyone so young in church nowadays. He hoped he wasn't here to pinch something.

Mrs. Fay's eyes opened and shone.

"My son!" she said in hushed tones, as if she could scarcely believe the words. Pritchard cast the boy another look. Surely he was too young?

The boy wandered closer, sprinting when he caught sight of the woman prone on the pew.

"Mum…"

Pritchard was dumbstruck. "She really is your mother?"

Mrs. Fay's eyelids flittered, she managed a thin smile. "You've been gone awhile."

"It's been years."

"Hundreds."

"Yeah…" His expression softened. "I'm back now though."

Probably been living it up in Spain by the look of his tan, Pritchard guessed. He had definitely been someplace hot.

"Is it really you? You could just be an illusion, made by M—"

"Mum. I promise it's me."

The old woman said a word he couldn't quite make out, something like 'floor-grid,' and then, "I'm so sorry for what I did. I've regretted it ever since."

Her son gave an indignant look.

"Really." She scrunched up her eyes; she was shaking, either from ill health or emotion. "I missed you. Some days, I'd—I'd imagine you were there. Not as the king, or even a knight, just my boy. If I was practising my necromancy, raising the dead from the depths, I thought of you there, ready to help in case I forgot the incantation. Or if I'd allied myself with a warlord, you'd remind me to poison his drink and steal his army."

Her voice dropped a little. "Or I'd pretend you were sitting next to me whilst watching telly." The embers crackled again. "And then I'd open my eyes, and I'd be alone."

The boy's eyes hardened. "You're not the only one who suffered. You treated me like nothing when I was kid. Never allowed to play at sword-fighting in the woods with the other children, just kept locked up indoors and told your tales." His temper raised slightly, his cheeks blemishing with red. "Everything you failed to achieve, your dreams, your…battles, you hoisted on me. You never let me have my own life."

"If you had your own life you wouldn't have had room for mine."

He ignored her. "But I've had a long time to think about it. I understand why you did it, and I turned out okay in the end." He sucked in a long breath. "I forgive you."

A solitary tear drifted down the woman's cheek. "Thank you." Her weakness seemingly disappeared in an instant as she sat up straight.

The boy turned to Pritchard. "You'll have to excuse mum," he whispered. "She gets…confused."

Pritchard nodded. He didn't need to be told that.

"Could you give us a moment? We'll be gone soon."

Pritchard mumbled something agreeable before his priestly programming took over. "Well, if you need anything come and see me anytime."

"Oh, no." The boy shook his head. "We'll be leaving the village. I think mum needs some new surroundings. Somewhere down *south*, perhaps."

Mrs. Fay looked crestfallen. "Can't we go up *north*?"

"Trust me, the south is much more you. You always preferred warm conditions."

Pritchard stood up and strolled over to the altar, looking the other way. His hunger was growing again but he tried to ignore it. He would give them a bit of time alone. Although not too long.

Soon, a gust of wind blew around him. He turned to the open door. Funny, it didn't look windy outside.

"Are you all right now, Mrs. Fa—?"

The pew where they had sat was empty. He shrugged. He hoped they had a nice time down south. Perhaps they were going to Cornwall; Mrs. Fay would like a spell there.

He wandered to his vestry at the back of the church where, to his great surprise, he found a freshly-made sandwich waiting for him on the table. Cheese, ham, and mayonnaise. One of the fundraising women must have left it for him. He might grow to like Little Emrys after all.

You will begin to like the village, Father. Just listen…

A glimmer of memory echoed in his head, like a distant call rebounding against the church walls. He had heard that recently, hadn't he?

A knock and a creak of the door broke his thoughts. A gaunt-looking octogenarian limped into the room.

"Can I speak with you, Father?" The man's frail frame lit up with a hopeful smile.

A moment of dismay flittered across Pritchard's face.

"Well, Mr...?"

"Penn, Arthur Penn."

"Well, Mr. Penn, I'm afraid—"

"Please, I need to talk to someone."

Pritchard frowned, digesting his second bout of déjá vu in as many minutes; Mrs. Fay had said that earlier. He hadn't wanted to talk to her, nor any of the villagers, since he had arrived. But he *had* talked to Mrs. Fay, he told himself, and it had done some good; the woman and her son had hated each other but, thanks to his guidance, were now moving on to warm pastures new. The village was a quaint place, really. And its people needed him to be there, to listen and to talk to.

The alarm slipped from his face, replaced by a broad, kind smile that found a more permanent home there.

"Of course, Mr. Penn, tell me all about it."

The Hammer and the Spear

Patrick S. Baker

October 10, 732, near Moussais, Duchy of Aquitaine

Charles, Prince and Warlord of the Franks, looked closely at the spear the old man held in his one hand. The old man had but one hand. The weapon was a standard Frankish winged-spear, with a finely-wrought leaf-shaped, iron-head about a *pes*, a Roman foot, long with two lugs at the bottom to prevent it going too deeply into an enemy. The only variation from the standard design was the spearhead had an opening through it and in that opening was the black iron spear-point from a Roman *pilum* bound in place by gold wire. The spear's wooden shaft was about eight *pedes* long.

"It is a fine weapon," Charles commented. "Why present it to me? Er…"

"He is Bedwyr Bedrydant, formerly *satellites* and *marshal* for *Arturus Rex*." The young companion of the old man said. "And I am Brother Bonaventure, humble monk and traveling companion to Bedwyr."

"Bedwyr Bedrydant," scoffed Carloman, Charles' 25 year-old son. "Bedwyr Bedrydant of Arthur's fame would be nearly a hundred and fifty years old."

"One hundred and fifty-two," the old man said as he suddenly stood and lifted the spear horizontally over his head.

An intense, holy, white light emanated from the spearhead, filling the tent, blinding the gathered Frankish, Burgundian and Aquitanian nobles. Now in the old man's place stood a handsome young man of noble bearing and warrior's build.

"I am Battle-Crowned Bedwyr of the Perfect Sinews, friend and follower of Battle-Lord and King Arthur Pendragon. After the Battle of Camlann, I was given charge to return Excalibur to the Lady of the Lake. While travelling back to the wounded

Arthur, I met King Pellam, the Fisher King, near Castle Corbenic. King Pellam gave me the Holy Lance, the Spear of Longinus, the Spear of Destiny. The spear holds the *pilum* point that pierced Our Lord Jesus Christ's side on the cross. The Wounded King knew he could no longer wield the Holy Spear, so he passed to me the obligation to find a warlord worthy of the weapon. Worthy to defend civilization. Charles, son of Pippin, Mayor of the Palace and Prince of the Franks, soon to be known as *Martellus*, the Hammer, is that worthy *Dux Bellorum*."

Bedwyr held the spear out, shaft first to an amazed Charles, who, not knowing what else to do, took the weapon. The light snapped off and the old Bedwyr returned. Then the old man sank down to the ground, dead. Father Boniface knelt beside the body and started to pray.

"Pippin," Charles said to his eighteen year-old son. "See to what the priest needs for Bedwyr's body."

The young man gently lifted the monk to his feet and then with the help of two soldiers removed the body from the tent.

A Frankish warrior stuck his head in through the flap.

"My Lord Charles," the soldier said. "There is a scout at the gate, he says the Moors are close."

"Bring the fellow in so I can get his report," Charles said.

"My Lord, the scout is one of Lord Eudo's men, an Aquitainian…" the messenger trailed off and looked embarrassed.

Charles quickly stood.

"My Lords," he said in his piercing battle-voice. "Enough of this. Lord Eudo is now our friend and ally. His men stand with ours in the battle-line against the invaders. Treat the Aquitanians with the respect they are due. Now let us all go hear what this scout has to say."

Without another word, the collected great magnates followed Charles from the tent and trooped toward the gate of the camp. Although the warlord wanted to run, he did not. It would not do for his men to see their *Dux* rushing around. He needed to set a good example.

At the camp's gate stood the scout and his horse. They were both covered in mud and grass. Rivulets of sweat ran freely down the young man's face from under his iron helmet. The horse's flanks and bit were flecked with foam. Someone had fetched the scout some wine and he was sipping carefully from a clay cup, like it was the finest vintage in the world.

"My Lord," the scout started to address Eudo of Aquitaine.

"Address the Lord Charles," Eudo ordered.

The young man look a bit confused. The enmity between the Franks and Aquitainians was long standing. In just the last year, Charles had raided deep into Eudo's territory twice, burned two of the *Dux* of Aquitaine's forts, and came back with a great amount of loot. Charles's Franks and Burgundians had been gathering for a third raid, when Eudo arrived at the Northerners' camp. The Aquitanian leader told the story of his terrible defeat at the River Garonne and of the Saracens looting and burning of Bordeaux. The two warlords quickly made an *amicitia,* an alliance of friendship. Charles then swiftly moved his army south to stop the invaders before they reached Tours.

"My Lord Charles," the Aquitainian scout turned to the Mayor of the Palace and gave a polite nod. "The Moors are advancing up the Roman road, less than a *mille* from our battle position."

"My lords, to your places. Battle awaits!" Charles said loudly and clearly.

Charles, Eudo and the great magnates moved to mount their horses. As a group they rode up the gentle rear slope of the hill to where some twenty thousand Franks, Burgundians and Aquitanians stood in line, nearly shoulder to shoulder, round shields resting on their legs, spears at slope arms.

At the bottom of the grassy slope the Muslims' light cavalry appeared, tough mountaineers from across the Pillars of Hercules on equally tough ponies. Next came the heavy cavalry, Arabs on big horses with long lances and long swords, wearing scale armor and using stirrups. Then came the infantry; spearmen, archers, slingers guarding the wagons carrying the loot of dozens of towns and churches. The Christians let out a low, angry murmur when they saw the collected booty from the holy places stacked on enemy carts.

"I gave the priest a wagon and three men to take the body into Tours to the House of the Blessed Martin," Pippin said, as he rode up to his father and brother. Then he added, "This is a excellent battle position."

The Christian battle-line ran for some three thousand paces just below the brow of a low hill with an open, grassy field to the front. On the right was the wooded valley of the River Clain and to the left was another heavily wooded area. The highly mobile enemy could not turn the Christians' flanks and Frankish leaders positioned just behind the infantry line on horses could see everything the enemy was doing.

While the men of the north watched, the Moors went into action. A ditch, rampart and palisade were quickly built around the wagons and carts holding the treasure. Then the Saracens moved into a five-part battle-formation. The vanguard were foot archers, with light cavalry in front of heavy horsemen. To the left and right were blocks of spearmen and archers ready to support the cavalry, or exploit a breakthrough. In the center, just behind the vanguard, a small number of well-appointed horsemen, messengers and subordinates, surrounded the enemy commander. Behind the commander, guarding the newly built camp, was a small unit of infantry.

"Shields up, spears ready!" Charles said, pitching his well-trained command voice to be heard many paces away.

The Frankish line rippled from the center to the flanks as the men picked up their heavy wooden shields and then brought their spears up into the favored over-hand striking position at the warlord's command. The men who could not hear Charles followed the example of their comrades to get ready.

Moorish archers jogged forward toward the center of the Christian line, closely followed by the light horsemen. At two-hundred paces the bowmen stopped, formed a double line, and raised their bows. The front rank of the Franks knelt and raise their shields over their heads, angled toward the enemy. The other ranks put their shields up, also toward the enemy. On a command, the Moorish archers let fly. Thousands of arrows arched outward and fell on the closely-packed ranks of the Franks. Most landed in upraised shields. A few slipped into the gaps and impacted the ground. Even fewer arrows hit men, mostly in the feet or shoulders. At least one unlucky fellow in the rearmost rank, who unwisely peeked around his shield, took an arrow in his right eye.

The arrow storm continued for what seemed like a long time. Then the hail of shafts stopped as the Moorish bowmen ran out of projectiles. Now the Berber light cavalry charged forward, shouting guttural battle-cries and shaking their javelins at the unbroken line of Frankish foot soldiers.

"Bowmen, make ready!" Charles shouted while the enemy horse closed on his line.

When the enemy horsemen were one hundred paces from the frontline the Frankish *Dux* shouted. "Loose!"

Now the European archers struck back. The European self-bows lacked the range of the Moorish recurved bows, but against the lightly-armored Berbers, with their small leather shields, they were deadly. The Christians' arrows fell like a lethal rain. Howling men and screaming horses tumbled to the ground. The survivors closed on the Christians, hurling javelins and curses at the solid lines of spears and shields. The javelins did little damage. Now the light horsemen turned and galloped away, hoping to draw the Christians into breaking ranks and charging after them. But the foot-soldiers stood still in their places, holding in place like a glacier in the far north.

The Arab heavy cavalry now charged forward. Riding leg-to-leg, the Moorish horsemen formed a solid mass of men and animals, long lances, and heavy shields. They shouted "Allahu Akbar" as they charged. The ground trembled as they thundered forward. The Franks gripped their spears tighter, and dug their feet in a bit deeper. The Moslem horses reared and skittered back, unwilling to crash into the barricade of iron points and iron men. A few Franks in the front line went down, impaled by the sixteen-*pedes* long spears of the enemy. When one infantryman fell, another stepped forward and took the fallen soldier's place. As the Moors came even closer, the Franks struck. They drove their 8-*pedes* long spears into men and horses. As Frankish spears broke, or were lost, replacements were passed forward.

The horsemen pressed on, the front ranks driven forward by the rear ranks wanting to get at the Franks. In the center of the battle-line, the infantry started to waver, as the seemly unstoppable wall of horsemen came on and on. A noticeable bulge formed in the back rank as the front line was pushed back, with Christian soldiers killed, or knocked back, by the sheer mass of the attacking enemy.

"Father," Carloman said and pointed at the spot about to give way.

"Follow me!" Charles shouted.

As he rode forward, Charles raised the Spear of Destiny and the holy weapon started to glow with an ethereal while light.

"Hold my soldiers," the warlord said in his battle-voice, as he slipped off his mount. "Hold I say, for Christ's sake, stand fast."

Holding the Holy Lance in one hand, Charles grabbed a man that was backing up and pushed him forward. He saw another start to turn to run and the *Dux* turned him around by the shoulders and kicked him in his arse, sending him back into the line. Four men now backed-up in a line; Charles wielded the Spear horizontally, put it in the small of their backs and shoved them all forward, toward the fighting. Charles's sons and his personal *comitatus* quickly joined him in pushing, shoving and sometimes kicking men back into formation. The pressure from the front finally relented and the line reformed. Charles remounted and scanned the now retreating enemy. The Moors fell back in disarray from the unbroken Christian line. The Frankish archers launched arrows at the backs of the enemy until they were out of range.

The battlefield now stank like a farm at slaughtering time. Crying, writhing, howling men and horses filled the grassy slope. The Frankish wounded were hauled back from the line, as they begged for water, or cried for their womenfolk, or for a priest.

The fighting paused as the Moorish archers raced back to their supply wagons to refill their arrow bags. The Christian bowmen did the same, sending one man in four back to the Frankish camp to get reloads for himself and his fellows. The unbroken spears of the dead and seriously wounded were gathered up and then given to those soldiers who had broken or lost their weapons. The lightly wounded were quickly bandaged by their comrades and then put themselves back into formation, and without being told, the men readjusted the line to fill in the weakened parts.

The Moors went back into their battle formations, this time the vanguard shifted to Charles's right, close to the River Clain.

"They're trying the right this time," Pippin said, his voice nearly squeaked with excitement.

Again the Moors started forward, again with the foot archers in the front, followed by the light and then heavy cavalry. The archers stopped one hundred and fifty paces from the battle line, just out of bowshot of the Christians, and formed into a division four ranks deep. The enemy arrows flew. The Burgundians occupied this part of the Christian line and they sheltered under their shields. But the arrows didn't stop falling. As the Moorish bowmen started to run out of projectiles, horsemen arrived from the supply wagons with more arrows, which were quickly distributed. The arrow-storm continued unabated. The sheer volume of shafts insured some got through the overlapping shields. Burgundians began to fall, wounded or dead by the never ending enemy volleys.

Count Chadoind, leader of the Burgundians, a scarred veteran, and old companion of Charles rode up to the Frankish leader.

"My Lord Charles," the Burgundian said. "Let me lead by horsemen in a charge against those bowmen. They are slaughtering my infantry, my men. I must strike back."

"My Count Chadoind," Charles responded politely and respectfully to the slightly older man. "I can see just as well as you what is happening. But you will accomplish nothing by a charge, except your death and the death of your horsemen."

"My archers?" Chadoind asked.

"They'll be twenty paces into the enemy's killing zone before they can shoot an arrow to any good effect," Charles shook his head. "And nothing would stop the enemy cavalry from riding them down."

Then the wily battle-lord stopped and smiled.

"My lord count," Charles said. "Take a quarter of your bowmen and move them through the woods to the right, but on this side of the river. They are to come in from that side and shoot three arrows each, then run like a frightened deer through the trees back to our lines."

Chadoind nodded and also smiled wickedly at the plan, wishing he had thought of it.

The Count collected one in four of his archers and took them back, out of sight of the enemy. Then he dismounted, along with half his *comitatus*, and led the group into the heavy woods. For what seemed long hours, but was only a few moments, the Moors incessant rain of arrows continued. Charles sat on his horse right behind the tormented Burgundians, ready to use the Holy Lance to keep poor bloody infantry in line, if needed. More Christians were down, those still standing began to slip, ever so slightly, rearward.

A flight of arrow erupted from the forest to the enemy's left. Several Moorish archers dropped, killed or wounded, by the unseen attackers. Now second flight of shafts plunged into the Muslim formation. More invaders fell and the others turned about to find their assailants. A particularly quick-witted group of about twenty Berbers charged at the woods, only to be mowed down to a man by the third volley of arrows. A few other light cavalry raced up to the edge of the forest and hurled their javelins. But the trees were too densely packed for the mountaineers to force even their tough ponies through.

The Moorish warriors milled around in confusion for just a moment and then at a single barked order the heavy cavalry charged forward. Not in one solid mass as before, but in smaller groups traveling at different speeds so they closed on the Burgundians in widely spaced packets.

The Christian archers shot, unseating a few of the Moorish horsemen. The Burgundian infantry roared, incoherently, as they struck back at their tormentors. They skewered the attacking Moors, while the Saracens lanced exposed Burgundians. The Christians' blood was up. Even now when their spears broken or were lost, often stuck into the guts of the enemy, the infantrymen drew their swords and axes and hacked at the invaders. Men and horses were wounded and killed. The Franks' favorite targets were the unarmored flanks and legs of the horses, as they followed the infantryman's adage when dealing with cavalry: "Horse down, man down." Whenever a Moorish warrior fell to the ground, he was set upon by a group of Burgundians, who hacked him to bloody pieces.

The Moors now recoiled from the carnage. This was no orderly withdrawal, but a sprinting, running, tumbling rout down the hill as the Saracens drew out of striking distance of the battle-maddened Burgundians.

As the enemy fell back, a party of Burgundians broke from the forest behind the Christian line. The four armored men carried Count Chadoind. The old count was dead, a javelin buried in his face. Charles called for a priest and went over to his old comrade-in-arms. The *Dux* dismounted, closed the Count's one open eye and said a brief prayer for the dead while crossing himself.

A loud murmur ran along the ranks of the Christians.

"Father," Pippin said. "They are saying the Lord Charles is dead."

The Frankish warlord took a deep breath and blew it out. He quickly remounted his horse and handed Pippin his helmet. The *Dux* cantered through the reforming Burgundians, putting himself in front of the Christian line, alone. Holding the glowing Spear of Destiny high, Charles rode slowly in full view of his men.

When Charles was about halfway along his line, a Saracen warrior broke from the leader's retinue and cantered forward on a large, fully-armored warhorse. This Moor was clearly a rich nobleman. His equipment was of the finest quality, with his armor and helmet highlighted in gold. This single Moor had not yet fought this day; his armor was clean and his horse fresh. The Muslim noble moved forward to challenge Charles to single combat.

Charles paused, watching the young Muslim warrior cross the battlefield. He shifted the Holy Lance in his right hand, as if he were going to charge the oncoming Saracen. Then Charles, son of Pippin, Mayor of the Palace, Prince and Warlord of the Franks, lifted his left hand high, showed the approaching Islamic soldier his *digitus impudicus*, turned and trotted his horse back though his men.

The Muslim warrior galloped up to just outside bowshot and

red-faced, he angrily shook his spear at Charles. The Frankish soldiers just howled in laughter.

The Moors now formed to attack the left of Charles's infantry line, where the Aquitainian contingent was stationed. Charles and his retinue placed themselves just behind the southerners' part of the line. Charles was concerned that Eudo's men, having already been defeated once by the Moors, would break easily.

"My Lord Charles," Eudo said as he rode up with his *comitatus*. "My *antrustione*, Abbo, is a local man. He tells me there is a path, wide enough for two horses abreast that runs through the forest and comes out behind the Moors' camp. Let me take some horsemen and attack it."

"Don't allow it, Father," Carloman spoke up. "Eudo is a coward and just wants to be away from the battle. He knows his men will not hold the line."

"You pup," Eudo said hotly to the younger man. "Call me a coward, will you? I was fighting and beating those *lupas* while you were still hiding behind your mother's skirts."

"Enough!" Charles drove his horse forward to separate the two men. "My Lord Eudo, take your men and follow your plan. Carloman, my son, you take your *satellites* and go with Lord Eudo, if you wish. I will stay with the Holy Spear and insure the line holds."

Eudo gave a curt nod and rode off with his men. Carloman hesitated, unsure whether to go or not. The young man decided, turned his horse and with his handful of followers rode after the Aquitainians.

The Moors took some time to organize for their next attack. Even the bravest, most aggressive warriors showed some reluctance in assaulting the solid line of infantry again after suffering two bloody repulses.

Late in the day, as long shadows fell across the field, the

enemy moved to their third attack. A commotion broke out near the Moors' hastily erected camp. Eudo and Carloman's men emerged from the forest, quickly dismounted and rushed at the unblocked entrance of the enemy palisade. The Frankish raiding party killed the handful of Saracen guards and poured into the camp.

The Moorish *Emir* seeing this sudden attack on his redoubt, dispatched a messenger to the force about to attack the Christian line. This force turned and hurried back down the slope, moving quickly to protect their loot.

Charles pointed the Spear of Destiny, now blazing to rival the sun, and ordered a general advance. Staying in their tightly pack ranks, the Christians stepped forward for the first time that long, bloodstained day. Step by step, they crossed the field, at last advancing on the enemy.

The Christian raiders, seeing the main enemy force coming at them, tumbled out of the Saracen camp, quickly remounted their horses and plunged back into the trees, before the fast approaching enemy could trap them.

The attack on the walled camp and the now advancing mass of Frankish infantry was all too much for the tired and disheartened Saracens. In drip and drabs, the Moors started to slip away. First the Berbers turned their ponies and ambled to the south. Then the heavy Arab cavalry also started to slip away toward their home. Finally, the infantry turned and marched quickly away. A few hundred remaining Muslim foot-soldiers, led by a tall and noble looking man in full cavalry armor, formed a thin line as a rearguard, in front of their now secure camp.

As the Franks approached, the enemy held its place. The Saracen general stepped forward. He struck at a Frankish warrior, who'd rushed ahead of his fellows. The Muslim's long sword, drove down the Christian's shield and wounded him badly in the shoulder. Two other Franks lunged forward and speared the Moorish leader in the chest. Seeing their *Emir* die, the remaining Moors lost heart. They turned and ran back into their walled camp, pushing heavy carts across the entrances, blocking them

The sun dipped even lower and night fell. Rather than conduct a dangerous night-attack against an unknown number of enemies in a fortified camp, Charles ordered his men to return to their own camp for the night.

The next day, the men of the north formed up just before dawn and moved on the enemy position. They burst through the flimsy wooden palisade, poured over the carts blocking the entrances and found the camp empty with much of the loot abandoned.

Thanking God for his victory, Charles took his army home, while Eudo's Aquitanian forces cautiously followed the defeated enemy.

October 22, 741 Quierzy-sur-Oise, Kingdom of The Franks
Lord Charles, Prince of the Franks, was dying. The old *Dux Bellorum* looked over at the Spear of Destiny as the holy weapon lay just within reach on a table near his bed. Since the great battle at Tours, the warlord won every battle he fought. He campaigned against the Moors of Narbonne, against the Frisians in the North Sea, and the pagan Saxons in Germany. At all times the Holy Lance helped and supported him.

Near their father's bed stood Carloman and Pippin, while in the corner of the room priests prayed for the dying man's soul. A young monk entered the room and went to take the Spear.

"Stop," Charles managed to croak. "What are you doing?"

"I'm taking the Holy Lance to keep it for the next soul worthy to wield it," the young monk replied.

"I know you," Carloman said as he stepped forward to block the monk from removing the holy relic.

"I am Brother Bonaventure, I was boon-companion to Battle-Crowned Bedwyr. Now, charged by God, I am keeper of the

217

Holy Spear."

"But my sons…?" Charles asked.

"My Great Lord Charles," the monk said gently. "One of your sons may be worthy, or not. One of your grandchildren may be worthy, or not. It is not for you, or I, to say. But rather the will of God shall determine who may have the Holy Lance and whom it will serve in the future."

The holy brother took the Spear of Destiny and without another word left the room, walking into the future.

Forsaking All Others

Elizabeth Zuckerman

We have not seen each other for five years.

He stands as I enter the room. I know the look on his face—how should I not know it, I of all people—the intense focus on appearances to mask inner turmoil. But I also know where it always cracks: the faint flare of his nostrils as he draws in his breath, the hair-thin pale line where his lips meet as he presses them together. Such beautiful lips, after all these years. He is still so beautiful. I ache at the sight of him. One hand reaches to press my heart, to still it, before I realize what it is that I truly feel. This ache in my heart, this emptiness in my limbs—it is the absence of what I always felt before. I used to tremble at the mere brush of his glance. Now I tremble because he is staring at me, as desperate as a thirsty man facing water, and my heart beats steadily as it never has in thirty years.

What becomes of love when passion dies?

It changes, I think, standing before him in my white robe. (I would have changed it for black—how I longed to change it—but I am a novice, old as I am, and not yet permitted the dignity of a nun's full black. I asked anyway, but the prioress shook her head, so sadly, and touched my cheek to wipe away the tear I could not hold back.) I do still love him—I wouldn't be myself if I did not—but I think more now of the three of us, between whom love was never a lie. Memories of his armor gleaming in the sun, of his hair tossed back as he pulled his helmet off, of his strong arms locked around me in hopeless need, flicker around me like tongues of flame too far to lend heat. But I remember him laughing with Arthur over a cup of wine by the fireside or muttering some wry observation about poor Kay's prickly jealousy, and I am warm and alive with love. For my friend that is gone; for the happiness to which passion blinded us, and which we can never have again.

In all my frightened imaginings of the future, I never pictured a world where I felt only a dear friend's love for this man. I am not sure, even now, which scares me more: the fact itself, or the comfort I feel at it.

"It is finished?" Lancelot asks at last, his voice catching in his throat from long silence.

I nod. "Just last week, they finished the smaller carvings. It's only—well, I know it's a lie, but I still think I would have struck anyone else if they had claimed him. I may have little right to him, but at least I have more than a stranger's."

"You have every right," he says softly. I don't care if it is true or not; it does my heart good to hear him say it. "Will you show me?"

I smile. "I think I would strike anyone else who dared to," I say, and now he smiles too.

We walk together, side by side, first over cold clicking stone and then soft grass that rustles under our feet. My hands are folded in the wide sleeves of my robe; his right, nearest to me, rests on his sword. Our hands took these positions out of sheer habit, trained rigidly to indifference when all we ached to do was touch. Now it's a relief to tuck my hands in swaths of fabric and not have to face how much has changed.

The midday sun presses my head down, steams my veil and wimple to my head. I glance at Lancelot; how he must suffer in this heat, clanking beside me in his armor and wool surcoat. I think of earlier times, how we would walk side by side in a garden, I in my white gown and he in his own bright silver laced with blue, and I have to laugh, or else I'd weep for what we lost. There's no time, now, to wash off the grime of the road; no sweet-smelling silks to skim the lines of our bodies; no queen among the flowers, no lover kneeling at her feet. Only a nun and a knight, walking with the slowing tread of middle age.

"What is it?" he asks, drawn by my short sudden laugh. "My

lady?"

I shake my head, not sure which utterance of his I am denying. "Nothing," I say. "Just…remembering."

"I am glad that you can laugh," he says. From another man, that would be an insult; from him, it is utterly sincere.

I never deserved him. I push the thought away. It is true. I did not deserve the love of even one great man, let alone the two greatest of the age. Such different loves, asking such different things of me. I returned them as best I could—I could not help it, for both my men were made to be loved—but they each needed all of me, and try as I might, I was only ever one woman. *Better,* I had thought often, crying silent bitter tears into my pillow so Arthur wouldn't wake at the sound, *that I had never seen either of them, or that they had never seen me. Better I had never been born than to hurt them so.*

But I had been born, and we had all seen each other, and love had followed on the heels of those sightings as sunrise follows midnight: inevitably, sweeping all before it. We had made our choices long ago. Better, truly, to live with them as we might than to wish them undone.

Lost in thought as I am, my feet stop before my eyes see why. They know the way, as they should; I come here so often that I have worn a path in the grass. Lancelot is still as stone beside me. It is as if the world holds its breath to see us reunited again.

It's a lie, I think. *A slab of carved marble, no matter how gilded and adored, is not my husband. If I make a joke, it will not smile and deepen the crinkled lines around its mouth. If I fling myself on it, it will bruise me.* It is part of my penance: to remind myself, every day, of the full depth of what I have lost.

"It looks like him," Lancelot breathes at last. I do not need to look at him to know that he is on the verge of tears.

"Bedivere carved it," I say. "He came here with the news. I suppose, in the end, he didn't dislike me all that much, to make sure I heard it first from him. He wouldn't leave his cell for days, even to eat, and when he finally emerged, it was to find the stone and begin work on this. I came every day—I wouldn't let anyone else tend to him while he worked—and by the end I think he knew I grieved as much as he did."

"Where is he now?" Lancelot asks. "I need to thank him for it."

"I don't know," I say. "He finished carving Arthur, then he left. In the middle of the night, without saying goodbye." I leave it at that. I understand—Arthur's oldest friend, if not his best, and proud for all he never sought fame, not wanting to bow to the woman who brought it all down—but I thought he might be willing to tolerate me, if not to forgive. His sudden departure hurt more than I had told even our confessor at the convent.

No matter. I can't blame him for judging me rightly. And to Lancelot, it's nothing. Already his strong jaw tightens in resolve. "He can't have gone far. I'll find him. He should not be alone."

How strange, that we should fear for our safety again. I forgot what it was like to hire guards and never travel after dusk. "I hope you do," I say.

He shoots me a sharp look—still eagle-eyed, undimmed by time—but says nothing.

Instead, he kneels in the grass before Arthur's tomb. I watch the slowness of his movements, the way he grips the rim of the stone for support, and I could weep for the lost years of our youth. Twenty years ago—ten years ago—he would have dropped in one fluid motion, hands clasped and head raised, so graceful it was a pleasure just to watch him move. And now the long legs creak with age, the beautiful mouth tenses in pain, the proud head bends as if his neck can barely hold it upright. Suddenly I ache to touch him, to caress that weary head, to hold him to me until he has strength enough to face whatever comes next.

But as I reach out, still so weak when tempted, he starts the slow careful process of standing, and I pull my hand back.

How often did we keep each other from the edge, unknowingly, as now? How many times did he turn away to answer a question or a challenge just before I tangled my fingers in his hair; how many times did I step across the hall as he was about to crush me to him? This is how we kept each other sane, I think, all those long years of unspoken agony. You sense the beloved's pain; you move temptation away.

My hand falls; my fingers curl around thin air, not him. Just as well. It would not be the worst wrong I have done my husband, but I do not want it on my conscience.

He has risen, and turns now to face me. Memory floods back, unbidden, unwelcome: Camelot at sunset, and the two of us facing each other in a garden of rose bushes. *"I have tried,"* he said, *"so hard. More than anything, I want not to love you. But I do. I'm going north tomorrow, to the coast. I had to tell you before I left."*

And me, my hands shaking so badly that I could barely lift them to his face, my heart pounding fast enough to force words out of my lungs in short frantic bursts of air: *"Oh God, Lance. You too? Not you too. I could bear it if it was just me."*

He hadn't dared to take me in his arms, not in the middle of the garden, even though we were alone. But he turned his head under my shaking hand and kissed my open palm, his lips warm and desperate, his eyes clenched shut as if to hold back tears.

Now we face each other again. We do not touch. I wait, not for the words unspoken below his courtly speech, but for his farewell. The absence of passion is a pain almost as great as passion itself had been, once.

It is his turn now to laugh, mirthlessly, in one sharp rush. "All this time," he says, "and I still don't know what to say to you. All my life, and one look at your face robs me of my wits."

"Lance, please," I say. My fingers clench on each other, digging hard enough to numb. "Not here."

"Where else?" he asks, jerking his head to take in everything:

the garden, steaming sweet-scented in the heat; the modest thatched roof of the abbey in the distance; the pale stone face of my carven husband, watching as impassively as ever. "And when, if not now? I know everything has changed; no one knows that better than you and I, who stood in the heart of what was. Too many good men have died, and one whose like will never come again. I know that. We know that. We can't go back; there is nothing to return to. But we must go forward."

He reaches through the folds of my sleeves and finds my hand. His own hand closes around it, warm and strong. "I love you," he says. "Love has never come easily to me, except with you and with him. He was our rock, but you were the sun, and I don't think you know how brightly you shone on us all."

Tears clog my throat and creep up toward my eyes. "I do not shine anymore," I say, and swallow hard. "None of us do, without him. He was the one who believed we could."

"You do," he says. "You always have. He's gone, and I will mourn him all my life, but we are here, and I love you. I know I'm a poor substitute, but I'm yours, even more than I was his." He takes a step, and suddenly he fills my eyes, blocking out the blinding glare of the empty white tomb. "Come with me," he whispers. "Life is more than regret."

He is right, and doesn't know how right he is. Here we stand, alone in a garden once more, and I feel only relief at the strange lightness in me where desire used to live. I can see him read it in my eyes, even as he cups my cheek and tips my head up for a kiss.

I have never before kissed him as a lie. For the sake of what was between us, and for what remains, I cannot do it now. I turn my face away, and hear in the sudden catch of his breath the breaking of his heart.

We stand, frozen in attitudes like figures painted on a wall, for some time; I don't know how long. I can't bear to count the seconds, to know how long he hoped before his fingers slacken on my face. He drops his hand; sunlight glares in my eyes as he steps away.

I look down at the grass around the tomb instead of up through the sunlight at him. It has always been my weakness to avoid what I have brought to ruin.

And he, poor beloved soul, differently loved now but loved no less—who knew of woman's love only what he had from me, who came as virgin to my arms as I came to Arthur's—if he looks at me now, what does he see? An old nun in novice's white, feigning a purity I never had? A demon with a loved face sent to destroy him? A queen in May, time dissolved in love? If I look at him, I will know how he sees me. But I cannot do it.

"I'm sorry," I whisper. "I will not ask for your forgiveness; I don't deserve it. But I am sorry, sorry for every instant of pain you have ever known that traces itself to me. I cannot love without hurting. And I can't go with you."

The sun is bright in my eyes. I shut them, pinching my eyelids down hard on tears.

"Why?" he asks. His struggling voice and the warmth of the sun on my face are my whole world.

So he does not know, or refuses to know. Then there is a kindness I can do for him still. A queenly way to send him from me; something to say that will not spoil all of our love, which was real, and has died. And if it's a lie of omission—lying too is loving, at times, in a way.

I open my eyes and face him, although I keep my gaze on the grass at our feet. "I will not leave this place and break my word," I say. "I won't be forsworn again. I pledged myself here for atonement, and there is so much still to atone for." It's not enough. Not yet. More truth is required, more pain for us both, to spare him that ultimate loss. "I betrayed my word for you once, beloved, and it cost us the world. We are not yet so old that we can't learn."

He bows his head as I raise mine. I cannot see the look in his eyes. "I don't understand," he says. "I may never. But I honor you for it."

And this is why I loved you, Lance. And why I cannot go with you. Obedient to the last, the loyal knight to his lady. The older I grow, the less I want obedience. I have had time, these five years, to think with a head unclouded by desperate youth. The arms I remember, the kisses, the flaming looks: those are Lancelot's, and perhaps always will be. But the words that ring in my memory, the smiles that strain my heart with pride even now in pale memory, the passionate mind always at work—oh, my lord, my king. You are gone where I cannot go, and I never realized how much I would feel your loss. When passion dies, friendship endures, and we were always friends. It is you I need beside me now, you I would walk with, you whose gentleness would move me where his aching need does not.

But when I open my mouth, all I say is: "And I honor you, and always will."

He looks up at that, and our eyes meet at last. In them I see myself: young and fair, more beautiful than I ever truly was, and remote as a star. I cannot be a goddess ever again; worship weighs my shoulders down. I am only a woman, as I have always been. I need more than his devotion can give me now.

He leaves, walking with a heavier step than when he came. I wonder, watching him go, if I have taken hope from him, if I've sent him out to die. I hope not. I want him to live and prosper, perhaps to love again if he can. Not to forget me—I have vanity enough left for that—but not to need me. I will not carry that burden, not when I need myself more.

And so here we are, my love, alone in the garden at dusk. You are cold stone, and I'm old bones, but here we are. Here we will stay, until time shreds us into dust. I will wait here for as long as it takes to earn you once more, and I will never leave you again.

Authors

Nicole Petit writes because no other job lets her sleep until noon. Fantasy is her forte, a sliver of genre right between urban fantasy and fairy tales. She writes the *Magic Realm Manuscripts* series and has curated the collections *Just So Stories, After Avalon,* and the award-winning *From the Dragon Lord's Library* series.

Colin Fisher is a writer of poetry and fiction who currently works in IT. Previous lives have seen turning his hands to the fields of archaeology and bookselling, and he has published poems with small presses such as Moonstone and Broom Cupboard. His short stories have appeared in a number of anthologies, such as *Ain't No Sanity Clause, Sanity Clause is Coming to Town*, and *To Hell with Dante*. He is the editor of two volumes of reworked fairy tales from Fringeworks Press entitled *Grimm and Grimmer*, with volume 5 forthcoming in 2016. He is currently working on a children's novel and is shortly to be published in a poetry anthology from Wyrd Harvest Press. He lives just outside London with his wife and two antagonistic cats.

Leigh Ann Cowan: I am in my second year of college, majoring in English and minoring in history. Between struggling to survive the harsh environment of the English Department, writing essays, and hiding in the library, I somehow found the wherewithal and strength to complete this piece, in great part due to the encouragements of my mother, my English Literature professor, and a few good friends of mine.

Amy Wolf's novel The Misses Brontë's Establishment is an Amazon Kindle Scout Winner. She has published thirty-eight short stories in the fantasy/sf press, including Interzone and Realms of Fantasy (2). She is a graduate of the Clarion West Writer's Workshop and holds an Honours Degree in English from the University of London.

Her fantasy series The Cavernis Trilogy will be published by Red Empress Press in early 2017.

She started her career working in the film industry at 20th Century Fox, Warner Bros., etc.

Originally from L.A, she is an economic refugee living in Seattle.

Thomas Olivieri, an enthusiast of long walks on the beach, chilly mornings, and strong pipe-tobacco, has written many short stories which have been published in numerous anthologies and periodicals.

He writes tales of love, death, and shipwrecks.

New publications (and occasional blog entries) can be found at this site:

https://redtomsmathomhouse.wordpress.com/

Jon Black is your basic absinthe & BBQ guy from Austin, Texas.

His previous jobs include archeological excavator, Benjamin Franklin impersonator, embassy worker, graduate assistant, newspaper reporter, pizza jockey, political speechwriter, small business owner, substitute teacher, and summer camp counselor...not always in the order one might expect.

He settled on writing as the one profession where he could work while wearing only his bathrobe or from his favorite coffeehouse (though not, it should be noted, both at the same time). For ten years he has been active in music journalism, ghostwriting, and freelance journalism. Bel Nemeton is his first fiction piece he dared show anybody.

The story is dedicated to his parents. His father, Merwyn (another name derived from Myrddin), is, like that legendary seer, a seeker after wisdom and mysteries. More than a little of his mother is reflected in Vivian Cuinnsey's adventurousness, competence, and intelligence.

Patricia S. Bowne enjoyed all kinds of folk tales as a child, but knights in armor and mysterious damosels were particular favorites. She's become more skeptical about all that war and jousting, but the fascination remains—along with a conviction that sometimes the best outcomes require putting down the sword. This story contains in-jokes for the ichthyologists in the crowd.

Other work by Pat, including the Royal Academy at Osyth series about faculty in a modern department of Demonology, can be found at www.patbowne.com or www.raosyth.com.

Claudia Quint writes fantasy, romance, and erotica when she isn't brewing wine, taking care of her society finches, and messing about in her garden. Keep up with her latest releases at claudiaquint.wordpress.com.

David Wiley is an author of science fiction and fantasy stories, choosing to write the stories that he would love to read. His short fiction has previously been published in *Sci Phi Journal*, *Firewords Quarterly*, *Mystic Signals*, and a King Arthur anthology by Uffda Press. David resides in central Iowa with his wife and their cats and spends his time reading, writing, and playing board games.

Christian Bone: A graduate of a Creative Writing degree from the University of Winchester, I am a fiction and non-fiction writer based in the UK. I have had several short stories and flash fiction pieces published in both print and online.

Patrick S. Baker: Patrick S. Baker was born April 9, 1962. He is a U.S. Army Veteran, currently a Department of Defense employee. He holds Bachelor degrees in History and Political Science and a Masters in European History. He has been writing professionally since 2013 when he was 51 years old.

His pieces in the speculative fiction field include non-fiction philosophical and historical works regarding the genre as well as short stories.

His nonfiction has appeared in *Medieval Warfare Magazine*, *Ancient Warfare Magazine*, *Sci Phi Journal*, and *New Myths*. His fiction has appeared in the *Sci Phi Journal*, *New Realm Magazine*, *Bewildering Stories*, and the *King of Ages* Anthology. In his spare time he reads, works out, plays war-games, and enjoys life with his wife, dog, and two cats.

Elizabeth Zuckerman got addicted to Arthuriana as a child and refuses to detox. She has previously published stories in *Footnote*, *NonBinary Review*, and *Timeless Tales*, and has blogged about Arthur (and other things) at storyseer.blogspot.com. In her free time, she makes costumes and hunts for a time machine. She lives in Trenton, NJ, with a gallant knight/court jester.

Preview

The Dragon Lord's Secretary

By Nicole Petit

Can't bear to leave the Arthurian world just yet? Check out Nicole Petit's *The Dragon Lord's Secretary*, which features Arthurian elements in an alternate, magical world connected to our own. Available now from 18thWall Productions.

Dear Mr. Great and Glorious Dragon Lord,

I am applying for a position you don't know that you need filled, that of your secretary. Before you reject this application, please consider the following. Who organizes and polishes your treasure hoard? Dragon claws are too large and imprecise. You require an applicant with thumbs. Who organizes your schedule? Dragons are too self-interested for this work. You require an applicant willing to write down your every meeting and make sure each one fits neatly into your calendar.

I believe I am this applicant.

I come highly recommended, and I would gladly direct you to my previous employers. Unfortunately, most of them have died. Not through any misfortune or anything caused by me. They died of old age, as mortals tend to do. If you would like confirmation of my abilities, please contact Mr. Winston Churchill. He lives at 28 Hyde Park Gate, London, England, Mortal Realm.

I have enclosed my resume. It is very long. See the attached. (Inside the box. The huge box. You can't miss it.)

Sincerely,
Miss Scarlet Chase

Chapter 1

Deep in the land where magic hides, in the court of the Dragon Lord, a war as old as Camelot raged. Down past the caverns carved by dwarven hands, laced with streams of gold, fire blazed and armor clashed. Past the cavern halls smoke smudged the tableau. It seeped, black and riotous, from the mouths of slain guards. Roars shook the roots of the mountain.

In the throne room, a Knight brandished his shield against the mighty Dragon Lord.

Gales of wind from great black wings beat against the small body of the Knight. A wave of his hand and the mighty winds turned, slamming with greater force against the dragon's great head. The beast snarled, unveiling rows of sharp teeth.

"SUCH MAGIC DOES NOT IMPRESS ME, CHILD OF THE WIND."

Each rumbling word beat the Knight's armor; the force of sound slammed against his ribs.

"That was no magic, lizard. That was a warning. I've killed two of your kind today. Release your captive and you won't be the third."

The Dragon Lord circled the Knight. "WARNINGS CARRY MORE WEIGHT WHEN YOU HOLD MORE THAN A SHIELD TO COWER BEHIND."

The golden blade attached to his whip-tail sliced through the shield and the power of its protective runes. The Knight howled, arm shattered by the force of the blow. The floor heaved beneath him as the dragon moved forward, each step causing tremors in the cave.

The jewel hung around the Dragon Lord's neck flared through the smoke. The massive gem was said to contain the flame of the very first dragon, a power more ancient than the entirety of the Knight's own race. The Dragon Lord towered over the fallen Knight, opening his jaws wide to call forth the ancient flame buried deep in his chest.

CRACK!

A whip made of the wind sliced through the roof of the Dragon Lord's mouth. Blood quenched the fire. The Dragon Lord reared back from his prey.

"Weight only burdens you, lead scales."

Blood continued to choke the Dragon Lord, but the fury boiling in his molten gold eyes said enough. Gold claws shot toward the Knight's chest. The Knight pulled back his whip and…

"I swear I leave the room for one hour and the whole place goes to pot."

From the secret tunnels behind the Dragon's Throne a young lady appeared. Curls of strawberry blonde hair escaped the tight bun and bounced across a pair of black rimmed glasses. Eyes the tangly green of spanish moss peered over the rims of her glasses. With a steady rhythm she tapped a pen against a notepad resting in one arm. The Dragon Lord stepped forward, his bloodied mouth hanging open. She gasped, resting the pen against her lips.

"Lord Almighty!"

The dragon smiled, his voice almost a purr. "Yes, Miss Chase?"

"Not *you*. The *merciful* one. Come down here, let me see." She crooked a finger. The dragon lowered his head, resting it against the floor. One slitted pupil kept a close watch on the Knight. The lady leaned in between his teeth, peering up at the wound. As she prodded experimentally with her pen the dragon writhed and snarled.

The Knight brandished his whip, "Step back, m'lady. I'll set you free from this beast."

Miss Chase pulled back, making notes on her notepad. "Beast is a horrible slur. It would be proper to call the Great and Glorious Dragon Lord Calix by his name, which just so happens to be the Great and Glorious Dragon Lord Calix. What, exactly, makes you think I need to be freed?"

The Knight stepped forward, laying a hand on her shoulder. His voice softened. "You're his slave."

She grimaced at the creases his armor made against her green blouse. With distaste she brushed off his heavy hand.

"Slave? Sir, I'm his secretary."

Chapter 2

"And then you have a meeting with the Elder Wyrms For Wyvern Equality at three."

"LEVIATHAN BURN IT ALL! NOT THOSE WALKING CASES OF SCALE ROT."

Heaps of gold shuddered under the force of Calix's bellow. Priceless and highly breakable objects tumbled from their piles. The secretary sighed as she walked beside him, struggling to keep her hair in its bun as the wind whipped up by the Knight grew wilder and wilder.

"Would you mind taking this fight elsewhere? I *just* alphabetized the dwarven artifacts."

"PRIORITIES, MISS CHASE! MY KINGDOM IS IN PERIL!" A burst of flame scorched Calix's collection of Dragon-proof armor. He fled into the deeper reaches of the Dragon Lord's hoard. Calix chased after to be met with a crack of the whip against his muzzle. He roared, and a furious lash of his tail cast an entire pile of gold into the air. A flick of the secretary's wrist and the gold hung in the air.

Miss Chase arched a brow. "Peril? A single mage?"

"YES, PERIL! YOU LET ONE PEST IN AND AN INFESTATION IS SURE TO FOLLOW." He leaned down close and cleared his throat. "This would all be much easier if you would just let me eat him."

Miss Chase lowered her hand, the gold fell back into a neat pile. "Or, you know, I could just use my—"

"NO. I'M THE HOST, HE'S MY UNWANTED GUEST. I'LL DEAL WITH HIM, NOT YOU." With a lash of his wings the Dragon Lord slid off, scattering treasures as he went. Miss Chase sighed and made herself as comfortable as she could in a particularly rickety golden throne. The cavern shuddered. Gales of wind knocked over her carefully arranged vases, and plumes of fire displaced her organization. Dabbing the tip of her finger against her tongue she flipped through the pages on her notepad.

"Make it quick, my lord. You have a board meeting in an hour."

"**BOARD MEETING? HELLHOUNDS TAKE YOU AND YOUR STRANGE PHRASEOLOGY, SECRETARY!**"

A furious roar, a scattering of gold, and the Knight was launched high into the air by a swat from Calix's claws. His tail twitched merrily, molten gold eyes glittering at the sight. Instead of the clatter of armor against floor Calix expected, he was met with a furious blast of magic. Not the wind he had come to expect, but a more dazzling sort of shockwave that could only come from…

Miss Chase yelped and rushed through the thin paths, stopping at the section she reserved for cursed items. She came to a shield of some long forgotten race (knocked woefully out of place) and stopped. It was metallic with a milky white gloss, and shaped like a chrysalis' wing. Much too delicate for its purpose. Miss Chase stared at it, tracing the thin lines with her eyes. These lines pulsed with a silver light that she never recalled being there before. Confronted with a strange new glow in the cursed items section of Calix's hoard, she did what any self-respecting secretary would. She tapped on it with her pen.

The shield quivered, the lights pulsed bright. "IN THE NAME OF ALL THE OLD GODS OF ATLANTIS, WHERE AM I? WHAT HAVE YOU DONE TO ME, BEAST?"

Calix threw back his head and laughed, drowning out the Knight's cries. Miss Chase gave a resigned sigh, adding a note at the very bottom of her to-do list:

Free Knight from cursed treasure.

Preview

The Whole Art of Detection

By M.H. Norris

Or, if you'd like to keep your reading centered on England's great heroes, you may enjoy M.H. Norris' *The Whole Art of Detection*. Adelaide Baynes finds a book that shouldn't exist, written by a man who couldn't have lived—*The Whole Art of Detection*, by Sherlock Holmes. The book changes her life, and puts her in conflict with dangerous forces…and a dead author.

Available now from 18thWall Productions.

Adelaide Baynes hated bees.

She hated the buzzing, that they could sting without warning, that they were an insect. She didn't care what her real reason was—she hated them. She could never understand why her hero insisted on keeping bees.

He *could* have stayed in London, with its access to amenities that one would *never* find here in the Sussex Downs.

But *no*, he moved to the middle of nowhere and raised bees.

And they were still here. Well, technically their great-great-great (and so on) grandchildren.

The bees were everywhere.

Holmes' hermitage was the only place, besides the famous flat in Baker Street, where Adelaide felt she could be near her hero.

Which is why she found herself wandering the woods two weeks before she would start classes at King's College. Covering more than twenty acres, Holmes' hermitage was a haven for the world's Sherlockians and Holmesians. As she entered the woods, she could hear the English Channel beat the cliffside, sounding straight out of a white noise machine.

Adelaide wandered away from the path, avoiding tourists so she could think. She hoped to take a few minutes and maybe sit where her hero might have sat and thought.

Everything was about to change. If she was perfectly honest with herself, she was scared. But then again, wasn't everyone?

Leaves crunched under her feet and she could hear the ever-present buzzing of bees. But the map told her that she was a good distance away from the hives. Part of her could get used to the fact that the height of summer felt like a nice spring day.

Others might not be used to it—because she was alone out there in the woods. Granted, she was a bit off the path and a lot of people were in the hermitage, watching a documentary on permanent loop in Holmes' sitting room (he'd hate that). But considering her parents had helped put it together, which was partially why she was here in the first place, Adelaide didn't mind skipping it. She'd seen it enough already.

Wandering away from the sound of the bees, she found herself above the channel. Water flowed about a hundred feet below her and off to her right was an abandoned beehive. Unlike the others, this one was falling apart as if neither bee nor man dared to come near it. Also, unlike the other ones on the property, this one was more of an antique, as if untouched by the Heritage Site beekeepers. It was silent. No honey bees roamed near it.

It didn't take an expert (though she was one, arguably, if by osmosis alone) to know what Holmes would do in this situation. So Adelaide went around the hive, trying to find out why it was abandoned. By bees, at least. There were over three dozen hives on the property itself, so what made this different? She studied the map and noticed she was at the edge of Holmes' property—but that still didn't help her figure it out.

She went up close to examine it. Greenery grew up against it, providing Adelaide with her first clue. The ones that made the honey the museum sold were clear of foliage all around.

So what made this one different?

The hutch went to her waist and she knelt down in front of it.

Silence continued to reign. A strong earthy smell met Adelaide, but it seemed it was the plants. Where had she smelled that before?

The hutch's lid crumbled in her hands. She winced, and peered in.

There were no bees, but there were spiders. A few crawled out of the hutch as Adelaide suppressed a shudder and peered inside. To her surprise, it looked as if this hutch had never seen any bees at all. Even one of the slides was misporportioned to the hutch. Where the rest held the traditional mesh, albeit missing honeycombs, this one was solid brown and thicker than the other ones by far.

Shrugging her backpack off her shoulders, she grabbed the partition and tried to lift it, surprised at how solid it felt. She met little resistance as she pulled it out—though a couple spiders took that as a chance to seek freedom. A few feet away, a log sat making an opportune chair, and she took the partition over to examine it.

To her surprise, it was a package wrapped in old brown oilskin. Twine kept the paper secured and Adelaide reached in her bag for the pocket knife her father bought her as a "you're starting college and in case of an emergency I want you to be able to defend yourself since I'm going to be an ocean away" present. It made quick work of the twine and she unwrapped the package.

A book sat inside the oilskin. The title appeared to be printed on the brown cover, at first, but after a second look she saw to be incredibly neat copperplate, a lost art.

The Whole Art of Detection
S. Holmes

No way.

There was no way she was holding what she thought she was holding. It was lost, or it didn't exist. Sherlockians and Holmesians didn't agree on much, but most assumed that what she might be holding, should it even exist, was lost and incomplete.

With shaking hands, Adelaide opened the cover of the folio—*book* wasn't the right word for this work of art—and there was a envelope attached to the back of the front cover in the same handwriting gracing the envelope.

Read if Convenient—If Inconvenient, Read All the Same

Adelaide had to take a few deep breaths trying to stop her heart from beating out of her chest. She let out a little laugh. This wasn't real, she was dreaming and would soon wake up back at the inn in Brighton.

Part of her hoped desperately that this was a dream. If it wasn't she had just made one of the greatest discoveries in the history of criminology, nineteenth and twentieth century history, chemistry, take your pick.

Opening the envelope, Adelaide found a couple pages of the same script.

> *January 6*
>
> *The Whole Art of Detection did not reach my publishers in London. The primary manuscript was destroyed (likely in my own fireplace). I am dead.*
>
> *You are young. Your parents are doting, yet distant, allowing you to traipse all about my property while they attend to their own business. You pride yourself on an unearned intelligence, compared only against your peers. You will do.*
>
> *Forgive an old man his sense of the dramatic. The dead have so few opportunities to impress, and I suspect this shall be my last chance to take part in that particular conjuring of mine.*

Now you explode with questions. Calm yourself. I have more than enough reason to deduce the above.

The persecution began while Watson yet lived. The highest class of criminals embarked on a campaign against us. Not against our persons, which were valueless, but against his notes, which were invaluable. The word of respected men already meant little by 1927—but accounts written, in the moment, with quotes and pasted-in evidence could convict many of the most powerful men, and families, at work in Europe.

For all our work—and veiled threats Watson made in his later romances—his papers were destroyed hardly an hour after his death reached Fleet Street, and when I was nearly within sight of Cox and Co.'s vaults.

What you hold in your hands, then, is not only the sole account of my career, complete with techniques, notes, and all required to know and utilize my methods, it is also the bane of all Europe's uncrowned heads.

Do not reveal this. Do not seek its publication, no matter how many decades lie between this missive and your discovery. My work will not make it to press, let alone to sale. You will meet their fury, as have I. Do not tempt the Krafthauser.

But if you wish, you may make use of my notes for yourself. You fancy yourself intelligent, as I have said. Then let this be the light toward true intelligence, guided by the greatest tutor. I shall be the Socrates to your Plato, the Aristotle to your Alexander, and, perhaps, the Holmes to your Watson. There is no conclusion more congenial to me than this.

Very sincerely yours,
Sherlock Holmes

With care, Adelaide tucked the note back into the envelope that was still attached to the front cover. She had just read words written by Holmes himself. When she'd wandered off to feel closer to the Master Detective, she'd never imagined anything like this.

A chime from her phone brought her back to the present and she looked down to see a text from her best friend, Nessie.

MOVIE'S DONE. WHERE YOU AT?

To which she responded, **OUT IN THE WOODS, ENJOYING THE QUIET. MEET YOU AT THE MUSEUM IN 10.**

What to do with the folio?

With great care, she slid it into her backpack and slid the paper back into the beehive. Adjusting it, getting used to the extra weight, Adelaide made her way back to the path.

10 Years Later

Dr. Adelaide Baynes shifted uneasily in the wings of the auditorium at her *alma mater*. Had someone told her that day in the woods that she would deliver the keynote at a Sherlock Holmes conference in London within the decade, she would have thought that they were crazy.

Well, maybe before she found the folio.

Her phone vibrated and she pulled it out to see a call from Nessie. Hitting the red button, she shoved it back into her pocket before straightening her blazer.

"It is my privilege to introduce this year's keynote speaker. Daughter of Clarissa and Louis Baynes, she has become one of the greatest voices in Holmesian research. Often quoted as saying she's 'a Sherlockian by birth but a Holmesian by choice,' Dr. Adelaide Baynes has put out annotated versions of several of Dr. John Watson's memoirs and is currently working her way through our favorite literary agent's related work—late trains, men with watches, and Napoleon's men indeed."

"In addition to her scholarly work, she is the co-owner of The Whole Art of Detection, out of Edinburgh, and an alumni of Cambridge. Dr. Baynes has not only become one of the leading experts on Sherlock Holmes, but follows in his footsteps with her own consulting detective firm. A most impeccable career. It is my privilege to welcome to the stage, renowned Sherlock Holmes expert and detective, Dr. Adelaide Baynes."

Adelaide made her way out, taking the stage to applause. The auditorium was packed and she could just make out people standing along the walls. Though she would never admit it, moments like these made Adelaide feel every inch of her twenty-eight years. Shoving those thoughts down, she made her way to the center of the stage, glad for the headset so she could roam the stage as she talked.

"Thank you so much for the warm welcome and having me as the keynote speaker at this year's Infinite Capacity Conference. I grew up coming to these every year with my mom and dad and to be here, on this stage, is truly an honor. Sherlock Holmes, the Master Detective, one of the greatest names in criminology.

"We have dedicated our lives to the study of this man, this man who seemed to be able to solve any case. Part of me wonders what he would think if he were here to hear how people all but worship him. He would harangue us for praising the painter rather than the painting, and studying the writer rather than his words. And yet, following this fallacy, we find he did not solve every case. We tend to ignore that fact because his record was truly amazing and his deductive reasoning skills were unrivaled."

Clicking her remote, she let her topic appear on the screen behind her. Her phone vibrated again and she ignored it as she launched into her lecture. "I have the privilege of speaking with you several times this weekend and, you can ask my partner, Nessie, I've spent the last few weeks agonizing over what order to put my lectures in."

"Sherlock Holmes is known for finding the obscure, critical details from observation alone. From people and the mannerisms to the environment around him, Holmes used his eyes to find the real clues. Over in the states, Dr. Cal Lightman and the Lightman Group help to solve cases using body language. While working on my dissertation on Holmes, I spent a few months back in the states, interning, seeking to learn body language from the greatest source. At least, of course, until some lucky soul discovers *The Whole Art of Detection*."

A polite chuckle from the audience.

"Holmes, unlike Lightman, understood that people and their body language are only a small part of what's necessary. People do not exist in vacuum. They are agents within an environment."

She scanned the first few rows of the crowd. All ages were represented and she smiled at her parents in the front row. "For example, my mom is trying to look like she is fully focused on my lecture, note that she hasn't looked away and eyes suggest intense focus, but I can tell she's also bursting with pride over the fact that I'm on this stage right now—note the blush. Not that I doubt she's listening. I understand, of course, that reading one's own mother is cheating."

The crowd laughed as Adelaide nodded to her mother and walked around. "We'll be primarily drawing from 'The Book of Life,' today. It's one of the few articles Holmes had printed before the public, before Watson became all but his only public outlet. Despite the esoteric title, Holmes outlined the basics of his rules for observation, such as…"

Adelaide left the stage with a satisfied smile on her face. One lecture down, three more to go. Checking her watch, she saw that she had just enough time to make it across town so she could attend Dr. Rosella Tassoni's lecture. It was purely a coincidence that the two were in the same place on the same weekend, but Adelaide had been hoping for a chance to see the famed Forensic Mythologist speak. After all, she was where Adelaide was now ten years ago. With any luck, Adelaide could have a career like hers.

Stepping out the back entrance of the convention hall, she waved down a taxi. Giving him the address of Dr. Tassoni's lecture, Adelaide pulled out her phone to return Nessie's phone calls. "You know I was giving my first talk just now, right?"

"It was important."

"I'm out of the office all weekend, I distinctly remember that conversation going something like 'oh don't worry Adelaide, I've got everything under control, I can handle a few days without you. Have fun in London, bring me back something fun.' So what's important you'd interrupt one of the crowning moments of my life?"

"A new case. An odd one. The Dutchess of Cambridge asked me to ask you to look into it while you were there. And aren't you going to Dr. Tassoni's lecture tonight?"

"I'm on my way now. What's this case?"

"Get her to sign something for me. I almost came with you just to see her."

"The case, Nessie."

"You're no fun."

"*Nessie.*"

"Right. Well, you know the Isaac MacGoraidh series?"

"Those mind-numbingly fantasy 'novels.'"

"It's a work of art."

"Sure it is. What does it have to do with our case?" Adelaide pulled out a notepad from her satchel and got ready to make notes.

"Nadine Jowett, the author, was found dead about a hundred miles away from the castle fans claim is Isaac's school's geographical match"

"Because Jowett made the two worlds overlap?"

"It served as an entrance and exit point into our world."

"Close enough. Have you got the police report?"

"It's in your email. Jowett was supposed to do a book signing here today and when she didn't show up, people got worried."

"What's the verdict from the Fiscal?"

"Pathologist is going to do the examination tomorrow."

"External or Dissection?"

"Don't know yet, when I know I'll let you know. But considering this is pretty high profile, I'm going to assume they'll dissect."

Adelaide opened her mouth when Nessie cut her off.

"And before you start complaining, yes, I know—no, you are not cutting your weekend short to come back to work *this* case. You've been dreaming of headlining that conference for years. Yes, I can go to the examination, yes, I'll record, and yes, I'm sure you can examine the body when your train gets here Monday."

Adelaide let out a sigh. "Take notes."

"Aye, aye boss."

Letting out a laugh, Adelaide watched as London rolled by outside her window. "In the morning, call Jowett's publisher here in the UK and get me an appointment for some time I'm free."

"The Duchess set it up for tomorrow night after your last talk."

"Excellent."

"Have fun tonight."

Adelaide nodded, even though she knew Nessie couldn't see her. "You too."

Hanging up, Adelaide looked at the brief notes she had taken on the case.

The car pulled up to the back door of the hall where Dr. Tassoni spoke and Adelaide quickly slipped inside. Checking her phone, she saw she had about ten minutes to spare and she made her way into the auditorium.

"Dr. Baynes."

"Isn't she speaking at that Holmes convention?"

"What is she doing here?"

Adelaide smiled and waved, hopes dashed that people would ignore her presence. She took a seat and pulled out another notepad, glad no one else would see evidence of the odd habit she had picked up. Maybe it was Watson's fault—after all he took extensive notes on all their cases.

The lights dimmed and after brief introduction that was similar to the one she had received a couple hours earlier, Dr. Rosella Tassoni came out and launched into her lecture.

Adelaide slid on her earbuds as she pulled out a folder the next day. Her morning talk had gone well, and the following question and answer segment was as much fun as nerve-wracking. Finally she could get to the report. Lunch lay out in front of her and she took a bite as she hit play.

"Today is the twelfth of June 2026 and it is fifteen minutes past eight in the morning. This is Dr. Lauralee Eldridge performing the examination of Nadine Elizabeth Jowett on the order of the Procurators Fiscal. In attendance are Inspector Don Linstead of the SCD and Miss Nessie O'Malley of The Whole Art of Detection, here on behalf of the Crown. If I might begin?"

There was a slight pause where Adelaide assumed Nessie and Inspector Linstead nodded. Dr. Eldridge continued through the preliminaries: height, weight, age, gender, race, hair, eye and liver color, and body temperature before moving on to the clothes that Jowett was found in. Adelaide noted that she was found in the same clothes that her assistant said she was wearing when she was last seen.

"On the temples there are what appear to be bite marks. Marks are about point six millimeters in length and a quarter of that in width in a slightly round shape. Continuing down the body, there are scratches on both the left and right side of her face as well as defensive wounds on her arms. Bite marks can be seen there as well. I am going to swab under the nails in case there is DNA evidence.

"Another thing of note is the presence of a web-like, slimey substance in the victim's hair as well as between the fingers. Source of webbing currently unknown."

Dr. Eldridge went on to describe how x-rays showed massive swelling in the brain as well as fractures in the skull due to whatever caused the wounds on the temples. She went on with the examination and Adelaide finished up her lunch as she got to her assessment of the cause of death—overdose.

Toxicology was outstanding as well as some of the DNA tests that Dr. Eldridge was running. She did confirm for both Nessie and Inspector Linstead that Jowett's death was a homicide.

Adelaide looked at her notes as the recording ended, trying to gather her thoughts. Off to the side, where one might put doodles, were questions she had to ask the pathologist when she got back to Edinburgh. Others were musings she had along the way. The wound and cause of death told conflicting stories but would reveal themselves in time. She shot off an email to Inspector Linsead. She wrote some of her initial thoughts as well as letting him know about her interview for that night.

That done, she put her tablet back in her satchel and made her way out to a book signing she had scheduled before her third talk of the weekend. At least this way she was getting to see a bit of the conference floor.

www.ingramcontent.com/pod-product-compliance
Lightning Source LLC
Chambersburg PA
CBHW060631260626
47161CB00008B/2862